Cupid

By: John Netti

Chapter 1

Everyone is a moon and has a dark side, which he never shows to anybody.
Mark Twain

Maddy Reynolds, 1978, Utica, New York

"Is Mr. Beretta feeling hot today, Maddy?"

"He's feeling really hot, Jake." The old sergeant laughed. Jake always asked the same question and got the same answer, but Maddy didn't mind, because being a range master at a police shooting facility was a lonely job, and she knew about lonely.

Each day, after her daughter got on the bus for school, Maddy would stop at the range to run through routines before heading in to work. It was a ritual that started when she was fourteen, and for Maddy, it was as essential as eating and sleeping.

She laid the black case on the same table as always, pulled out the Beretta 9-millimeter, checked to make sure it wasn't loaded, and walked over to lane three. When she popped in the magazine, she felt herself step out of the personality known to her family, friends, and coworkers to become a very dangerous person. Few people knew that person; Jake was one, and she had sworn him to secrecy about her shooting skills.

It was a day for holster, long-range draw-and-fire drills. Fifty or one hundred yards, it didn't matter. Maddy was a High Master Shooter, and her scores were always off the charts.

"Got time for a cup of coffee before you go?" Jake asked as she packed up her weapon. "I've got a fresh pot brewing."

"Love to, but not today. Maybe tomorrow."

"I'm going to hold you to it. By the way, rumor has it you've made detective."

"That's one true rumor. I start next week."

"If my calculations are correct, that makes you the first woman detective in the Oneida County Sheriff's Department."

"Your calculations are right on the money." She smiled.

"Well, congrats then. I guess that means you'll be working under Captain Zepatello."

"Yep, he's the one who hired me."

"That's a good thing, Maddy. He's an awful hard ass. Ex-military. He runs the place like a combat unit but takes good care of his people. In the long run, you'll be better for it." The old man handed her a clipboard; she signed it and, as usual, hers was the first name at the top of the sign-out sheet. "You have a good one," he said as he took it back.

"See you tomorrow, Jake."

Chapter 2

Nigel, 1954, London

Nigel's room was his sanctuary, the only place he felt safe, and his friends were in his rock collection because rocks didn't talk back. He felt protected in his private place, but when he ventured outside of it, dragons appeared, spat fire, and attempted to devour him. He often spent his afternoons joking with Green Opal, but after a beating, the only one who could comfort him was Jade.

"You're ugly," or "What a fat pig you are," were the types of insults he endured from Mother and Gertie. For the longest time, he ignored them, believing they didn't really mean it, but in time, he realized they hated him.

Gertie was only eight but made Nigel feel small. She possessed the power to bring Mother's wrath down on him, and whenever she lurked about, he grew fearful, because she always drew blood. Although he was big for fourteen, Nigel paled compared to his mother. She had the punch of a heavyweight, wore a massive ring with a blue stone on her right hand, and wasn't afraid to use it. *I'd rather get kicked in the balls by a mule than hit by that baby,* he once told Green Opal.

"Someone's at the front door. Answer it, Nigel!" Mother yelled from her room.

"Can't Gertie get it? She's right downstairs."

"You do it! Now!" Nigel set aside his rock collection, jumped down the steps to the front room, and, as he passed by Gertie playing on the floor, asked, "Is that a new toy Mother bought you?"

"Yes, it's a tea set. She gave it to me yesterday." Her haughty tone added to his irritation. *Mother showers her with gifts for no reason.*

When he opened the front door, Paul from down the street stood on the step. Freckled-faced, a smile like a broken fence, Paul always looked ridiculous in Nigel's eyes. "A few kids are going to the playground. Wanna go?"

"Sure. Hang on; I'll be right back." Nigel ran up to Mother's room, but her door was closed. "Mother," he said through the closed door, "can I go with Paul to the playground? Mother. Mother, are you in there." A faint moan grew louder until, like an orchestra, it reached a crescendo, and ended with a deep voice grunting out, "Oh baby."

Shit, she has a man in there again. Nigel turned in disgust, walked back down, and forced a smile on his face as he cracked open the front door. "Oh, Paul, Mother is taking Gertie and me to the zoo today. I completely forgot. Thanks for asking, though." He closed the door quickly, leaned his back against it, and stared at the floor. The words his father spoke the night that he left drifted back into his mind: "Get out of this place, boy, before they kill ya."

Gertie's mocking voice sailed in from the next room. "'Mother is taking Gertie and me to the zoo.' Why would she do that when she just took me last weekend? And oh, by the way, it was terrific."

Nigel's boiler was already at maximum pressure, and Gertie's mean words popped its valve, releasing a torrent of energy that propelled him toward his sister. His intention was to explode her face with his foot, but at the last second, an ounce of reason nudged him off course. His kick blasted ceramic cups, saucers, spoons, and a tea kettle into a thousand tiny pieces. Nigel tried to quiet Gertie's train-whistle scream. "Quiet, Gertie. Please," he begged. She looked at him, unable to hide the glee in her eyes as she howled even louder.

Mother's door slammed, and Nigel's heart stopped as he watched the stairs. A fat man leaped down the risers with his shirttail outside of his pants. He stopped at the bottom, stared at Nigel and Gertie, raised an eyebrow as though he was looking at a two-headed dog, and chuckled. The man shook his head, turned, and walked out the door. Gertie resumed her feigned hysteria, in a blatant attempt to have Mother eviscerate him. "I'm sorry, Gertie. I'll give you my piece of chocolate cake if you stop screaming." The door upstairs slammed again, and this time Nigel knew it was Mother.

Mother's feet pounded on the stairs as she ran down. Her loose-fitting nightgown flowed behind her, breasts bounced, and her hair spiked as though she'd been in a wind tunnel. "You're a no-good piece of shit just like your father," she shrieked. "I should have put a coat hanger up my twat and gotten rid of you when I had the chance."

Nigel was stunned and stood in disbelief as his mother lurched at him with her fists clenched. When she smashed his face, the blue stone of her ring penetrated his cheekbone, lightning bolts flashed, and a hundred screaming freight trains echoed through his head. Nigel fell into murky darkness. When he opened his eyes, Mother was halfway up the stairs with her arm around Gertie's shoulder. Blood and tears dripped from Nigel's face. It felt like the time Mickey Jennings flung the ice-ball that clobbered his jaw. It hurt just as much, except that Mickey said he was sorry.

Each whimper added to Nigel's physical pain, but it didn't compare to the pangs of abandonment that twisted in his gut. *It's one thing for her to hate me and another to punch me,* he agonized. *I wish she had killed me before I was born.*

Deeply shaken, Nigel felt the emotional glue that held him together coming undone. A steel door within him opened, and a river of unfamiliar memories flooded out into his consciousness. He found himself drifting back in time, standing in a cage, alone in the dark. The smell of a dirty diaper rose from his wet, cold crotch. He screamed for someone to come, but no one did. He dropped and rolled to his side, put his thumb in his mouth, and gazed into the darkness.

A flash of light startled him, and a red, glowing dot moved up and down. Plumes of smoke made his nose itch, and when the red speck glowed bright, he saw a hand, a ring, and a blue stone. Excited, he stood up, held the wooden bars, and called out, "Mummy, Mummy." But when mummy didn't come, he cried himself into exhaustion and collapsed. The steel door slammed shut, and Nigel left his dream-like state. He looked around at pieces of pink ceramic spread out on the floor, wiped the blood and snot from his face, stumbled up to his bed, and fell into sleep.

Chapter 3

I am so glad it's Friday. Maddy pulled up to her house, grabbed a pizza box from the back seat, and plodded up the stairs, keys clenched between her teeth. A fresh autumn breeze brushed up against her face and reminded her that winter was on its way. *There's so much I need to do around here before the snow flies,* she thought. She tripped on one of the broken pieces of concrete and thought how the old place was too much for a divorced mother living on a cop's salary. *If Grandma hadn't willed to me, I'd sell it.*

She opened the front door. "Hey, kids," she said as she rushed past Amber and Samantha to the kitchen with arms full. "My God, it's seven thirty? Sorry I'm so late. Who's winning?"

"Amber is killing me, Mrs. Reynolds."

"I just bought a hotel on Park Place," Amber said.

"You kids must be starving."

"Naw, we've been snacking on chips." Amber held up a bag of Doritos.

"Can you stay for pizza, Sam?"

"No, I better go. My Mom has dinner waiting."

"Take a couple of slices for later. Before I forget, let me get your money. Thanks for helping me out tonight. I needed to get my reports to the D.A." Maddy returned from the kitchen and handed Sam an envelope with money in it and two pizza slices wrapped in tin foil. "Thanks, Mrs. Reynolds. How do you like your new job? I read that article that said you are the first woman detective in the Oneida County Sheriff's. How cool."

"She loves it," Amber piped up. Maddy tried not to interrupt the flow of conversation as she hung up Amber's coat, put her book bag in the hallway, and carried empty glasses from the living room to the kitchen. "Every night since she made detective, she comes home, puts on sweatpants, eats, pours a glass of wine, and reads reports. How boring!"

Maddy laughed. "Yeah, I do like it. It's what I've always wanted to do. But I still have a lot to learn. It's only been a couple of months."

After Samantha left, Maddy and Amber sat at the kitchen table and dug into the pizza.

"So, what are your plans for tomorrow?" Maddy asked.

"Dad wants to take me to the zoo, but it's not his weekend, so he has to ask you."

"Do you want to go?"

"Only if I can bring a friend...I think Abby's around tomorrow. What about you? What will you do if I go with Dad?"

"What will I do? I'll tell you exactly what I'll do. I'm going to be the laziest person in the neighborhood. That means no reports; I might sleep in; I might eat junk food; I might not even take a shower. Maybe I'll make progress on my new puzzle. What do you think of that?"

"I'll tell you what I think of that...I'll believe it when I see it," Amber said with a giggle.

When they finished, Maddy wrapped the leftover slices and put them in the refrigerator. "Let's go up early tonight, pooch. I'm exhausted. I can read to you for a while if you want."

"No, that's okay. I have a magazine."

Lying in bed, Maddy tried to focus on her latest Stephen King novel, but the sound of Amber's television turned her thoughts to her daughter. She tiptoed down the hall, cracked opened Amber's door, and inched her way over to the bed. Amber lowered the magazine and smiled when Maddy sat next to her.

"Whatcha looking at?"

"Just thumbing through *Teen Magazine*."

"Anything interesting?"

"Not really."

Maddy put her hand on her daughter's arm and said, "Honey, I don't feel like I'm doing well at keeping all the balls in the air lately."

"What do you mean, Mom?"

"You know. I missed your school concert a few weeks ago, and now I have to reschedule your dentist's appointment for the third time, things like that. We don't have time together the way we used to."

"It's okay. Don't worry so much."

"I miss our talks. I don't want the job to take 'us' over." Maddy leaned over and hugged her daughter, snuggled her head up against her shoulder, and said, "Nothing is more important to me than you."

When she returned to her room, she pulled out a leather-bound book and wrote, "Dad, I wish you could have known your granddaughter. She would have made you proud." She closed the diary, placed it on the nightstand next to her father's Chicago Police Detective badge, and switched off the lamp.

"How about bacon and eggs this morning?"

Amber pulled up a chair at the table. "No, thanks, I'll just have Cheerios. Do you know what the weather's supposed to be like today?"

Maddy opened the newspaper to the weather page. "Let's see. It says, 'overcast, then sunny and then, oh crap, snow."

"Snow! Really?"

"That's what it says. I guess I better try and get the storm windows on this weekend."

"Dad said he'd help with that."

"Tell him thanks, but I can handle it."

The phone rang. "I'll get it," Amber said. "It might be Abby." She pulled the long cord over to her chair. "Hello. Just a minute." She covered the receiver and handed the phone to her mother. "It's for you. It's a man."

"Hello."

"Hi, Maddy. Sorry to bother you on the weekend, but I've got something I'd like you to handle. Can you meet me at the office?"

"Sure, Zep. I'll be there in an hour." She hung up and frowned. "I guess you were right; it doesn't look like I'll have a relaxing Saturday after all. It's a good thing Jack wants to take you to the zoo."

"What do you have to do?"

"Zep said he wants me to handle something, but he didn't say what."

"What kind of name is Zep?"

"His name is Frank Zepatello. Everyone just calls him Zep. He's a captain and my boss. He's the one who pushed for me to be the first woman detective, which is a big deal in this day and age. Come on, let's finish up and get dressed. I'll drop you off at Dad's on the way to work."

"Aww, Mom. I like to relax on Saturday mornings."

"Sorry, honey."

Chapter 4

"Sit down, Maddy." Zep put his feet up on his desk, took a sip of coffee from a Styrofoam cup, and set it down. "Thanks for coming in. I know it's Saturday, and you've been putting in a lot of hours lately, but something's come up I think you're ready for." He picked up a folder from the desk and handed it to her.

"An eleven-year-old girl has gone missing. Her name is Sarah Benning. Over the last few years, we've been to the house several times; domestic disputes, runaway issues, but no violence."

He put his feet down, folded his hands on the desk, and said, "The kid usually shows up in a day or two, but this time it's been six nights and the mother is beside herself. She's an alcoholic and gets ornery when she drinks. Shit has hit the fan since the husband moved in with a woman half his age. According to the interview conducted yesterday with the mother, Sarah's been acting out worse than normal ever since the father left. It's all in the report," Zep said as he pointed to the folder in Maddy's hand.

"Trick Diaz did the interview?" Maddy asked when she saw his name on the report. "I thought he transferred into the K-9 unit."

"Do you know Trick?"

"We partnered last summer for a few months."

"Well, don't tell him, but he's been accepted. It's just a matter of paperwork. Any questions?"

She glanced at the folder one more time and said, "Nope, got it."

"That's it, then. Just do your best and keep me posted."

Maddy walked out and thought, *my first real assignment as a detective.* She reached into her jacket pocket, felt for the brass Chicago Police

Department badge, held it in her hand, and whispered to herself, "I did it, Dad."

The Benning place was on the county line. As Maddy drove, a gray October sky set off by orange and red trees brought back memories of autumn in Chicago when she was a kid. But the beauty ended when she pulled up to the Benning house. *I can't believe anyone lives in this shithole.*

Yellow paint flaked off wood clapboards, and the side porch was propped up by a piece of lumber. A woman in her fifties with long, gray, stringy hair, came to the door. She wore dirty overall jeans and a faded green flannel shirt with holes in the elbows.

"Are you here about Sarah?" the woman asked.

"Yes. I'm Maddy Reynolds from the Oneida County Sheriff's. You must be Martha."

The woman looked at her and twisted her face. "You're a detective?"

Aww geez, here we go with that female shit again. "Yep," Maddy said.

"Oh well, come on in," Martha said as she opened the screen door and told Maddy to have a seat.

Maddy sat in an old, cushioned chair. Worn-through fabric exposed stuffing on its rounded arms; an empty bottle of vodka stood on an end table next to her. "I know you explained everything to Officer Diaz yesterday, but would you go through it again one more time for me?"

Martha cleared her throat, sat up, and brushed the hair from her face. "Last Monday after school I told Sarah she had to come with me to Herkimer to help get a load of firewood. With winter coming, I can't afford oil, so I try to heat with wood. But Frank, the asshole, oh, excuse me, my ex-husband, told Sarah that he and his bitch girlfriend wanted to take her to the movies to see Cinderella. Of course, Sarah wants to go with them, and I end up the bad guy. So, Sarah gets all pissed off when I say 'No,' storms out of the house, and I haven't seen her since."

"Do you have any idea where she might have gone?"

"She has a few friends from school, but none of them have seen her. Sometimes she runs to Frank's when she's in a snit, that's her father, and sometimes she'll go to Mary Thompson's. She lives just down the road. Frank ain't seen her either. When I called Mary, she said Sarah stopped by that day for a little while, then left. The only other place she's been that I know of is Utica. That's where she went last time. She hitchhiked there and stayed for three days."

"Do you know where in Utica she went?"

"Nope. She wouldn't say. But I hope she didn't go there again. That's no place for a child."

Maddy spoke as she wrote in her notebook. "Has Sarah talked about meeting any new people? You know, teachers, friends, neighbors?"

"Nope."

"Have you noticed her acting differently in any way?"

"Other than being a little shit, not really."

"Can I take a look at her room?"

"Oh, she's not in there." *No shit*, Maddy thought to herself. "I just want to look around. We might find something that'll give us an idea of where she's gone."

Martha balked, put her fingertips together, and appeared pensive, as though she was about to choose one of three doors on a game show. Finally, she said, "I guess it'll be all right."

She led the way to a room off the kitchen. *Oh my God,* Maddy thought when she walked inside the bedroom. *This place isn't fit for a dog.* Damp and musty, the room reeked of mouse droppings. Broken windowpanes covered with plastic and water stains on faded yellow walls painted a picture of neglect. A sleeping bag draped over a twin-bed, half lying on a filthy floor. *Poor kid,* Maddy thought to herself.

On a pillow lay a small photo of two adults and a child with their heads together, smiling. "Who's this?" Maddy asked.

"That's me, Frank, and Sarah, six years ago. It was all different then. We had jobs. But when GE moved out, everything hit the shitter."

A plaque of a girl kneeling with her hands clasped in prayer, looking up to heaven and a tear running down one cheek, lay next to the photo. The inscription on the bottom read, "Dear God, I know you are always with me. Please comfort me and make my sadness go away. Amen." *This kid sounds depressed.*

Maddy walked over to Sarah's dresser and rummaged through odds and ends scattered on top. She held up small scraps of paper, flyers, notes from teachers, gum and candy wrappers, ballpoint pens, hair clips, combs, and even arms and legs from broken Barbie dolls. She pulled open the dresser drawers and found two empty, one with mix-matched pants and tops, and another with a few pairs of underwear and socks. "It doesn't look like there's anything here to go on. Can you give me Sarah's description, as well as the addresses of her father and the Thompson woman?"

"Well, Sarah's about four seven and weighs about ninety-five pounds. She has brown eyes and dirty blond hair."

"Can you remember what she wore?"

"Hmm, let's see. Sarah wore black pants and a purple dress down to her knees. Over that, probably her black sweater-coat that zips in the front. She always carries a purple-and-white beaded bag with a rag doll inside."

When they walked back into the kitchen, Martha grabbed a utility bill from the top of a bread box. On the back, she wrote down the addresses. As they left the kitchen, Martha kissed her fingers and gently placed them on a picture of Jesus taped on the refrigerator.

She's going to need his help, Maddy thought.

"Are you Mary Thompson?" Maddy stood in front of a black woman sweeping leaves off a porch.

The old woman straightened up and smiled. "I am the woman. Or at least what's left of her." She leaned back, rested her weight on the broom, and eyeballed Maddy up and down. "You look like the law."

"I'm Detective Reynolds from the Sheriff's Department. I'd like to speak with you about Sarah Benning."

The woman's lips curled sadly. As she paused, her cheeks drooped, and the light that had beamed from her eyes faded. "I was just about to have a cup of tea. Why don't you come and join me?"

They walked through a dining room with uneven floorboards and burgundy wallpaper that had been scrubbed clean. An old Stickley table and chairs, perfectly kept, gave Maddy the impression that Mary once knew the more beautiful things in life. Mary gestured to Maddy to take a seat as she walked to the stove, poured the tea from an already hot kettle, and placed two cups on the table.

"What is your relationship with Sarah?" Maddy asked as Mary sat down.

"Well dear, sometimes Sarah needs a mama and every once and a while God asks me to be that mama. You know, just for a few hours, to help her through a bad day. Last Monday was one of those days."

"Can you tell me what happened?"

"Sarah walked in about six thirty and didn't say much. I said, 'Would you like some warm apple pie that I just made this afternoon?' Her eyes lit up, and she said, 'Yes.' She sat right where you're sitting now, took Jenny from her bag, and leaned her right there." Mary pointed to a sugar bowl. "Jenny's the old rag doll I gave her a long time ago."

"Then, Jenny and I watched Sarah eat her apple pie and ice cream. You'd think the child hadn't eaten in a month. When she ate it all up, she took my hand, held it in hers, and asked if I'd pray with her. I nearly cried. She looked at me with those big, sad brown eyes, and I said, 'Sure, honey.' She bowed her head and said, 'Please God, make Mom and Dad love each other again.' That was all. She got up, put Jenny back in her bag, and walked out the door."

Mary's account was so absorbing that Maddy forgot to take notes.

"I've watched the Bennings grow into a family over the years, and then, over the last few, fall apart. It happens all the time around here.

Once, they were a happy family. But when the jobs go, troubles come. First, the alcohol, then the bickering about money, and before you know it, there goes the car down the road to the watering hole, sometimes staying away for days. It doesn't take much of that before the marriage goes too, and with it, the little family. Finally, comes the broken child. That's Sarah."

Mary had set a hook in Maddy's heart and so she asked Marry where she was from.

"Now, you didn't come here to ask about me, did you?" Mary said with a laugh.

"No," Maddy said sheepishly.

"Well, I don't mind. I grew up in South Carolina. I married the man of my dreams when I was nineteen. Ben was smart and went all the way through high school, which is rare for colored folk where I come from. His best friend was a white boy who convinced him to take a job at the General Electric factory in Greenville. Eventually, Ben got transferred to the Utica Plant. By that time, we had three children, now all grown up and doing fine. But Ben got sick ten years ago and passed. Now it's just me here with my letters to the grandkids, all far away, and my memories. There's not much more to it than that, dear."

In less than an hour, Maddy had come to feel like she had known Mary her entire life.

"Would you like more tea?" Mary asked.

"Oh my God, it's getting late. No thanks. I have to go."

When Maddy walked out on the porch, clouds had cleared, and the sun beamed down from a blue sky. The scent of autumn filled the air, and a soft yellow carpet of birch leaves lay beneath her feet. Before she got in her car, she looked back and saw Mary on the porch sweeping leaves again. "It's a beautiful day," Maddy shouted.

Mary stopped and looked over. Her white teeth stood out against her black face as she said, "Every day the Good Lord makes is a beautiful day. You find that child, Miz Reynolds, you find her."

Chapter 5

It's not hard to see who got the best of that divorce. No wonder Martha's so bitter, Maddy thought as she drove up to Frank Benning's house. Sarah's father lived in a sprawling ranch, surrounded by trimmed lawns and expensive landscaping.

"Can I help you?" an attractive woman asked when she came to the door. Maddy introduced herself and asked for Frank Benning. "I'm Cindy Featherstone, Frank's fiancé. He's up at his hunting lodge. Can I be of help?" She was in her late twenties, slender, had long black hair, and wore a burgundy workout outfit with spotless white sneakers.

"Maybe," Maddy said after she introduced herself. She stepped into a large ornately decorated room. *Someone has money, and I don't think it's Frank,* she thought. She sat in an oversized white leather chair and marveled at hand-painted murals of dancing ballet figures in tutus and oblong wood carvings of African warriors. *Holy shit, this room is worth more than my house.* She opened her notebook and asked, "Did you know that Sarah left home Monday and hasn't returned?"

"Oh, dear! I didn't. I was afraid something like that might happen. I knew Frank wanted to take her to the movies and thought there might be trouble over it."

"Martha said an argument about Frank and you taking Sarah to see Cinderella is what led to Sarah walking out."

"Martha hasn't done well since Frank moved in with me. She's bitter and takes it out on Sarah. I wasn't in favor of the whole Cinderella thing. I knew Martha would react badly, but Frank insisted."

"Does Sarah come here often?"

"Frank has visitation rights every other weekend, but since it's only a twenty-five-minute walk from Martha's house, Sarah comes and goes all the time during the week. She has her bedroom and a key to the house. Sometimes we'll come home to find cookie crumbs in the kitchen and know that she's been here."

Maddy jotted down a few words. "When did Frank go to the lodge?"

"After Martha told Frank that he couldn't take Sarah, he got agitated. When I came home from my class, there was a note saying he'd gone up north. That was a little after six o'clock."

"Is there any chance Sarah is with him now?"

"I suppose it's possible," Cindy said as she tossed her hair back. "He might have seen her on the road and picked her up. There's no phone up there, but I can give you the address and directions if you want."

Maddy tore a piece of paper from the notebook, handed it to Cindy with a pen, and asked her to write down the address.

"If Frank did bring Sarah with him, would he have let Martha know?"

"Probably not. He was terribly angry with her."

Maddy took the directions and said that if Sarah didn't show up by the next day, she'd be back to speak with Frank.

The weather had turned bad while Maddy was interviewing Cindy, and when she opened the door to leave, a blast of cold air blew in her face. As she drove down the road, snow began to fall, and within minutes, she could barely see a car length ahead. While she focused on keeping the car on the road, in the back of her mind thoughts of Sarah lingered.

Here's a kid living in poverty with an alcoholic mother at one house, and right up the road, her father is living high on the hog with a woman half his age who looks like she belongs in Hollywood. The kid probably doesn't know which end is up.

The phone rang as she was about to turn onto the expressway. "What ya got, Maddy?" Zep asked.

"I just left the father's place. He took off to his hunting lodge on the afternoon Sarah was last seen, so I spoke with his girlfriend. I also interviewed the mother and a neighbor. Nothing new came out of it, except the possibility that Sarah is with her father. The lodge is up in St. Lawrence County. There's no phone, but I have an address."

"I'll contact the Sheriff's up there and ask them to check it out. It's nearly five. There's nothing more for you to do right now, so why don't you go home. Al Ramirez is working tonight. I'll have him call if anything breaks."

As they hung up, the snow intensified. *I hate this weather. One minute the sun's out, and the next, you can't see your hand in front of your face.* She pulled into her driveway, and snowflakes pelted her face as she bulled her way up to the front door. She stepped inside, turned up the thermostat, and kept her coat on as she stood near an old, cast-iron radiator to warm herself. The phone rang. She rushed into the living room and picked up the receiver. "Mom, you won't believe what I saw at the zoo today." Amber's voice was high and shrill.

"Tell me."

"A new baby elephant. Today was the first time that people got to see her. She's so cute! I want one."

Maddy laughed, "You're too funny. It sounds like you had fun."

"Abby came with us, and it was a scream."

"Any plans for tonight?"

"Abby's staying for a sleepover, and Mom, did you see the snow? Do you think maybe we won't have school Monday?"

"You never know. You guys have a blast tonight. Let me talk with Dad, please.... Love you."

"Hey, Maddy," Jack said.

"Jack, I'm investigating a missing kid, and I might have to work tomorrow. Can you keep Amber if need be?"

"Not a problem. She's been a peach all day."

"Thanks. I'll let you know what's going on tomorrow when I know more."

After she hung up, she knocked off a dish of leftovers from the fridge and trudged her way upstairs to the comfortable chair next to her bed. She grabbed her book and cozied up to read, but her mind was on autopilot and started to analyze everything she'd learned about the case.

That plaque on Sarah's pillow worries me. Maybe she killed herself. God knows she has reason to be depressed. She could have jumped in the river. Shit, we might never find the body. I've heard of kids her age hanging themselves. Maybe we should search the woods around her house.

Her mind raced as she went down to the pantry, pulled out a bottle of Merlot, and poured a glass. She sat in the only chair at the dining room table and emptied nine thousand pieces of her new jigsaw puzzle, *Tempest on the Sea*. She propped the empty box cover-up on an easel in front of the table where it was visible from every angle, and carefully scrutinized the picture.

A lone ship faltered in a storm, its masts tilting to nearly forty degrees. Waves crashed over its bow. Black, ominous clouds swirled overhead. In the far distance, a small break in the clouds let through streams of light that rested on the smashing sea. *There's something very odd about this,* Maddy thought as she tried to pinpoint what disturbed her about the puzzle. Then she recognized it. Barely noticeable, in a window of the ship, stood a silhouetted figure of a man. His features, almost indistinguishable from the shadows of the room he was in, gave Maddy the feeling that he enjoyed all the chaos, and maybe had even caused it.

What the hell is he doing there?

She sorted through the puzzle pieces but couldn't find the one with the man. "Ahh, I see. Your creator has made you difficult to find."

Maddy then focused on cloud pieces. She selected, sorted, and organized them into piles by shades of black, white, lavender, and gray, then placed them where they'd likely belong. When the wine began to muddy her thinking, she knew it was time to quit. Before she went up to bed, she stood before the easel and said, "Rest assured, I will find you."

Chapter 6

Maddy woke up the next morning to sunlight bursting through her window. She rolled over, shaded her eyes, and looked at the alarm clock. "10:12! Shit, I must have zonked." When she threw back the covers and got out of bed, a puff of cold air blew over her body: *Damn, it's cold in here. I never put the storm windows on. Should have let Jack do it.* She wrapped herself in a robe, walked to the window and gazed out. The reflection of sunlight glistening off several inches of snow pained her eyes.

She meandered downstairs, put on a pot of coffee, then grabbed the Sunday paper from the porch, and scanned the headlines. While she sipped her coffee, she wondered if Zep might call with an update on Sarah Benning. When it was almost noon, and she hadn't heard anything, Maddy decided to call Zep at home. "I hope I'm not bothering you."

"Not at all, Maddy, what's up?"

"I was wondering if you heard anything more about the Benning girl."

"No. Still no word from St. Lawrence County. Until we hear back, all we can do is sit tight. I'll call you if anything changes."

With Amber still at Jack's and nothing more she could do on the case, she thought about taking care of the storm windows. *No way am I doing that now.* She lay on the living room couch, covered up with a quilt, and drifted off into an afternoon nap. The phone rang. She opened her eyes, startled.

"Maddy?" Zep said, seeming excited.

"Yeah, I'm here," she said groggily.

"They reached Sarah's father at the hunting lodge. She's not been with him. Frank is back at his house. Can you get over there and interview him before it gets too late?"

"Sure thing."

"Let me know how that goes."

Maddy scrambled to get dressed, brought along a cup of the now-cold morning coffee in a mug, and started for Frank Benning's. When she arrived, she knocked on the door. It felt like an hour but was probably seven or eight minutes before a bearded man with long hair came to the door.

"Are you Frank Benning?"

"Yes," he said nervously, eyes bugged out of his head and the veins on his neck bulging. Before Maddy could get a word out, he snapped at her. "Do you know where my daughter is?"

Maddy stepped back. "Can I come in?"

"Oh...oh, of course." Maddy came in out of the cold and stood in the front hall. Cindy walked in from another room with her hands clasped together; her calm from the day before had disappeared.

"Mr. Benning, I don't know where Sarah is. I've come here to get information from you. I realize you are both anxious about her. I'm trying to put together the pieces so I can figure out where she might be and bring her home. If you don't mind, I have a few questions." Hesitantly, Frank agreed.

Maddy sat in the same chair as she had the day before. Frank and Cindy sat across from her. "What time did you leave for your lodge on Monday?"

"A little after seven p.m."

"Which route did you take when you left?"

"Route 5 West." Frank's face tightened; his lips curled, and his irritation was evident.

"Sarah left a house up the road about 7:05 p.m.," Maddy said. "The only road she could have been walking was Route 5. Did you see her?"

"What are you getting at?" Frank snarled; fists clenched.

Caught off guard, Maddy took a moment to compose herself. "It seems you should have driven right by her."

"I didn't see her!" he shouted. Cindy put her hand on Frank's shoulder.

Maddy remained quiet and looked at her notebook for a few minutes to give Frank a chance to calm down. Then she asked to see Sarah's bedroom. "Sure," Cindy interjected. They walked through the house to a room off a long hallway. A neatly made bed with a yellow comforter that had designs of orange butterflies resting on green plants stood in the middle of the room. On the desk, a goldfish bowl with blue pebbles had two giant angel fish that swam gracefully inside. A poster of the Marx Brothers with silly faces hung on a wall over the bed. Its frame matched the oak desk and the headboard of the bed.

"Does Sarah keep a diary?"

"Not that I know of," Frank said.

While Maddy asked questions, she opened drawers and shuffled items around on the dresser. "Where are some of the places Sarah has run away to in the past?" she asked, as she tried to keep the conversation alive while looking through Sarah's things for clues.

Cindy chimed in, "Once she tried to hitchhike to New York City on the Thruway, but the troopers picked her up and brought her home. Another time she went to Utica for a few days."

"Do you know where she stayed in Utica?"

"No, she just ended up coming home."

On a small bookshelf over the desk, a red wooden apple with a removable top caught Maddy's attention. She picked it up, took the lid off, and found a bunch of different colored elastic hair ties. Knick-knacks and books lined the shelf. Maddy thumbed through a few books. When she picked up *The Box Car Kids*, a valentine fell out onto the desk.

It seemed vintage and looked to Maddy to be from the nineteen-thirties. A naked cherub stood on a heart with a bow and an arrow ready to be released. The inside read:

My lady fair at Valentine,
When lovers pledge anew,
I send to you, to have and hold,
A loyal heart and true.

It was signed, "Mark."

"Do you know who gave her this?" Maddy asked as she handed it to Frank. He looked at it and gave it to Cindy. They both shook their heads.

"As far as I know, she doesn't know anyone named Mark," Frank said.

An alarm went off in Maddy's head. *Child predators groom their victims*, she recalled. *They give them little gifts and ask them to keep secrets.* She turned to Frank and Cindy. "It would be best if we go into another room. I have to call in a forensics team to go through this room with a fine-tooth..." But before she finished, Frank exploded.

"What the hell is this all about? Do you think I had something to do with this?" His face was red, and his hands shook. Cindy put her arm around his waist, trying to console him.

"I didn't say that, Mr. Benning. If the valentine was given to Sarah by someone whose intentions were not good, there might be other evidence here." Frank stormed out of the room.

"You know, he's not normally like this," Cindy said. "It's just that he's so upset about Sarah right now."

"Of course," said Maddy. She called Zep from the kitchen as she kept an eye on Sarah's room to make sure Frank and Cindy stayed out.

"I don't think we can rule out foul play, Zep."

"What do you have, Maddy?"

"I found a Valentine in Sarah's room. The father and his girlfriend hadn't seen it before. It was signed 'Mark,' and they don't know a Mark."

"Did you find out where in Utica she went the last time she took off?"

"No one has any idea."

"Okay. I'll send Forensics over, but make sure you keep them out of that room. We don't need Frank Benning washing it down with Clorox right under our noses."

By the time the forensics team finished with Sarah's room, it was almost nine thirty. Maddy smoothed things over with Frank and Cindy as best she could before she left. It was after ten thirty when she finally walked in her front door, and she called Jack to say goodnight to Amber.

"Sorry, Maddy, she's asleep."

"Shit! Tell her I'll call tomorrow."

She put on her sweats and favorite black sweater, the one with the holes in the sleeves, and a pair of loose-fitting wool socks. She went downstairs, poured a glass of wine, and proceeded to the Tempest on the Sea. But when she looked at the thousands of puzzle pieces, her mind said "No" and wanted instead to analyze the case, so she let it.

Martha has a lot of pent up rage. Is it possible that under the right circumstance, she might harm her child? And Frank is wound up so tight he might blow a gasket over anything. How is it that he didn't see Sarah on the road? I need to know more about that guy. I'm not sure about Cindy. She'll cover Frank's ass no matter what, I think. But the question is, just how far will she go? Then there's Mary, sweet Mary. She has no motive and is as kind as they come. But it's the valentine that's scaring the shit out of me.

Maddy's thoughts became heavy from the wine. She walked up to the bed, pulled a journal from her nightstand drawer, and wrote: "Sarah wanders the streets tonight, her whereabouts unknown, and I'm worried about my child too, right here within my own home."

Chapter 7

The next morning Maddy decided to pick up cinnamon rolls on her way to work. She pulled up to the Friendly Bean, a boutique-style bakeshop and restaurant. It was a place that always put her mind at ease. *I need a Friendly Bean fix today*, she said to herself as she got out of the car.

Rusty was the heart and soul of the Bean. He was the owner and kept the place lively with humor and witty chitchat. Less than a block from headquarters, it was almost always filled with cops. "Did you see what our brilliant Mayor is up to now?" or "When will they ever fix those potholes on Main Street?" were typical conversational topics that lightened everyone's spirits before heading in to work.

When Maddy opened the door, a tapestry of aromas—cinnamon, fresh bread, and newly brewed coffee—greeted her.

"There she is. Now my day is made." Rusty's loud voice rang through the restaurant from the front counter, where he sat with a few customers. "How ya doing, Maddy?"

"Doing well, Rusty. How about yourself?"

"As good as can be expected for an old fool," he chuckled as he walked over.

"What's good today?" she asked as soft reggae music played in the background. It felt like valium to her soul.

"Well, let's see, in addition to our world-famous cinnamon rolls, today we have a raspberry tart, cheese Danish, blueberry muffins, and apple pie, just like mama used to make," he said, as he smacked his lips.

"Hmm, I'm afraid I'm going to be an old fuddy-duddy and go with the cinnamon rolls. I'll take a dozen." Artie, who worked behind the counter, started to fill her order.

"Why don't ya have a seat and chat a bit?" Rusty asked.

"I have a few minutes, sure." She sat at his table, and Artie placed a cup of coffee on the table for her.

"So, how is Amber doing these days," Rusty asked.

"She is entering the "boy" stage," Maddy laughed, "and it scares me."

"We all went through it, Maddy. Does she have a particular boyfriend?"

"Not yet, but there's a boy named Ben that she talks about all the time."

"'Deep as love, deep as first love, and wild with all regret,' the words of Tennyson are so true, aren't they?" Maddy grimaced at the thought of her daughter being in love, but she remembered how it was when she was Amber's age, and indeed it was beautiful.

"Well, I guess I'll just have to muddle my way through it," she said. She glanced at her watch. "Oh, my God, I really have to get going." She reached for her purse to pay for the coffee.

Rusty put his hand on her wrist. "The rolls and the coffee are on me today."

"You're too kind, Rusty," Maddy said as she walked out of the restaurant. It felt like she was walking out of a great movie. As she pulled into the department parking lot, she was startled to see Al Ramirez rushing to his car. "What's going on, Al?" she asked when she rolled down the window.

"Zep will fill you in. You better get upstairs. He's waiting in his office." Al's unshakably calm demeanor was shaken. Maddy left her placid feelings from the Friendly Bean in the parking lot, and when the elevator door opened, she stepped into a room of deadly serious people rushing around the office.

What the hell's going on? She dropped the cinnamon rolls on her desk as she hurried to Zep's office, where he stood with his arms folded and his coat on.

"They found the body of a girl that fits Sarah Benning's description at a construction site. Come on, let's go, you drive." Maddy felt sucker punched. Her heart pounded as they rushed to the car. On the way, Zep asked, "Have you ever been involved in a child murder case before? It can get the best of even the most seasoned detectives." It was not the time to open up childhood wounds, so Maddy remained silent.

When they pulled up to the construction site, the scene screamed of a tragedy—flashing lights, squad car doors left open, and men in hardhats from a construction crew racing in the same direction. It looked like something out of *The Blob*, but it wasn't, it was real. Maddy's thoughts ran wild. *It's not a car accident; it's not a fire—it's a dead kid we're going to. Can it be Sarah?*

Maddy lost Zep among a sea of men in hardhats. Their necks stretched up, trying to look above the person in front of them. Their heavy work boots made a sloshing sound in the mud as they seemed to dance for a better position to get a peek at the spectacle.

"Sheriff—make way. Sheriff—make way," Maddy shouted. The further forward she moved the stronger the foul smell of urine, feces, and disinfectant grew. She saw a small opening in the crowd just ahead and edged her way into it. A man down on one knee looked down into the mud, vomiting. Another man stood near with a hand on his shoulder as if trying to console him.

As she neared the front of the mob, a middle-aged man on her left nudged her. She turned and looked into his tear-filled eyes. He outstretched his glove-covered hand, and on it was a pair of little girl's underwear, soaked in blood, with the crotch ripped open. "I found these," he said. Maddy's body stiffened, and her eyes widened. She backed away, too stunned to say or do anything, then turned and forced her way forward until she finally broke through.

The naked body of a girl lay on the floor of a portable toilet. Her skin was waxen white, and a reddish-brown streak of dried blood ran from her buttocks to the floor. Toilet paper, strewn about like streamers in the aftermath of a New Year's Eve party, was everywhere, and a cake of urinal disinfectant soap leaned up against the girl's head. A rag doll lay nearby, and a torn purple dress, several feet away, was sopped in the mud. *That's Sarah Benning*, Maddy acknowledged to herself. *And that's her doll, Jenny.*

Maddy's arms and legs lost all strength, her insides shuddered, and her core became as cold as winter as she squatted next to the body. A feeling of unreality shrouded over her. For a moment, she forgot where she was. The stink of the portable toilet gathered in her throat, and she began to gag. Suddenly aware of dozens of men gazing on like vultures eyeballing roadkill, she got up, turned to the crowd, and screamed, "Somebody cover her."

The men jolted back at the shrill of her voice. A few looked away in shame. A man standing nearby held a blue plastic tarp. Maddy ripped it from his hands, shook it open and gently floated it down over Sarah's body. She lowered herself with the tarp to one knee and then looked down into the mud. The touch of a hand on her shoulder startled her; jerking around, Maddy saw Zep. She felt the muscles in her face contort, and tears run down her cheek. She then bolted to the car and buried her head in her arms.

After he gave directives to bring the scene under control, Zep came over to Maddy. Like a coach encouraging his star quarterback to get back on the field after throwing an interception, he said, "Come on, Maddy, there's a lot to be done now. These guys will take care of the scene. I need you to complete your report with as much detail as possible and get it out to law enforcement in the area." Maddy unburied her head. "When you finish, get back over to Mary Thompson's and find out if there's anything more she can tell us."

The humiliation Maddy felt disappeared. Her thoughts moved from guilt to following orders, and it was what she needed. Implicit in Zep's words was the notion that all cops are human and break sometimes; when they do, they have to get back up and keep moving.

By the time Maddy left the construction site, the sky had darkened. As she drove back to the office, she struggled to fight off images of Sarah on the floor of the portable toilet. She finished her report and headed back out to Mary Thompson's. As she arrived, snowflakes swirled around in the wind. Mary sat on her porch. She wore a heavy black coat with her hands buried in the pockets. Her gaze was far away, and her face etched in stone. Before Maddy uttered a word, Mary spoke. "I know why you're here. I don't know anything more than what I told you yesterday."

Maddy stopped. The wind blew snow in her face and flakes attached to her eyelashes. "How did you hear?" she shouted over the sound of rustling leaves.

"News travels fast around here, especially when it's bad."

"I'm sorry. I know you cared a great deal for Sarah."

"You know, I've heard it said that to harm a child is to make an angel cry. Today, there must be a host of angels crying for little Sarah. Although I must say, the poor thing is happier now with the Lord than she could ever be in this world."

Maddy looked down, turned, and started to walk back to the car. She heard a voice behind her shout, "Be careful. I have a bad feeling that things are going to get a lot worse before they get better."

Chapter 8

Nigel, 1954, London, England

"Ouch." Nigel winced as he pulled the bandage off the hole Mother had put in his face. "God, that's ugly," he said out loud, looking in a mirror at the bloody mess. He gently touched around the edges of the wound, and fearful it might get infected, pulled out a bottle of distilled water and washed it.

Nigel had remained hidden in his room all night, and the next morning the popping sound of a VW engine sent him to the window. He saw Mother's VW Bug sputtering down the street. *This is my chance; I have to get out of here.* He ran to the kitchen, stuffed a handful of Cheerios in his mouth, and took off on his bicycle to Paul's flat.

"Oh my God, what happened to your face?" Paul's mother shrieked when she opened the door.

"I fell off my bike."

"Oh, poor dear. Step inside, let me put something on that." Reluctantly, he walked in and let her put iodine and a fresh bandage on his wound.

"Stay for lunch, Nigel," Paul's mother said sternly. "We're only having tuna fish sandwiches and tomato soup, but I insist."

Famished, Nigel agreed. A bowl of peanuts on the kitchen counter caught his eye, and Paul's mother noticed him gazing at it. "Go ahead, help yourself," she said. He took a hand full, put some in his mouth, and the rest in his pocket.

"I never get to have peanuts at my house because my sister has a peanut allergy."

"That's very dangerous, you know."

"What do you mean?"

"Well, a person with that kind of allergy can die with just the smallest amount of peanut."

"I knew peanuts could make her sick, but I didn't realize they could kill her."

"It's true, so be sure to wash your hands before you leave."

Paul's mother peppered Nigel with questions during lunch. "What does your father do? How is it I never see him? Which church do you go to? I see your mother leave the house late; does she have a night job?" *What a pain in the ass*, he thought.

As Nigel slugged down the last of his milk, Paul asked if he wanted to play some chess. "Now, Paul, that's not fair." Paul's mother interrupted and turned to Nigel. "Paul's won the regional chess tournament for his age group three years in a row. He's been playing a long time. Why don't you boys go outside and ride your bikes; it's a beautiful day."

"I'd like to learn how to play chess," Nigel said.

"Great. Come on; I'll show you how."

In the den, two thickly padded black leather chairs stood up against a table with inlaid gray and white marble squares. White and black chess pieces, nearly the size of billiard balls, were lined up on each side like two armies about to face off. Paul explained the concepts behind chess as he held each piece and described its movements on the chessboard.

"It's a game of strategy, Nigel. The goal is to keep your king safe while you figure out how to entrap your opponent's king. When you get good, you think several moves ahead and anticipate your opponent's moves before he makes them. If you have a response planned, you'll crush him."

"Very interesting."

"Come on, let's play." Paul looked at Nigel like he was about to devour an ice cream sundae. Nigel knew Paul was eager to beat him, but he was willing to take a licking to gain the knowledge of strategy, the hallmark of chess.

The match progressed slowly, and Paul thought a long time before each move. But for Nigel, it was like returning a serve in a ping pong match; he responded quickly. Nearly an hour and a half had gone by when Paul's mother stuck her head in the door. "You boys are quiet in there." She looked at her son and said, "Are you okay, Paul? You don't look well." Paul didn't answer.

After several minutes of contemplating a move, Paul reached out, picked up his Queen, hovered it over Nigel's king, and said, "Checkmate!" He slumped back in his chair, let his hands fall to his side, and appeared relieved to have averted an embarrassing loss to a novice.

The second game went differently. "Shit!" Paul shouted in frustration several times. Nigel knew what Paul was thinking: "This isn't supposed to happen. I should be killing this guy," and when the game ended in a stalemate, Paul yelled, "Damn."

"Paul!" his mother shouted from the kitchen. "That's enough chess for today."

Over the next week, Nigel spent afternoons at the library reading up on chess strategy and was amazed at how much there was to know. When he met Paul for another match, it lasted nearly four hours. Although Paul won, Nigel did not see it as a setback, but as a mark of his progress. It wasn't the game itself that mattered, but the ability to manage situations strategically and achieve the outcomes he wanted.

Within just a few weeks, Nigel defeated Paul. He reached over, grabbed his queen, held it over Paul's king, and said, "Checkmate." In Nigel's head, however, he said, "Checkmate, motherfucker," deriving pleasure in Paul's misery as he watched his eyes glare, and his face turn pink.

For Nigel, it was as though he had attained a new weapon. It was the power of thought unencumbered by feelings, and he believed that its applications went far beyond chess and to uses he had only begun to imagine.

The sun was descending behind the houses as Nigel rode his bike home after his victory. But it wasn't chess that was on his mind; it was

Mother and Gertie. *I wonder if they're in there.* He leaned his bike up against the back-yard fence, stuck his head in the kitchen, and found the house eerily quiet. He crept upstairs, opened the door, and in shock, seethed as he gazed at his ransacked room. Torn out pages from his journal strewn on his desk, gems from his collection scattered on the bed, and the lapidary polisher left running, pointed to Gertie as the culprit.

"Where's Jade?" He said out loud. "You just couldn't leave things alone, could you, Gertie?" He started for the door, then suddenly stopped. The words, "Think chess," popped into his head. He realized that he was in a chess match with Gertie. *She made the first move. Now she wants me to respond by blowing up. Sure, that's what she wants. Then Mother will get involved, and I'll get a beating. Well, I'm not going to take the bait.*

Nigel sat on the floor, put his hands over his face, closed his eyes, and took deep breaths, repeating to himself over and over, *don't take the bait.* When his anger subsided, he began a search for Jade. Thinking strategically, he imagined the carpet was a chessboard and searched each square before moving to the next. Within minutes he found the beloved stone under the bed.

The notion of harnessing the power of thoughts over feelings gave Nigel a sense of control that he had never had before. *I can accomplish things I never imagined.* Then it hit him: *I could even kill Gertie!* He mulled the thought over throughout the day, but by the next morning, when he saw kids riding their bikes in the sunshine, it had left him.

Maybe Paul's up and would like to go riding. He headed to the yard to get his bike, but Gertie's shrill voice came from inside the house and caught him off guard. "Mother, Nigel ate my Cheerios and left the box open. Now they're stale." He froze. Mother's bedroom door slammed, and he heard the sounds of heavy feet thud down the stairs.

"I'm going to kill that bastard," he heard her say. "Where is he?" she asked when she reached the kitchen.

Nigel bolted for his bike, hopped on, and went for the street. He pumped the pedals as fast as he could, but it felt like he was barely moving.

Mother screamed, "Get back here." He looked over his shoulder and saw her running behind him in her bare feet and a nightgown. He stood on the pedals and pushed with all his weight, and when he was finally at a safe distance, he heard her scream, "Wait till I get my hands on you."

Tears and snot blew back on his face as he pulled away. He turned in to an empty wood lot, dismounted, and walked his bike back to where no one could see. He got off, knelt, and retched. It felt like the time he had food poisoning, but nothing came out. Nigel wished he were dead. He rolled on his side and stared past the trees into nothingness. *What am I going to do now?* He closed his eyes, and his mind drifted back to the dark place within himself. "Mother hates me and wishes me dead." The door inside blew open again, and feelings that smelled as rank as dead animal carcasses overwhelmed him.

"It's not fair," he wailed. "I didn't do anything to deserve this."

The door that had opened only slightly before was blown off its hinges and pent-up rage poured out like a tidal wave. *I can't keep on this way. I have to do something. If I run away, they'll only catch me and send me back.* He remembered to think strategically, like in chess, and the notion of killing Gertie returned. *But will that make any difference?* He answered his own question. *Gertie is at the bottom of every beating I get. If she's not around, I'll just stay out of Mother's way. She'll probably leave me alone.*

The sun cast long shadows in the patch of woods. Nigel found a candy bar in his jacket, sat up, and ate it. He listened to the breeze blow through the treetops and wondered how he might kill his sister and not get caught. Every possibility that he thought of pointed right back to him. He began to rebuke himself. *This is stupid; it can't be done.* He felt like he was drowning and needed someone to throw him a lifeline. Then it dawned on him: someone had, and of all people, it was Paul's mother. *Peanuts!*

For several weeks, Nigel made himself invisible in his house. He recorded observations about Mother and Gertie's daily rituals in a notebook and tried to identify patterns in their behavior. *I think I've got it;* he concluded one night. *Breakfast, that's the best time to get peanut powder into Gertie.*

After researching allergic reactions to peanuts at the library, he determined that it would take ten minutes for Gertie to die by asphyxiation once she ingested the crushed-up nuts. Critical to his plan were the calculations of time. *Gertie eats breakfast in the kitchen at 9:00 while she watches Howdy Doody. On certain days Mother goes into the bathroom about 8:45 to take a shower and comes out about 9:15. That gives me enough time to get the powder in the cereal milk while Mother is distracted and before Gertie goes into the kitchen. The problem is, Mother is inconsistent about the days she goes in the shower at that time.*

Nigel studied Mother's showering habits carefully. He recorded her routines before and after a shower and hoped to predict the days she went in by eight forty-five. *That will give me enough time.*

After gathering all the data and analyzing it thoroughly, he realized that *Midnight Matinee* was the key. *On mornings after Mother stays up late to watch Midnight Matinee, she enters the shower about 8:45. Now I have everything I need.*

Chapter 9

Nigel was almost asleep, and somewhere in the haze between wakefulness and slumber, he heard music. It was a television commercial. Gradually he awakened and realized it was Mother's television. The clock read 11:57 p.m. *This is it!* He jumped out of bed, put his head to his door, and listened. It was the theme music of Midnight Matinee. He ran to his dresser, opened the top drawer, grabbed a vial of powder that he had ground from the peanuts that he'd taken from Paul's house, and reached under his bed for two empty milk bottles.

Quietly, he crept down the stairs to check the refrigerator for milk. *There's more than enough*, he thought, then returned to his bedroom and waited for the television to turn off. *Perfect. Now to be patient and wait until morning.* He couldn't sleep. His mind raced, and as he stared at the ceiling, he thought about turning back. *But if I do, I'll just be a punching bag again for Gertie and Mother. I have no choice but to do this.*

When light gathered outside his window, Nigel got up to look at the street below. A soft rain fell, and he wondered where he'd be by the end of the fateful day. At a little past six a.m., he went down to the refrigerator with the two empty bottles and poured a cup of milk in each, then returned to his room. Just a few light taps on the glass vial slid the peanut powder into one of the milk bottles. A few stirs and shakes, and he was ready to go.

"Right on time," he thought when Mother walked into the bathroom at 8:52 and the shower water began to run. Gertie played in the living room. When he heard her walk into the kitchen and turn on the TV, he softly said, "Perfect!" He slipped the bottle of tainted milk under his loose-fitting shirt, and calmly walked back to the kitchen, opened the refrigerator door, and swapped the peanut milk for the untainted milk. Laughing at a commercial, Gertie ignored him, and he walked back up to his room. When he closed the bedroom door, his heart accelerated, and it took several deep breaths to calm it down.

Okay, Gertie, now fill your bowl with Cheerios and watch Howdy Doody. As if he had magical powers, Gertie seemed to follow his commands. From the top of the stairs, he listened to the sounds of the cereal bits striking a bowl and he could hear the shower water running as well. A tingling sensation in his abdomen turned into exhilaration as his plan executed. Nigel expected to hear death sounds from Gertie but instead heard only silence. *Shit, what's going on. Maybe I didn't use enough peanut powder.* When the shower water stopped running, his stomach dropped, and he ran back to his room.

The air in his lungs felt thin, and it was hard to breathe. He didn't have a plan for things going wrong. But then a loud crash, a thud, and the tinkling of silverware hitting the ceramic floor washed his fears away. *That was Gertie,* Nigel thought excitedly. It was a critical juncture, and plenty could still go wrong. *Please stay in the bathroom, Mother.* If Mother came out at that moment, she would hear Gertie, save her, and his scheme would be exposed.

"Mother! Mother! Nigel! Someone help me," a muffled, raspy voice cried out. *Stay in the bathroom, Mother, stay in the bathroom, please,* Nigel thought. The fan in the bathroom was loud and always drowned out other sounds. *I don't believe Mother can hear her.*

Nigel waited the required ten minutes, peeked out his door, and was relieved to find Mother still in the bathroom. He flew down to the kitchen with the untainted milk in his hand. Gertie was lying face up with her eyes bugging out in their sockets, mouth open and vomit smeared around her lips.

He took the tainted milk from the counter, put it in a plastic bag, and replaced it with the untainted container. He snatched up the cereal bowl from the table and the silverware off the floor, put them in a seperate plastic bag, and replaced them with untainted items. To make Gertie's breakfast appear as if it had been eaten as usual, he rinsed out the cereal bowl with water, and poured in some good milk and a little cereal from the box.

Suddenly struck with a bolt of fear, Nigel heard the bathroom door open and Mother's door shut. *Don't panic, Nigel, just follow the plan; just follow the plan!* a voice within him said. He took the bags with the tainted contents to the back garden and shoved them behind a loose clapboard. The rain had stopped, the sun shone, and Nigel casually walked to the front of the house to sit on the step. He pulled a handful of rocks from his jacket pocket and began to polish them with a rag.

Time dragged as he waited for Mother to discover Gertie. He scolded himself to stop looking at his watch and to act naturally. As the minutes passed, his stomach tightened, and he had to fight the urge to go back in the house, discover the body himself, and call out to his mother. Then a shrill voice shrieked, "Help, help, help, help!" It brought him both relief and fear. When he went inside, he tried to act genuinely panicked, but Mother didn't seem to buy it and did not look at him.

"Oh my God," he said, as he tried to stay in the role.

Mother kept her face turned in the other direction, held Gertie in her arms and moaned, "My poor baby," over and over.

"I'll call an ambulance." Nigel dashed to the phone and said something that he wished he hadn't. "Poor Gertie." With her eyes fixed wide, Mother lifted her head and glared at him. *She knows.*

As he waited at the front step for the ambulance, a tingling sensation grew in his abdomen, then moved to his genitals, made them throb, and he ejaculated. *How did that happen?* He felt his face grow warm, and he looked down to check for evidence on his trousers, but there wasn't any.

When the ambulance arrived, two medics got out, Nigel pointed to the inside of the house and they rushed in, and he followed. One put an arm around Mother, lifted her to her feet, and said, "Come, let us work on her," and helped her to the next room. The other cleaned vomit from Gertie's face and tried to revive her. *It's way too late for that*, Nigel thought, quite satisfied that he had waited the required amount of time. His greatest challenge at that moment was to hide his delight. He walked back to the front steps where he could be less visible, sat with his face buried in his hands, and pretended to cry. When Gertie was in the ambulance, Mother told the medics that she wanted to go along.

"What about your son? There's not enough room for both of you," a medic said. Mother grimaced, said nothing, and hopped in the back before the ambulance sped off.

Nigel had no plan for what came next. *Now what?* He wondered as he sat in the living room. A sense of anticipation slowly faded into monotony. He felt like he should be doing something, but didn't know what. He wracked his brain and thought, *What would someone do in a situation like this? Geez, I need to call the fucking hospital and check on Gertie's condition.*

A woman with a smooth voice came to the phone when he asked about Gertie. "My sister came to the hospital this morning, and I'm really worried about her."

The woman said, "I'm afraid your sister didn't recover. I'm so sorry. We've been trying to sort things out here with your mother, and well," she hesitated and started to stumble over her words before she finally said, "someone will be out to speak with you soon. Please be patient."

Sort things out, he repeated to himself. *What the fuck does that mean?* Half an hour passed before Nigel saw a brown Ford with two people inside pull up to the front of his house. He tried to look despondent when he answered the door. A man and a woman dressed in plain clothes stood outside. "Can we come in?" the woman asked. Nigel brought them into the living room, where they sat down.

Feigning a cracking voice, Nigel said, "I called the hospital, and they said Gertie died. I just can't believe it."

The woman detective waited for him to compose himself, then asked, "Can you explain what you were doing at the time of the tragedy?" He put his hands to his head and propped his elbows on his knees. "I was polishing some rocks on the front stoop when I heard Mother scream."

"Your mother said you hated your sister," the male detective said in a harsh tone. Nigel looked at him, and a surge of anger bubbled up inside.

Chapter 9

"We had our disagreements, and she was an awful pesky eight-year-old, but she was my sister, and I loved her."

"Can we look around?" the woman asked.

"Sure."

The man went to the car and brought in a box labeled "Sample Collection Kit." The detectives spent a long time in the kitchen while Nigel waited anxiously in the living room. The sounds of cupboard doors and drawers opening and closing made him start to question himself. *Did I forget anything? I can't remember if I replaced the towel I used to wipe the floor.* On and on, his mind raced. He reviewed each step of his plan until he was interrupted by another knock at the door.

"Hi. I'm Diana Nelson, and I'm a social worker." She asked to come in, and they sat across from each other in the living room. She tried to strike up a conversation. "I'm very sorry for your loss, Nigel."

Nigel looked down with as sullen an expression as he could muster.

"I have been with your mother, and needless to say, she is beside herself with grief."

I'm sure she is, Nigel thought.

"Strangely, and I am sorry to say, she doesn't want to see you."

He looked at her, faked surprise and hurt, then put his face in his hands and pretended to cry. Diana came over and sat next to him and put her arm around his shoulder. "I don't know what was happening among the three of you, but the death of a family member can bring out feelings that we don't know we have. That must be what is happening with your mum."

With his guts in turmoil, Nigel thought, *Get away from me, lady.* Finally, she walked back to the other chair, opened her briefcase, and pulled out a folder. "It appears that except for your father, who lives in the United States, you have no family nearby to stay with. Until we can sort things out, you'll have to live with a foster family."

"Can't I stay here?"

"You're only twelve, Nigel. We can't leave you here alone. You'll have to go into foster care where we can begin family therapy and start working you back to living with your mum.

Bullshit, he thought.

That evening, after several hours in the social services office, Nigel was taken to the Nelson family for temporary foster care until a permanent solution to his family circumstance was addressed. Tim and Brenda Nelson were the foster parents and seemed okay to him. They didn't ask much, only that he be present at mealtime and respectful to the rest of the family. They had three kids of their own and made a temporary home for three others, all younger than Nigel.

So, this is how a typical family operates? he thought after a few days at the Nelsons'. It was enlightening to see family members getting along respectfully with one another. Ten-year-old Eric took a liking to him and would ask to play checkers. He accommodated, but deep down, he was envious that Eric had it so much easier that than he did.

One morning, Brenda came up to Nigel's room and told him he had a visitor. He walked downstairs, and in the front room, a man in a leather coat stood looking out the front window with his back to him. Brenda left them alone.

"Hi Nigel, remember me?" the man said when he turned around. Nigel felt a vague sense of familiarity, but he could not place him.

"I'm your father. It's been a long time, I know, but I'm here to take you with me to live in Chicago." Nigel didn't know what to say. Inside, his emotions bounced around like a pinball, hitting rejection, anger, warmth, and excitement.

"A lot has gone on behind the scenes that you don't know about," his father said. "Your mother thinks you killed Gertie and has tried to have you prosecuted. The police haven't found enough evidence to support her claim, so you're out of the woods. Gertie died of an allergic reaction to peanuts. The police concluded that her cereal must have gotten contaminated at the factory." Nigel felt an air of unreality flow into the room.

"The thing is...well, your mother wants nothing more to do with you."

Nigel thought it was odd that he felt pain when his father said that. He knew Mother hated him, but the words hurt none the less.

"I know I left you behind in that awful situation when you were little. I'm sorry. But I couldn't take you where I was going. You were too young. But if you want to come with me now, I have airline tickets right here in my pocket. It's up to you."

"Yes. Yes, I'll come."

"All right then, get your stuff and let's blow this popsicle stand."

Later that afternoon, as they flew over the only city he had ever lived in, Nigel looked down from the plane at the houses below. A feeling of elation overcame him. *I did it,* he said to himself, and at that moment, felt he could do anything he put his mind to.

Chapter 10

Maddy, 1978, Utica, New York

"Are we almost ready to eat, Mom? I'm starving," Amber whined when she walked into the smoke-filled kitchen, drawn by the smell of hamburgers sizzling on the stove.

"Almost." Maddy tried to carry out the motions of normalcy for Amber's sake while images of Sarah's body intruded into her thoughts.

"Are you okay, Mom? You don't look well."

"I'm fine, just a little tired."

The stench of feces and urine that lingered in her olfactory neurons caused the ground meat to smell spoiled, and all of her movements required extra effort, as though she had a hangover.

"Mom, tell me what's wrong!" Amber insisted.

Maddy knew she couldn't fake her feelings for long. "When we finish eating, help me with the dishes, then we'll talk." After they ate and the last of the silverware was put away, they walked into the living room and sat across from one another.

"So, what is it, Mom? You look like you did the day you told me Dad and you were getting a divorce."

Maddy spoke from her gut. "Remember the other day when I told you I was investigating a runaway girl?"

"Yes."

"She was found dead today. Her name was Sarah, and she was about your age. She was murdered, and I think she suffered a great deal before she died."

Amber got up without saying a word, walked over to her mother, and put her arms around her. "That must have been terrible. I can't imagine what it must have been like."

Mother and daughter comforted one another, and when Maddy started to nod off, she noticed that Amber had already fallen asleep. "Come on, honey. Let's go up." Once Amber was in bed, Maddy came back down and stopped by the pantry, grabbed a new bottle of wine, and brought it to the living room, where she sat in the dark.

She was filled with guilt and began to play prosecutor against herself, as though she was on trial. *You missed something in your investigation, Ms. Reynolds. Why didn't you stay on the case 24/7? Why didn't you request roadblocks around the area? Perhaps a car with the child might have been stopped, and she'd be alive today. You should have followed up further on Sara's trip into Utica. Your first case and look what happened. Are you sure you're cut out for this job, Maddy Reynolds?*

The phone rang and interrupted Maddy's self-flagellation. *I'm not in the mood to talk with anyone right now*, she thought sulkily, and let it ring. But something deep inside tugged at her until she finally picked up the receiver.

"Maddy," she heard a familiar voice.

"Is that you, Sherlock?" she asked.

"Yes. I was just sitting here working on my puzzle, and you popped in my mind. How's it going?"

Maddy had met Harvey at an international puzzle conference years earlier. He was an avid puzzle enthusiast like herself, lived in San Francisco, and although he was quite a bit older, they had a lot in common and had become friends. Harvey was the most analytic person she'd ever known, and she had nicknamed him after Conan Doyle's famous sleuth.

"I've had better days. How about you?"

"I'm Okay. Have you started that new puzzle yet? What's it called? 'Stormy Sea'?"

Maddy laughed. "'Tempest on the Sea.' Yeah, and it's bizarre."

"How so?"

She described the ship and the shadowy figure. "I've never seen anything like it before. The man looks like he's controlling the storm from within his cabin. It's weird."

"That is odd. I wonder what it means."

"Okay, Sherlock, what do you think it means?" she said in a slightly sarcastic tone, sensing his analytic mind kicking into gear.

"Well, are you involved in anything nefarious?"

His words sent a chill over her body. It was as though a window had opened, and a cool breeze entered the room. Caught off guard, she remained silent, then asked, "Why do you ask that?"

"Sometimes, a puzzle finds its way to me for reasons beyond my understanding. If you ask me that shadowy figure is symbolic of a diabolical force."

Shit! Maddy thought. *How does he do that?* Her voice cracked as she started to speak and she said, "Sorry, Sherlock, I'm tired, and I have had too much wine. You caught me on a bad day."

"Would you like me to call at another time?"

"No, no. It's just that there's so much happening that it's hard to know where to start."

"Try the beginning."

Like a truth serum, the wine did its work, and although she knew she shouldn't discuss the case, she opened up.

"I was given my very first assignment the other day. An eleven-year-old girl had run away, and I was assigned to track her down. This morning she was found dead, brutally raped, and her body discarded like yesterday's newspaper." Maddy's tone increased in intensity as she spoke. "Harvey, she was just eleven! Amber's age!" She sat on the couch, elbow on her knee and a hand propping up her head, and she strained to pronounce each word as tears flowed down her face. Harvey remained silent.

"I'm sorry, Sherlock," she said painfully. "I guess I'm questioning whether I'm cut out for this."

Harvey finally spoke. "Evil is all around us, Maddy. The worst day of my life was when I sent a squad of men on a mission of questionable importance to check out a village." Harvey was a major during the Korean War, one of only a few black men to reach such a rank at the time. His wounds put him in a wheelchair, though this circumstance only seemed to make him wiser.

"The men were captured and tortured to death. I was there when they found the bodies, and until that moment, I didn't realize that human beings could do such things to other human beings."

Maddy could hear Harvey's voice lower and become raspy as he talked. "Once you see with your own eyes what evil can do, you're never the same." A long pause followed. "Listen to what I am going to tell you, Maddy. You must do the work you're doing. You have been chosen for this mission. You must shake off yesterday and keep pursuing this monster."

In a tired voice, drained of all energy, Maddy exhaled a heavy breath, and said, "Thank you." After several moments of silence, she added, "I need to get to bed—nice talking to you. I'll be in touch. Goodnight, Sherlock."

"Goodnight," Harvey said. "And Maddy..."

"Yeah?"

"Beware of the man in the ship."

After she hung up with Harvey, Maddy stayed on the couch with the lights off. Tired, but too wired to sleep, her mind drifted back in time to a Halloween night when she was twelve. The scent of a bonfire filled the air, and kids laughed and paraded up and down her street in costumes. A strange, odd-shaped moon hung above.

"Hey, Maddy," a voice called out to her as she sat on her front step. Janet, her best friend, dressed as Athena, the Greek goddess, broke away from a group of goblins and ghosts and ran up the steps to where Maddy sat holding her stomach.

"What are you doing here? I thought you were trick-or-treating with your dad."

"He's not coming."

"Does he have to work late?"

"No. He's been injured."

"Gosh, I'm sorry." Janet reached into her bag of loot, pulled out a handful of chocolate kisses, and handed them to Maddy. "Want some? They're your favorite. They'll make you feel better."

Maddy took a few pieces and opened one. "I'm worried about my dad. He's in the hospital. Someone's on their way to get me."

"He'll probably be okay, Maddy. The doctors here are excellent. Try not to worry."

"Yeah, I hope you're right."

A pair of headlights pulled up. "I've got to go, Janet." The two friends hugged, and Maddy ran to the car. She hopped in and turned to her father's partner, "What happened to my father, Uncle Bob?" Bob Bennett was also her father's best friend, and Maddy expected honest answers, but instead, he hesitated and stumbled over his words.

"Your dad, well, he's injured," he said, then hesitated and added, "Badly."

"What happened, Uncle Bob?" she screamed in frustration.

"He was stabbed."

Maddy gasped and, for a moment, couldn't breathe, then yelled out, "Will he be all right?"

"I don't know."

"You don't know? Where was he stabbed?"

She watched Bob's face strain as he wrestled with his words. "In the back of his neck."

Maddy thrust her face into her hands and whimpered, "My poor daddy," then turned to Bob. "Why didn't you stop it? You're his partner!"

"I was on a special assignment today and wasn't with him. Another detective went in my place and was killed. I'm so sorry this happened. I wish I had been there."

A long silence passed before Maddy spoke. "Did they catch the guy?"

"No, he got away."

She turned toward the window and gazed absently out at buildings and people zipping by. Trick-or-treaters swarmed the neighborhood streets as Bob drove to the hospital. One, dressed as the devil, looked right at her when they passed by. As he followed her with his eyes, goosebumps ran up her arms like droplets of ice. She had heard stories about evil spirits that came out on Halloween night and wondered if that devil was one. Spooked, she looked over her shoulder into the back seat to make sure it was empty.

Maddy's thoughts turned to what might have happened to her father. "Why was Dad after the man in the first place?"

Bob's lips tightened, and again he seemed to struggle to find the right words. "You're upset right now," he said. "Maybe we should talk about this later."

"I want to know, Uncle Bob, please tell me."

He pushed himself back in his seat and took a deep breath. "He killed little girls...at least two. Maybe more."

The words, "He killed little girls," ricocheted around in her brain like a cue ball on a pool table. She fell back in her seat, and with her mouth opened, she thought of the devil who had stared at her. *Maybe he stabbed Dad and wants to hurt me too.* Aware that she was becoming unraveled, Maddy tried to calm herself, and stayed silent the rest of the way to the hospital.

When they arrived, they stopped to check in at the front desk in the lobby. "James Reynolds is in the ICU," they were told. "Since you are immediate family, you are allowed to visit him."

Bob led the way to the Intensive Care Unit, and when they reached the double doors, Maddy stopped dead in her tracks. "What's wrong, Maddy?"

"That's where Mom was the night of her accident. She died in there."

"You don't have to go in if you don't want to," Bob said as he put his arm around her shoulder.

"I'll go. I need to see Dad."

When they walked in, a nurse who seemed to be expecting them said, "I'm Sally, I'll bring you to your father." A sicky-sweet, disinfectant smell filled the air of a large, brightly lit room. They passed by ten or twelve patients lying in beds, connected by wires to machines that buzzed and beeped.

Sally stopped at a bed and began reading a chart. After a minute or so, Maddy grew impatient and asked, "Can we hurry to my dad? I want it to see him."

"Honey, this is your dad."

"This is my father?" she blurted out—a body with white, waxy skin lay before her. The man slept on his stomach with a bandage around his neck. Maddy felt lightheaded and grabbed the bed rail. Bob reached over, held her arm, and helped her into a chair.

"Put your head between your knees," Bob said.

"Are you alright, honey?" Sally asked.

"I'll be Okay."

Finally, she looked up, began rubbing her father's arm, and placed her head on his shoulder. Although he was unconscious, she was comforted by just touching him. She felt something rough just above the back of his wrist and inspected it. Dried blood had crusted around an open cut. Concerned, she got up to see if there were other wounds. She found a red spot on the bandage around his neck the size of a quarter. When she realized it was blood, she called out to Sally to come over and stop the bleeding. To Maddy's relief, when Sally had finished, the red spot was gone.

After about ten minutes, she heard Sally softly say, "We need to prep your dad for surgery now, but you can have another few minutes." Bob, who was standing nearby, walked away, and Maddy pulled her chair up closer to her father. She leaned over and whispered, "I love you, Dad. I'm wearing my costume. It's a good one this year. I am dressed in your old street blues and was going to surprise you tonight. I was going to tell you that I've decided to become a detective someday, just like you. I promise I will." She felt Sally's hand on her shoulder, stood up, and rubbed her dad's arm one more time. She bent down, kissed him.

Sally directed Bob and Maddy to the waiting room and said that the surgeon would find them when it was over. The room was a large, brightly lit place, cheerfully decorated in soft shades of mauve and blue with landscape paintings on the walls. *It would be better if they painted it black,* Maddy thought to herself, as she felt darkness grow inside her. A half dozen families whispered among themselves as they sat clustered together. One by one, doctors came to the waiting room and spoke with a family. Sometimes the family members would smile and laugh, but a few times, they appeared upset by the news and began to comfort one another. In time, all gathered their things and slowly walked out. After four hours, only Maddy and Bob remained.

Negative thoughts began to haunt Maddy as she stared at the clock. She wanted to be optimistic, but with every passing minute, her longing for her father grew, and she feared that she'd never see him again. As she stewed, a short, stout man with blue scrubs walked in and shuffled over. "I'm Dr. Black," he said and looked away as he spoke. Maddy's heart sank. His voice was low and barely audible; he seemed to be avoiding something. "Your father's wound was very severe. The weapon severed nerves critical to sustaining life functions." He looked at the floor. "We did everything we could. I'm sorry, but we couldn't save him."

Maddy screamed, "That can't be!"

"I'm sorry, I'm very sorry," the surgeon said as he seemed to dance in place nervously. Maddy wailed, and Dr. Black looked at Bob as if to say, "Do something."

Bob looked toward Maddy and said with his face contorted with anguish, "There is nothing anyone can do now. Your father is with God."

She felt betrayed. "How can you say that, Uncle Bob? You're his best friend!"

"Yes, I am, and I love him. And I know what he would want me to do right now. He'd want me to help you understand what has happened, and I am going to try. But you have to let me help you."

Maddy cried uncontrollably and fell into Bob's arms. Her agony found new depths until her body was drained of all strength and unable to stand. Bob helped her into a chair. She saw the surgeon turn and walk away with his head hanging low as if he were defeated by an opponent far more powerful than himself. A woman dressed in street clothes came over and sat silently next Maddy as she sobbed, and at the right moment, in a voice as smooth as a lullaby, she said, "My name is Sheila. I'm a social worker. Would you like to see your father?"

Maddy looked up, wiped the tears from her face, and said that she would. *Maybe he's sleeping, and they just don't realize it,* she began to think. *He's a very sound sleeper.* Sheila led them to an empty room with a high ceiling. Its lights were dimmed, all except one. It shined down on a body. Maddy edged up and gazed at a man on an examination table lying on his back, covered up to his neck with a white blanket. Sheila walked out and left Maddy, Bob, and the man alone. The body resembled her father, she thought, but also it didn't. The skin was tight and shiny, and something seemed fake about it.

Maddy sat motionless on a chair next to the table where the man lay, gazing in its direction, but not directly at the corpse. She took her father's patrolman's hat off and held it as she rested her hands on her lap. Flaccid and hunched over, she felt as if she'd been waiting hours for a bus that never came.

Finally, Maddy stood up, walked to the body, looked down, and blurted out, "This is not my father!" and ran out of the room. Bob caught up with her in the parking lot. They got in his car without a word, and he drove off. As the vehicle climbed the entrance ramp to the highway, Maddy looked for the moon, but didn't see it. A clock on top of a tall building read, 3:23 a.m. How strange, she thought, *It's a new day, yet there's no hope, only sorrow.*

"Your grandmother from Utica has been notified and will be flying here into Chicago tomorrow morning," Bob said. "Tonight, you'll stay at my house, but first, we'll go by your place and pick up some clothes for you."

When they drove down her street, all the houses were dark. Scattered pieces of broken pumpkins, left by mischievous boys having Halloween fun, seemed odd to her. It was as though she had gone to Mars, and the world went on without her. The lights were still on in her house and the black address book that she used to call her father's work when he didn't show up lay face down on the couch. "Do you want me to wait down here while you go up and get your things?" Bob asked.

"Can you wait just outside my room?" Maddy didn't say it, but she was extremely afraid.

When she had finished in her room and was about to leave, Maddy stopped at the front door. She turned to look into the darkness of the house behind her. It was the only home that she'd ever known. *Oh my God,* she thought, *I'll never live here again.* On the way to Bob's house, she gazed out the window and wondered what might become of her. The enormity of the thought was too much, and she pushed it from her mind.

Later, as she lay in the darkness of a strange bedroom, she wondered what had happened to her father. She didn't believe the corpse at the hospital was him. As she wrestled with her thoughts, her brain became unbearably heavy until finally, she gave up, rolled over, and fell asleep.

The next day her grandmother arrived from Upstate New York, and the days that followed passed like a blur. Maddy couldn't wait until the funeral was over, and as she looked back, her only memory was when she was to place a white rose on her father's casket. When it came to her turn, she could not do it, for to her, it meant letting him go forever. Instead, she wrapped it in a tissue, shoved it in her pocket, and knelt and touched her forehead to the casket. Silently she said, "I promise, Dad, I will follow in your footsteps."

Within days, Maddy was to move to Utica to live with her grandmother. The Saturday after the funeral, they drove to meet movers at her house. They passed familiar places—schools, stores, churches, and playgrounds—and her only thought was, *This is so unfair.*

When they walked up the steps of her house, the pumpkins that she and her father had carved still sat on the porch. They had become wrinkled, and their funny faces were shriveled into scary monsters. Inside, furniture had been shoved together and the place reminded her of a used car lot. Boxes stacked high in the living room were marked "silverware," "bathroom," "breakables." Rolled-up rugs piled along a wall looked like cut tree trunks waiting to be hauled off by loggers. Her house was as disrupted as her life, and a sinking feeling in her stomach grew.

Maddy selected the items she wanted to keep, then went to the porch and sat on a step to wait for Bob Bennett, who wanted to say goodbye. He arrived, walked up, and sat next to her.

"How are you, Maddy?"

"Okay," she softly said as she looked down.

A silence settled over them until finally, she spoke. "Uncle Bob, I'm sorry for the things I said that night." Bob put his arm around her shoulder. "Do you think I can come to visit you sometime?"

"Of course. We can write and talk on the phone, too."

"I'd like that," she said. "And Uncle Bob, will you let me know when you catch the man who injured my dad?"

"I will."

When the movers came out to the porch, she watched her grandma put the key in the door. When the lock clunked shut, Maddy felt something come to an end.

After reliving the saddest and scariest night of her life, Maddy drifted back to the present. It was a night that had shaped all that followed and haunted her teenage years with fear and anxiety. She'd had to fight hard to overcome them, but ultimately attained the courage that she had come to rely on as an adult. Over an hour had passed since she had hung up with Harvey, and it was late. Emotionally spent and physically exhausted, she stood up, trudged slowly across the room, and walked up to bed.

Chapter 11

Boy, the wine kicked my butt last night. Maddy stood to wait for an elevator in the lobby. *I've got such a hangover.* The sledgehammer that pounded in her brain had begun to recede to a dull ache, although everything around her still seemed fuzzy.

"Hey, Maddy," a voice called out as she waited for the doors to open. Allison Van Dyke walked up to her, smiling.

"Hey, Allison," Maddy said to the tall, slender brunette with long hair, as she tried to snap out of her funk. "I hear you're going to be the second woman detective in the Oneida County Sheriff's," Maddy said with a smile.

"Okay, go ahead, rub it in," Allison said. "You beat me."

"So, when will you be finished up training?"

"Just a few more weeks, so you better get those old fogies prepared for me." After the two stopped laughing, Allison said in a softer tone, "I heard you were on the scene yesterday when they found Sarah Benning's body. It must have been awful."

"Indescribable," Maddy said. She closed her eyes briefly, and the image of the body flashed before her. While they chatted, Maddy noticed Bud Renshaw and another old-timer detective staring at them with smirks on their faces. Bud had a reputation as a redneck and a bigot who disliked minorities and especially women detectives. Zep had forewarned Maddy about guys like him when she took the job. He said changing the culture was one of his top priorities, and that Maddy's coming on board was an essential first step.

Maddy ignored Bud and turned to Allison. "Let's go shooting again."

"I feel a little out of my league going shooting with you. And besides, I'm not a member of that fancy club you belong to."

"We can go to the department range. Jake's there every morning."

"Do these people know you're a High Master shooter?"

"No, and please keep it under your hat." Maddy looked at her watch. "Oh shit, it's almost eight thirty. I have to get to a meeting." As the elevator door began to close, leaving Allison in the lobby, she said, "I mean it; let's get together soon."

Crowded around a table of pastries and coffee, detectives swarmed like bees. *I need the coffee, but not the calories.* Maddy grabbed a cup of high-test and took a seat.

"Okay, people, listen up." Zep stood in front of the room and waited for the chatter to die down, then gave an overview of the Benning case. He finished with a stern warning. "I don't have to tell you the reaction this is going to have in the community. I want all inquiries by the press directed to me. That's an order. Anyone who violates it will be looking for another job." Then, to Maddy's surprise, he said, "Maddy Reynolds was investigating the case before the body was found. Maddy, can you give us a rundown on what you know?"

All heads turned. Unprepared to speak impromptu in front of a group of over twenty men, she felt her heart race and struggled to catch her breath. She took a slow, deliberate sip of coffee to give her heart a chance to calm down, and then called upon a few old tricks she'd learned as a teenager when she struggled with anxiety. She imagined everyone was in their underwear, kept her eyes focused on the clock in the back of the room, and took three deep breaths before she started in. Slowly, she began to speak.

Like a stenographer reading back testimony at a trial, Maddy described every detail of the case, from the moment it was called in as a "Missing Person" to the time the body showed up in the portable toilet. Nearly finished, she glanced over at Zep, and he was smiling. Two other detectives, however, glared at her. One was Bud Renshaw.

Before dismissing the meeting, Zep directed everyone to check in with the administrative assistants in the back of the room to pick up their assignments. As Maddy moved with the crowd, Zep pulled her and Al Ramirez aside. "Why don't you two meet me in my office in ten minutes?"

"Okay," Al said. Maddy just nodded.

"What do you suppose he wants with us?" she asked.

"I think we'll be working with him directly."

Zep wasn't particularly close to any of the detectives; he seemed to treat them all about the same—all, that is, but Al. "You seem pretty tight with Zep," she said as they waited in Zep's office.

"War does that to people."

Maddy looked at him quizzically. "We were in Nam together," he said.

Zep walked in with papers in his hand and sat at his desk. "The FBI is checking into cases that involve valentines. They have Sarah's, but it'll take a few days to hear back. Ditto on the lab samples from her body." He thumbed through a spiral notebook on his desk. "Al, you know what you have to do, right?" Al nodded. We also have a guy at the construction site who has a criminal record. Maddy, why don't you interview him, and when you finish, come back and give Al a hand."

Zep said he had to get to a meeting and started for the door, but before he left the room, he stopped. "Oh, Maddy, we set up an appointment for you to meet with Dr. Sidney Myers tomorrow morning. He's a criminal psychology professor at Syracuse University. He's a little weird but good at what he does. We need a profile of our guy."

Maddy and Al were left sitting in the room, and she asked Al, "So, what is it that Zep wants you to do?"

"What I do best—research. My new home will be the basement file room for a few days, so when you get back, that's where I'll be."

Al's a strange character, but I kind of like him, she thought as she walked to her car. Clouds had begun to cover a blue sky. The wind had kicked up, and cold air found its way into the vehicle as she drove. *It's going to be an early winter,* she thought; she turned the heat up and headed back to the construction site.

The sign in front of a trailer read, "Briganti Construction—Site Superintendent." *Funny, I didn't even notice that yesterday.* Before she walked up the steps, she stopped and looked over at the portable toilets. Her mind flashed back to the sights, sounds, and smells from the previous day's nightmare. Before the terror and sadness rushed into her mind, she pushed them out of her head. She walked inside, where a heavy-set man with a white hardhat was arguing with someone on the phone.

"I don't give a good goddamn. You gotta send me another guy." He waited, then said, "Not my fucking problem. Your union promised me the men I need. One of your guys didn't show up today, so you have to send me someone to take his place." That got Maddy's attention. "That's right, the guy's name is Hawk Jenkins. He didn't even call in." He listened, and said, "Okay then, have him here by noon," and slammed the down the phone.

Surprised to see Maddy when he turned around, he said, "Oh, I didn't see you come in."

"I'm Detective Maddy Rey..."

"I know who you are," he interrupted. "I remember you from yesterday. I don't think I'll ever forget yesterday." He slumped in his chair, his voice became low, and he looked like a little boy who couldn't find his puppy.

"I came out here to talk with Billy Spires, but I heard you mention this Jenkins guy who didn't show up for work today. I'd like any information you can give me on him too."

"Spires works with the iron crew. You can find him on the west side of the site. As far as Jenkins goes, I don't have anything. Most of these guys just come here to work. I don't ask questions."

"You must have some payroll information on him."

"Some of these guys, even if they belong to the union, want cash only. If we have an address back at the main office, it's probably fake, but I'll check. You might want to ask Billy; I see him eating lunch with

Jenkins sometimes." Maddy put on a hardhat and set out for the west side of the building to find Billy Spires.

A crane roared as it hauled iron beams five stories into the air. Its black diesel fumes poured through a long pipe that rose behind a man in the small glass cab who operated the monster machine. Men on the highest beams walked back and forth as though they were on the ground. Each time a beam reached them, they caught it and guided it into place.

Maddy signaled a man walking by to stop. "Where is Billy Spires?" He couldn't hear her, so she repeated herself much louder: "Where is Billy Spires?"

He shouted back, "Up there," and pointed to the men walking on beams high above. "Why?" he asked.

"I want to speak to him."

The guy looked up, cupped his hands around his mouth, waited for the right moment, then screamed, "Hey, Billy. Someone wants to talk with you."

All the men on the beams looked down at Maddy. One whistled, and another said, "Whoa Billy, way to go." The man who Maddy had stopped apologized. "Don't mind them. They're not used to seeing a pretty woman out here."

Maddy's face flushed warm. It had been a long time since anyone told her that she was pretty. When Billy climbed down, they walked to a quieter spot. She introduced herself and said that she had some questions about what had happened the day before.

"Why are you talking to me? Do you think I had something to do with it?" Billy leaned back and defensively stretched out his hands with his eyes wide opened.

"I have no reason to think that. We're just checking anyone with priors. I noticed you had some trouble with the law a while back."

"I did, but that's all in the past. Or maybe it's never in the past," Billy said with some resignation in his voice. "I went through a crazy time when I was nineteen after my father died. I went wild, stole a car, and got a DWI.

But I've been off probation now for over five years, and there's been nothing since."

"I can understand how losing someone when you're young can knock you off course," Maddy said empathetically. "Where do you live, Billy?"

His facial muscles softened as he pulled out a pack of Luckys from his shirt pocket. He offered one to Maddy, and when she refused, lit one up and took a drag. "I live at Akwesasne, or the St. Regis Reservation, as you might know it. I'm a Mohawk."

"Do you have family there?"

"My whole family's there; wife and three kids."

Maddy smiled. "How old are your kids?"

"Twelve, eight, and three...all girls."

"I have a twelve-year-old girl too...quite a handful, aren't they?"

"Yes, ma'am. They take after their mama, that's for sure."

"Look, I just have a few questions, so bear with me." Billy leaned back on a steel beam and lifted a foot against it. "The foreman said you eat lunch with Jenkins sometimes. What can you tell me about him?"

"He's a strange one...a lot of bullshit."

"What do you mean?" Maddy opened her notebook.

"He likes to talk big. But a lot of what he says is pure bullshit. Just last week, he said he was going to bring in his new .44 Colt to show me. But the next day, when I asked him where it was, he acted like he didn't know what I was talking about."

"Do you know where he lives?"

"He's been staying at the same motel as me when we're here, but I don't know where he calls home."

Maddy wrote quickly, trying to keep up with Billy as he spoke. "What's he like?"

"Well, he keeps to himself most of the time and doesn't talk with anyone, except me, although I don't know why. He's up and down like a roller coaster. One minute he'll be all happy, whistling and joking around, then something sets him off, and he gets all pissy. One time when we were working near each other, we talked, and everything was fine. Then, for no reason, he got up, took a hammer, looked at me like he wanted to cave my head in, and hurled it at the shithouse door. I swear I have no idea what I said to piss him off."

Maddy wrote down, 'Mood swings; explosive temper, potentially violent.' "What else can you tell me about him."

"That's pretty much it, other than I heard him peel out of the motel parking lot in the middle of the night." Maddy took down the name of the hotel where Billy and Jenkins stayed, thanked him, and said she might have more questions later.

Within five minutes, she pulled up to a white building that had ten doors that opened to a parking lot with a sign out front that read: Sunrise Motel, Vacancy, Rooms from $19.99. A short, heavy man sat at a metal desk in the office. "Need a room?"

"I'm Detective Reynolds. I'm looking for Hawk Jenkins; have you seen him?"

"Oh, I'm Ben Crabtree. I own this place. Jenkins took off in the middle of the night, and in quite a hurry too. But he slipped the money for the room under the door."

"What room did he stay in?"

'Eight."

"Did he leave a forwarding address?"

"No, they never do."

Crabtree walked Maddy to Room 8, unlocked the door, and apologized for not having cleaned it.

"You'll have to stay outside while I look around," she said.

The room smelled like the toilet of a dive bar. The stench of body odor, spilled beer, and cigarette smoke nearly made her queasy. Empty Black Label beer bottles littered a nightstand and beer stains, still wet, spotted the rugs. Two empty pizza boxes on the floor next to the bed with partially eaten slices were open; damp towels lay strewn on the bathroom floor.

Maddy's eye caught a glimpse of something sticking out from under the bed. She walked over and picked up a magazine filled with photos of pre-pubescent girls engaged in every possible sex act with older men.

This might be our guy, she thought. Before she contaminated the room any further, she walked outside and marked it off with yellow crime scene tape. Crabtree gawked out the window of his office like a pervert trying to get a cheap thrill. She walked back and asked if Jenkins had anyone with him since he'd been there.

"Does this have something to do with the girl they found dead yesterday?"

"Just answer the question."

"No, I haven't seen him with anyone."

Maddy called Zep from her car and told him Billy Spires was clean, but another guy didn't show up for work and took off in the middle of the night. "He also had child porn in his motel room."

"I'll send the forensic guys over. Stay there until they arrive and make sure no one gets in that room. Then head back over to the construction site. I'll have someone meet you there who can put together a facial composite of Jenkins."

Maddy arrived back at Briganti Construction a little past noon, but the person she was to meet hadn't arrived yet. She walked through the half-built building looking for volunteers willing to assist in putting together the sketch. When she returned to the trailer, a middle-aged detective named Tony DiCarlo sat in his car with the engine running, eating a sandwich. He opened the window, and Maddy caught a whiff of his sandwich. *What the hell is he eating, fish guts?*

"Let me finish my sandwich," Tony said. "Then we can get started."

DiCarlo interviewed a half dozen volunteers and masterfully used the Identi-Kit tool to put together a sketch of Jenkins. As the face began to emerge, it was so ugly and scary that Maddy questioned DiCarlo about its validity.

"Are you sure you haven't dramatized this?"

"Listen, detective; I put them together according to the way they tell me."

Maddy scrutinized the face. Dark, curly hair hung down over a sizeable square forehead that had deep wavy wrinkles above bushy eyebrows. The whites of bulging eyes, set off by black pupils, seemed to glare with unrelenting hatred. *The son-of-a-bitch looks like he wants to leap right off the page,* she thought.

The jaw, broad and square, protruded beyond all other attributes on the face, except for a large, round, full nose. A six-inch scar traversed the right cheek from ear to chin.

"Jeez-Louise, we can't put this in the newspaper. Kids will have nightmares for a month," she said to DiCarlo.

"Sorry, Lady. Not my problem."

The face reeked of violence, volatility, and chaos. Maddy told Zep that if the sketch made it to the front page, they'd have a public panic on their hands. He agreed, and the image did not get released to the press, only to law enforcement.

When she left Zep's office, she headed to the basement to look for the file room where she was supposed to meet up with Al. The below-ground portion of the old building was like a dungeon from the Dark Ages. Brick walls and stone floors lined long corridors. The walls, recently covered with glossy light-blue paint, gave Maddy the impression that the color was either somebody's idea of a joke, a misguided attempt to make the place look cheerful, or a great deal from a going-out-of-business sale. The oil-based paint smell was so strong, she thought she'd be high or dead by the time she found Al. After several left and right turns, she popped her head into a room where Al was sitting at a long table, reading reports.

"Where's the torture chamber?" she asked.

Al looked up and laughed. "This is the file room," he said. "And yes, they may have had a torture chamber down here at one time," Al said in such a serious tone that Maddy wondered if he might be right.

"Just kidding," he said.

Maddy smiled, intrigued by his dry sense of humor. *There's more to him than meets the eye.*

Al proudly explained the library. "Records of cases going back to the eighteen-hundreds are still down here," he said as he went on about the method used to categorize files and how the old, yet efficient, indexing system worked. It seemed to Maddy that Al knew the file room like an auto mechanic knew a slant-six engine. *No wonder Zep picked him to do this work; the guy should have been a librarian.*

"Have you found anything?" she asked.

"Of the men in the area who are known child molesters, three are possibilities. They are all on parole or probation. One has fled. I need to do a little more digging, but I should have a report tomorrow."

He's in his mid-forties and good-looking, yet there's no ring on his finger. He must have a girlfriend. As it approached time to go home, she helped put boxes of files back on shelves. "I think my daughter is getting sick of pizza for dinner, but she's going to have it again tonight because I don't feel like cooking. How about you, any kids?"

"No, never been married."

Shit, maybe he's gay. I hope I didn't offend him.

"I'm sorry, I didn't mean to pry."

"I'm not offended. I have a strange background for a cop. I used to be a Catholic priest."

"Holy shit! Oh, sorry, I mean…"

Al laughed. "Don't worry; you won't go to hell. And besides, I haven't been one for a long time."

"How did you end up becoming a cop?"

Chapter 11

"I joined the army as a chaplain. After I was discharged and returned to the states, my life turned to scrambled eggs. The war did a job on my head. I lost my faith for a while, then my reason for living. I left the priesthood and was hitting the bottle pretty heavy, almost ended it, until one night, Zep saved me. He came down to Scranton, where I'm from, and stayed until I got through the worst of it."

It was unusual to hear such honesty from a man she had just met, but Al's authenticity and ability to be vulnerable helped her feel at ease.

"How did you end up here in Utica?"

"When Zep made captain, I'd been sober four years. He offered me a job as an analyst, and I took it. After that, I moved up in the ranks to detective."

"Do you live with someone?" Maddy cringed after she spoke and rebuked herself for asking such a personal question. But it didn't deter Al. He remained painfully honest.

"My mother is frail and can't care for herself anymore, so I moved her up here a few years ago. We live together. She makes good company," Al said, paused a moment, then added, "and great chili."

I like this guy, Maddy said to herself. "Thanks for sharing, Al. It helps me. To be honest, I haven't exactly felt welcome around here since I made detective."

"That will change in time, Maddy. Be patient. Zep is determined to make it change. That's why he picked you to be the first woman detective. He carefully followed your work as a cop. Zep believes you have enough courage to tough it out. He'll have your back when shit hits the fan. So will I."

Maddy felt a warmth when she talked with Al. Being with him was like standing next to a wood stove in a cold room. It was the first time she felt accepted since she started as a detective. Feeling more comfortable, she decided to share something that had bothered her all day. "Shouldn't we be doing more to catch the murderer?" she asked. "It feels like we're not doing enough."

Al smiled. "I used to think like that too. It took me a long time to trust the process. I learned that from Zep in Vietnam. If one of our units was hit bad, my reaction was to pursue the enemy immediately. But as captain, Zep had responsibility for the lives of the men. He never backed down from a fight but hated to put their wellbeing at risk unnecessarily. He'd say, 'We respond, we don't react. Reacting gets you killed.' He'd think things through, come up with a plan, then execute it to a T. A lot of us are still alive today because of it." Al had Maddy's undivided attention.

"Zep planned our response to the murder before we met this morning. Each detective has an assignment, it's our job to carry it out as best we can, and trust the process."

Maddy walked with Al to the elevator to leave for the day. She looked forward to getting home and away from the dark cloud of the investigation. When she stepped outside, a bitter October wind whipped into her face. *Damn, I don't think I'll ever get used to this.*

Chapter 12

The appointment with the criminal psychologist was at ten thirty a.m. at Syracuse University. At nine fifteen, before Maddy left for the one-hour drive, the phone rang, and Dr. Myers's secretary asked if she'd mind meeting at King David's for lunch, instead. "Sure, I love Middle Eastern food." She took down the directions and a description of the professor, then worked with Al to kill the extra hour before she headed out.

As she approached the University area in Syracuse, she saw a huge hill covered with buildings that sparkled in the sun. Medical centers, dormitories, and lecture halls.

Maddy snaked her way in and out of one-way streets, found an alley, and a sign that read, "King David." She parked in front of the restaurant and stepped out into comfortably cold autumn air. Students walked purposefully to classes, and it reminded Maddy of when she was that age without a care in the world except the next exam. When she entered the restaurant, a bald man with a red goatee was sitting at a table near a window eating while looking out at the street.

"Excuse me, are you Dr. Myers?"

"Yes. You must be Detective Reynolds."

"I am. Thank you for taking the time to meet with me."

Maddy stood next to the table, and Myers rudely said, "Well, don't just stand there, have a seat, why don't you."

What an asshole, Maddy thought.

Myers wasted no time cutting to the chase. "I understand you want a profile of a suspect. The murderer of Sarah Benning, I assume. I read about it in the paper. There wasn't much detail." He took a sip of his soft drink, forehead wrinkled, and appeared annoyed.

"That's correct."

"Your secretary didn't tell me who you wanted to talk about," Myers said. "It would have been nice if you people had told me in advance."

Now I know what Zep meant when he said the guy is weird. "Sorry you weren't better informed." Myers frowned and didn't accept her apology.

A waitress came over and asked Maddy if she'd like to order. Her stomach in knots from her brief interaction with Myers, her craving for hummus and tabouli had left her. "Just water, please."

"What's been your involvement in the case?" Myers asked sharply.

"I was investigating it as a 'missing person' and was at the scene yesterday."

"Not a pretty sight, was it?"

"No, it was not."

"So, now you're here looking for a profile of the perpetrator and think it will help you to find him?" he said sarcastically. "Am I right?"

"Yes. Yes, you are."

Myers took a few bites of his falafel sandwich and another sip of soda. He took his time chewing as if Maddy wasn't there and, after he swallowed, didn't speak or make eye contact for a minute or two.

What a dick! she fumed inside.

Finally, as though he had just remembered her presence, he said, "Have you ever been involved with a child killer case before?"

Maddy wasn't about to share the story about her father with such a person, and said, "No."

"Why did you become a detective, detective?"

Here we go, welcome to The Dr. Myers Show," she thought. "I'm keeping a promise," she said.

"To whom?"

Maddy wanted to say, 'None of you fucking business,' but just smiled.

After a long silence, Myers dropped the question-and-answer session and said, "Tell me what you know about what happened to Sarah Benning." With that, Maddy pulled out her notebook and pen.

"Sarah was eleven and from a home with a great deal of turbulence: estranged parents, mother an alcoholic. After an argument with her mother, she stormed out of the house, which was common behavior for her. Normally she'd show up again within a day or two."

"But not this time," he interrupted.

"No, not this time. We are waiting for the lab and medical examiner reports to come back, but it appears she was raped, sodomized, and strangled."

"Where did they find the body?"

"On the floor of a portable toilet at a construction site."

"Poor thing," Myers said, put his sandwich down, took off his glasses and rubbed his wrinkled forehead. "Did he leave a calling card?"

"A calling-card?"

"Some killers will leave something behind as a way to claim responsibility."

"We found a vintage valentine in Sarah's bedroom. It was signed 'Mark.' Her family has no idea how Sarah got it and didn't know who Mark could be."

"Either the card is somehow unrelated, or your boy is extremely cunning...to find a way to get the card in possession of the victim before the murder; very cunning."

Maddy wrote furiously and tried not to miss a thing.

"Was there sperm?"

"We won't know for sure until the lab report is back."

"Did they find prints or tracks or evidence of any kind?"

"No."

"Hmm. Off-the-cuff, and without knowing anything more, I'd say your killer is a male between thirty and forty-five, very intelligent, raised by an abusive mother, and has complete disdain for women. He is probably not originally from this area, and has done this before."

"Why do you think he's done this before?"

"Because he's too good. It takes practice to leave no clues. Your boy seems to have already fine-tuned his skills somewhere else. Right now, he is right where he wants to be, feeling very safe in his anonymity. He enjoyed reading the headlines this morning about what he did and relishes listening to the ladies in the checkout aisle at the grocery store talk about how they're going to keep their kids locked up from now on. He loves all the chaos." Maddy thought about the man in her puzzle.

"But most of all," Myers said, "he enjoys waiting."

"Waiting? Waiting for what?"

"To do it again."

"How sure are you of that?"

"One hundred percent."

Dr. Myers turned his attention back to his sandwich. Maddy wanted to leave, but thought she better wait for him to finish and sat quietly. Then, as if he'd snapped out of a coma, Myers said, "This guy you're after, he's not your ordinary impulsive killer. A lot is going on with him. He has a plan or a strategy of some kind, and he enjoys executing it to perfection.

"What do you mean?"

"It's like he staged a performance. He put the gruesomely violated body of a child in a place where he knew it would be seen and have its greatest impact. Had he buried her in the woods, the body might never be found. But that's not what he wanted. It's showtime. He's making his debut and saying, 'I'm here.'"

Maddy knew what Myers meant. She felt it at the construction site when they found Sarah. It was as if everyone present was the audience, and a master choreographer was standing somewhere behind a curtain watching their reaction to his creation.

When Myers finished, she thanked him, left the restaurant, and, as she walked to her car, wondered how the old blue-collar town was going to respond to a vicious serial killer lurking around in its back yard.

Chapter 13

It was a beautiful afternoon, and Maddy decided to take the back roads home to Utica after she met with Myers. The countryside was alive with autumn colors as she meandered through the winding roads, reflecting on how events of recent days had brought a dark cloud over her life. She hoped that nature's beauty might revive her spirits and bring her some peace of mind.

Apple orchards, one after another, appeared beneath fiery hills. A lone produce stand was the only visible structure in sight. Maddy decided to stop in. It was red, long and narrow, and had three open garage doors that faced the roadside.

She pulled into a gravel parking lot, got out, and an aroma of apples and fallen leaves greeted her. They brought back memories of playing in her parents' back yard in autumn, as a child. When she walked in, bushel baskets filled with different colored apples lined the walls. Two large kegs of apple cider used for filling plastic jugs sat on an old picnic table. *Oh, I want some of that,* she said to herself.

Pumpkins and gourds, artistically grouped in a circle, had been arranged on the dirt floor by someone with a great deal of patience and an artistic eye. Old snowshoes, plows, fishing poles, and two double-barrel shotguns hung on one wall and on another wall, black and white photographs of people from the past reflected a proud family tradition. The apple stand seemed frozen in time.

"Can I help you?" a woman dressed in denim overalls asked.

"How about a jug of that cider?"

The woman reached for a jug but was distracted by a bald man in his fifties. He was talking to a young girl of about fourteen at another display table. Unshaven and with tattoos of spiders on the backs of his hands, the man seemed more like a cult member than someone out looking to buy apples. The girl, who looked like the woman and was probably her daughter, leaned over a bushel to fill a bag with apples as the man tilted his head to look down her shirt.

"Excuse me," the woman said to Maddy, walked over to a tall man with long hair. She spoke a few words, and he looked over at the girl. *That must be the father.* He stopped stacking pumpkins, turned to his daughter, and said, "Go help your mother while I take care of this gentleman."

The man with the tattoos stepped back, turned his head like he just got caught stealing, walked out, and drove off. *If Sarah's parents had been looking over her like that, she might still be alive today,* Maddy thought.

On her drive back to Utica, Zep called to ask how the interview with Myers went. "He thinks the murderer is probably not from the area because he's too good at what he does to be new at it."

"I thought about that. He's probably right. What else did he say?"

"He said that he's sure he'll strike again."

"Shit. I think he's right about that too." Before they hung up, he gave her an assignment for the next day. "Tomorrow, I'd like you to take the Jenkins sketch to the people you interviewed before we found the body. Maybe we'll get a hit."

By the time she got home, it was after six thirty. Amber had already eaten leftovers with Samantha while doing homework. That was fine with Maddy because she wasn't hungry and wanted to make an early night of it. After tidying up the kitchen and saying goodnight to her daughter, she walked to her bedroom, changed into a nightgown, and crawled under the covers. Before she turned off the light, she pulled out her journal and wrote, "I'm falling into a valley of darkness and can't find my way out."

The next day Maddy felt she was in a funk. She had missed a few days of shooting practice, so she stopped by the department range before work. Except for Jake, the place was empty. As she set up her weapons, she heard a voice behind her say, "Do you mind a little company?" She turned and saw Allison.

"Not when it's good company."

Allison pulled up a stool across from her and checked her revolver, but when she saw Maddy's three handguns, two of which were semiautomatics, she said, "You know, I've wanted to ask how you got to be such a good shooter."

Maddy rested her hands on the table, looked out at the empty range, and began to reflect on her childhood. "When I was a kid, I lived in a prison of fear. At night, I saw faces in the shadows of my bedroom and called them 'Shadow Faces.' I'd stay awake until the morning light drove them away. Sometimes I'd run into Grandma's room and jump in bed with her."

The more Maddy talked, the more she remembered. "One summer afternoon I sat in Grandma's yard writing in my journal. I must have been about thirteen. Everything was fine until I noticed the sun getting low in the sky, and I began to shake. Long shadows from trees stretched out across the lawn toward me, and I couldn't move. All I could think was the Shadow Faces would be coming soon."

She remained quiet for a few minutes. "Maybe my fear had to do with my parents dying in separate tragedies. I'm not sure. Poor Grandma. She didn't know what to do with me. That day she covered me up with a blanket and stayed with me until morning."

Maddy stared at the floor. "Being in constant fear is a terrible way for a kid to live. I didn't do the things other kids did: no dances or sleepovers. I never went to summer camp. I felt haunted as if someone were coming to take my life away like my parents' lives had been taken. That's where guns came in."

She took a deep breath and paused. "Yes, guns. My favorite TV show was Honey West. She was a detective and had a gun. It was her equalizer against the bad guys, and I wanted one."

Amazed that she readily shared parts of herself she'd never spoken to anyone about except for Harvey, Maddy continued. "I became obsessed.

I felt having a weapon would give me power over death. I begged my grandmother to let me join a gun club. I'd say, 'You can take me, and I can learn to shoot.' That's how it began. Grandma gave in, and from then on, I virtually lived at the club."

Allison seemed enthralled with Maddy's story. "To see how you handle yourself so confidently now, I would never have thought you went through all that as a kid."

"Learning how to shoot was the beginning of controlling my fear. It helped me feel safe. In time I kept a gun in my nightstand next to my bed. Still do. Finally, I was able to sleep in my room alone. Shooting wasn't a sport for me; it was a medication."

Maddy was surprised when Allison leaned over without saying a word and put her arms around her. She felt a deep bond of friendship with a woman she barely knew. After they finished their shooting routines and were about to leave, Allison said, "Let's do this again soon."

Maddy smiled. "I'd like that."

How do I show a mother the face of a monster who may have killed her daughter? Maddy struggled with the thought as she walked up to Martha Benning's front door with Hawk Jenkins's sketch. She knocked, but there was no answer, so she peeked in the window—empty beer bottles scattered on tables and no sign of Martha. *Probably passed out. Too early for her. I should have come here last.* She got back in her car and headed to Frank Benning's.

The sun had started to show itself in the distance, but darkness was growing inside of Maddy. She rang the doorbell, and Cindy answered. "Can I speak with Frank?" she asked solemnly.

"Sorry, he is in town making funeral arrangements for Sarah."

"Oh, of course." How are the two of you holding up?"

"Frank is taking it real hard. He hasn't slept since it happened, and I'm worried about him." Cindy had seemed like a phony to Maddy when they first met, but her false attitude of superiority was gone.

"How about you? How are you doing?" Maddy asked.

Cindy looked away. Maddy knew she was trying to hide her tears, and soft sobbing, like the cry of a kitten, prompted her to put her hand on Cindy's arm. She turned, laid her head on Maddy's shoulder for a moment, then pulled back and took a tissue from the sleeve of her sweater and wiped her face "I never thought anything like this would ever happen to someone I knew," she said as in a quivering voice. "Sarah was such a sweet little girl, but so lost and so unhappy. Losing her is devasting to us all. Martha has been on a drinking bender since the day it happened, and Frank has withdrawn from me. I am afraid he might be using again. I'm not sure our relationship will survive this."

As tenderly as she could, Maddy said, "I have a composite sketch of a man who is a suspect, and I'd like you to look at it. It might be disturbing."

"Okay," she said, wiping her eyes with fresh tissue.

Cindy glanced at the sketch and winced. It was as if she were looking at a dead rat. "I'm sorry...no, I've never seen that person before." Maddy took the sketch back and got up to leave. "I don't think Frank has seen him either. It would disturb him a great deal to see that face."

Maddy nodded. "I sure understand that," she muttered as she left the house and headed to see Mary Thompson. When she pulled into Mary's driveway, Maddy saw the old woman standing next to a fire, holding twigs and small branches in her arms and occasionally dropping a few into the flames. The sight of Mary surrounded by smoke gave the illusion that she was standing in the clouds.

"Can't stop working, can ya?" Maddy said.

Mary laughed a halfhearted laugh. "I thought I'd take advantage of the sun. How are you, Maddy Reynolds?"

"I think a better question would be, how are you?"

"I'm just waiting to exit," Mary said.

Maddy gave her a quizzical look and wondered if she was ill.

"The way I figure it, there are three kinds of people in this world. Some are still waiting to live their lives, and most of those never will."

She put another handful of sticks in the fire. "Then, there are those who live every day fully. There's only a few of them. The rest of us are just waiting to exit. Take me. I've lived my dreams already. Now I'm just biding my time waiting to leave this old world.

"Don't get me wrong," she went on. "I love to see that old sun come up in the morning, and the flowers bust through the earth in spring. I love the little children too! Yes, I do, with all their wondrous imaginings and curiosities. But when I see what happened to Sarah, I say to myself, I have lived too long, and I am just waiting for my time to go."

The wind stirred. Smoke swirled around her, as rays of the sun fell on her worn purple dress like a spotlight. *She looks beautiful,* Maddy thought as the unusual woman fed the fire with small wood offerings. Mary was grieving in her way. It was a philosophical way, a spiritual way, and Maddy was hesitant to speak. Finally, in a gentle voice, she said, "Mary, I'm sorry, but I have to ask you to look at a sketch of a suspect. He's pretty fierce."

Slowly, Mary bent down and placed her bundle of branches on the ground. "Let's go up to the porch, dear." They sat on a bench next to each other, and before Maddy pulled out the replica of Jenkins's face, she saw a Geometry textbook on the floor next to her. "Catching up on your math?" Maddy asked, kiddingly, as she handed the book to Mary.

"Oh my." Mary said, "Jodi must have left that here."

"Who's Jodi?"

"She's a young girl who used to live around here. She stops by for a visit sometimes."

"Well, I hope she doesn't walk this road alone until we catch Sarah's…" Maddy was about to say "killer" but stopped herself. "You know, the person who harmed Sarah."

"I'm not too worried about Jodi," Mary said with a coy smile.

Maddy wondered what she meant but didn't ask. She opened the folder with the Jenkins sketch and handed it over. Mary looked at it for a long time. "What do you suppose happened to this man to make his face so filled with hate?" She handed the drawing back and said, "No, honey, I've never seen him before."

After she left Mary sitting on her porch, she spent the remainder of the afternoon stopping at grocery stores and gas stations in the area showing people the sketch, but no one recognized Hawk Jenkins. She stopped at the Friendly Bean just before closing time, and, except for Rusty and Artie, the place was empty.

"Strange time for you to be here, Maddy," Rusty said when she walked in. "Would you like something to go?"

"No, I am here on business."

"Oh, what did I do now," he said as he laughed.

Maddy managed a smile. "I'd like you to look at a sketch of a suspect in the Sarah Benning case...you too, Artie."

"Oh my, of course...come on out from behind the counter, Artie."

She pulled out the sketch and placed it on a table before the two men. Artie recoiled at the sight, shook his head, and said, "Haven't seen him, thank God."

Rusty just stared. Maddy turned to him for a response. "You know that's not a face you forget easily. It's vaguely familiar, but not recently. I don't think it was here. I can't place where it may have been. I guess I'm not much help."

As she stood up to leave, Rusty said, "I'm not sure about the man in your sketch, but I do remember something that might be important. About a month ago, a guy was in here several mornings in a row. He acted strangely. He stared at women, and I even had a customer complain to me. She said he made her feel uncomfortable."

That got Maddy's interest, so she pulled out her notebook.

"About a week later, he came back with a young girl about twelve. I remember thinking the girl didn't look at all like him and didn't act like she was his daughter. He hasn't been back here since."

"You've seen the picture of Sarah Benning in the paper. Did the girl look like her?"

"I'm not sure."

Maddy's interest was piqued, and she asked Rusty if he'd meet with a sketch artist.

"I'll do my best."

"We'll have someone over here in the morning. Thanks."

When she returned to the department, she told Zep that she had come up empty except for a possible new lead from Rusty. "Turns out, no one's having any luck," he said. "Tomorrow, I'm sending people to construction sites around the state where iron is being erected. Jenkins was an ironworker; somebody has to recognize him."

As she headed for the door, Zep said, "Oh, by the way, the reports from the medical examiner and lab came in. The cause of death was strangulation, and, just as we thought, Sarah was raped and sodomized before he killed her."

Maddy shook her head. She felt emotionally spent, and with her mind on overload, she was unable to process anything more. Just then, Al walked in, plopped himself in a chair, exhaled, and said, "Sometimes I just can't believe people. The more I know about them, the less I want to know."

"What's going on, Al?" Zep asked.

"So, I find the name of a guy who was convicted of raping a seven-year-old girl in Erie County five years ago. The case was overturned because of a Miranda violation, so I tracked his whereabouts since then and found out he's living here Utica. His name is Randy Ballinger. I do a little more digging and find out he works at Cedar Crest Elementary School as a fifth-grade teacher's aide. Can you believe that shit?"

Al sat up in his chair, more animated than Maddy had ever seen him. "Then it dawns on me, 'Ballinger,' that's the name of the Superintendent of Schools: Miriam Ballinger. And holy shit, guess what, he's her nephew."

"No shit," Zep said.

"Oh, wait, it gets better. Guess where Sarah Benning went to school? You got it, Cedar Crest. Is it me, or has the world gone crazy, putting a pervert like that in with those kids?"

Maddy looked at Zep's reaction and watched as he changed positions from sitting back in his chair to leaning forward with his elbows on his desk, writing in his notebook. When he looked up, he said, "I know Miriam Ballinger. Al, when you go to the school in the morning to interview this guy, I'll be at the Board of Education speaking with his aunt. If we don't handle this right, it will turn into a shit storm."

Then Zep looked at Maddy. "Since most of the ironworkers in New York are unionized, here is a list of unions to start checking out tomorrow to see if anyone recognizes Jenkins. Leave sketches behind too."

Al piped in again, "I've checked every record that I could think of, and I can't find anyone named Hawk Jenkins. It's must be an alias."

Maddy went back to her office, grabbed her briefcase, and started down the hallway to go home. Al walked out of his cubicle to do the same. They rode the elevator, and Maddy said, "It's horrifying how many pedophiles there are out there."

"That's one disease I don't think I'll ever get my head wrapped around," Al said.

It seemed like each day, the investigation created more questions than answers. Maddy was tired and just wanted to spend a quiet evening with her daughter. "Night, Al," she said.

"Night, Maddy."

Chapter 14

The next day Maddy set out to visit unions throughout Upstate New York. Wallkill was her first stop. It is located between two American jewels, Woodstock and New York City, and the congestion near the great city gave her a sense of awe and reawakened her awareness of the world outside of slow-moving Utica. The sounds of tires on the road, a constant humming of truck engines, and the smell of exhaust fumes made her feel part of something bigger than herself with an energy all of its own.

She planned to show artist sketch of Hawk Jenkins to as many ironworkers as possible and work her way back from the eastern edge of the state toward Central New York. Her final stop was a meeting on Thursday at Local 60 in Binghamton.

Frustrated by a delay in the meeting time, Maddy ended up too tired to drive back to Utica when it ended after seven thirty, and she decided to stay an extra night. Down in the mouth and missing her daughter, she called Jack's when she got to her room, but there was no answer. *Shit, Amber has a basketball game tonight.* In her room with nothing to do, she decided to call Zep and get caught up on the case.

"Hey, Maddy. Any luck?"

"No one recognized him, but I left a ton of flyers behind and asked people to post them. What happened when Al interviewed Randy Ballinger?"

"Al said the guy had a strangeness about him that he's seen in other child predators. He was cocky and even admitted dodging a bullet in the Buffalo rape case. Although he didn't come right out and say it, he as much as admitted that if it weren't for a cop screwing up reading him his Miranda Rights, he'd be in jail. Pretty ballsy, I'd say."

"What about his aunt...the superintendent of schools?"

"She's in total denial," Zep said. "Her nephew has her hoodwinked. She thinks he was set up and that everyone's out to get him. Not only do we need to look at him as a suspect in Sarah's murder, but as a threat to the kids in that school."

Then Zep shifted focus. "So, what's your plan with Jenkins?"

"I want to give it a few days to see if there's any response to the sketches. Something's got to turn up; the guy can't just vanish in midair. By the way, did we get the sketch back of the guy that Rusty saw at the Friendly Bean?"

"Got it yesterday. It's on your desk." Zep's voice trailed off, and he sounded tired. Before they hung up, he said, "Try and get some rest this weekend. Spend some time with your daughter. Don't let her get lost in all this crazy shit."

Zep's words hit her hard. When they hung up, she called Amber again, and this time she answered. "Hi, it's Mom. How are you?"

"I just got back from my game. Mom, you're not going to believe what happened."

"What happened, honey?"

"We were losing through the game and were down by one point with ten seconds left. Coach called a time out and called a play where Jamie was to take the last shot, but she missed, and the ball came to me. I put it up, and it went in. I can't believe it. We won the game, and everyone came over and hugged me."

"Aww honey, I'm so proud of you," Maddy said, her insides twisting. *I can't believe I missed that.*

"When are you coming home, Mom?"

"I'll be back tomorrow before dinner. You'll have to catch me up on everything that's happened since I've been away." When she hung up, the tightness in her stomach evolved into a heavy sadness. It was as though achieving her lifelong dream of becoming a detective had the damaging side effect of keeping her from her daughter.

Chapter 14

Maddy drove back to Utica in the morning and went directly in to work. When she walked into her house after work that afternoon, Amber sat on the floor, playing cards with Samantha. She popped up like a jack-in-the-box, ran to her mother, and smothered her with hugs and kisses.

"I missed you so much," Amber said. "You won't have to go away again, will you?"

"Not if I can help it."

Chapter 15

Maddy was glad to get back to the daily routine after the week-long trip around the state and felt a bounce in her step when she got off the elevator, like the first day on the job. When she got to her desk, a pile of papers awaited, and a note at the top of the stack read, "Call Bernie Pasternack, Albany Business Agent, Iron Workers, Local 12."

Pasternack answered right away. "One of our guys recognizes the face on the flyer you left. Dominick Cavallo is one of my stewards. He's out on the job right now, but I can have him call you when he gets back."

While she anxiously awaited the call from Cavallo, she read through the other messages and separated them into two piles: *crap* and *potential.* When she finished, only one note was in the 'potential' pile. *All these are bullshit,* she thought. Frustrated, she stopped by Al's cubicle. "Are you having any luck with your leads?"

"Well, three of the four guys are out of contention. One is dead, another is doing time in Elmira for robbery, and it looks like Randy Ballinger has a pretty solid alibi. He was in the hospital recuperating from hernia surgery on the day of Sarah's murder. This dude, Robert Flack, is still in play, but I can't seem to locate him. Today I'll go through financial transactions to see if I can dig something up on him. How about you?"

"I got an ironworker in Albany who recognizes the Jenkins sketch. I think it's a longshot, and if that fizzles, I've got nothing."

"Time is working against us," Al said. His phone rang. "It's for you," Maddy said she'd take it in her office.

The call came through as she reached her desk. "Hi, this is Dominick Cavallo. I saw the picture of the guy you're looking for, and I'm quite sure it's someone I worked with a couple of years ago."

"Do you remember his name?"

"He called himself Hawk."

"Do you know where he lives or anything about him?"

"He was quiet. I have no idea where he lives. But I can tell you who we worked for. It was the Eastern Construction Company. They're out of Syracuse."

"Think hard. There must be something else about the guy that you remember."

Dominick hesitated. "Let me think." He was silent for a moment, and finally said, "Wait...wait, I know. I saw him walking out of the VA hospital here in Albany about a year ago. He must be a veteran."

Maddy finally had something to go on. When she hung up, she called the construction company, but it had gone out of business. She tracked down the ex-office manager, who told her the company records had been destroyed in a fire. "Maybe you should try the IRS. They should have our W-2s."

How the hell does one deal with the IRS on an issue like this? Her next call was to the Veterans Administration in Albany. She got bounced around from one administrative assistant to another until finally, she got to the hospital CEO, Marvin Keene.

"Thank you for taking my call, Mr. Keene. I need your help. There has been a gruesome murder of a child here in Utica, and a key suspect was a patient at your hospital. He goes by the name of Hawk Jenkins. We need whatever information you can give us on him."

"I'm sorry, Detective, but we don't give out confidential patient information."

"You don't understand. We think Jenkins will kill again, and we need to speak with him as soon as possible; it's imperative."

"I'm sorry, Ms. Reynolds, we have our protocols."

"A girl was raped and sodomized and then strangled. Doesn't that mean anything to you?" At the end of her rope, she felt like she was alone in a real-time nightmare. *Doesn't anyone else care about stopping this guy?*

Keene, unmoved, said, "I suggest your attorney contact our hospital attorney." Then he said goodbye and hung up. Maddy had just hit two bureaucratic brick walls, one with the IRS and the other with the VA. She told Zep, and he said he'd hand both situations over to the legal department for follow up. That was it. Maddy had been stopped dead in her tracks by the government. Exasperated and without any new leads to pursue, she reverted to the mindless task of looking through old files trying to identify similarities to Sarah's case.

When she left for home at five thirty, darkness had fallen, and the wind chill factor had reached negative ten degrees. As she walked to her car, her head felt numb, and her body ached from the rawness of the penetrating cold.

Over the next six weeks, each lead seemed to die before it went anywhere, and with no feedback on Jenkins, Maddy became bogged down, investigating petty thefts and domestic conflicts. As winter reached its depths and the snowbanks climbed as high as the roof of her car, she became a regular at City-Wide Liquors. Three or four nights a week on the way home from work, Maddy stopped in. Later in the evening, she'd pour a glass of wine and escape to the bizarre world of *Tempest on the Sea*.

Although she did her best to keep up with Amber's school activities, occasionally she'd forget a basketball game or a band concert, and each time, she would beat herself up with guilt. Sarah Benning also preyed on her mind. For Maddy, the case was unfinished business and continually crept back into her thoughts. She couldn't shake it. Occasionally when she worked on *Tempest*, the man in the window reminded her too much of Sarah's killer, and she would have to stop.

Each day going to work was like swimming against a strong current, and she dreaded it. One morning she got out of bed, and frost was built up so thick on her bedroom window that she could not see out. The wind bitterly howled and rattled the glass. A wave of despair grabbed her. It was like the undertow of a mighty ocean wave dragging her into its murky darkness.

All hope drained from her being. She gave up her fighting spirit, and fell back onto the bed and curled into a fetal position. She pulled the covers over her head and wailed, "What the hell is wrong with me?"

"Mom, I need to get a dress for the Father-Daughter Valentine's Day Dance on Friday night."

"Amber!" Maddy barked as she drove her to school. "Today is Wednesday. Why didn't you just wait until Friday after school to tell me?" Maddy looked over at her daughter's startled face.

"I'm sorry, I wasn't thinking," Amber whimpered. Then, as if she remembered why she hadn't said anything sooner, Amber lashed back out at her mother. "And besides, you never have time to talk with me anymore. You're either too tired, cooped-up in your room, or reading reports. You missed my parent-teacher conference the other day, and Mrs. Chapman has to send you a letter to reschedule it. That embarrassed me."

That hit Maddy hard. She pulled the car to the curb and put her head on the steering wheel. *I can't believe I did that.* She tried to hold back tears as she stammered, "I am so sorry. I...I...I..." nothing came out.

"You don't have to say anything. I'll be okay. Come on, get me to school before I'm late."

The realization of how Sarah's case had brought her into such a dark place rattled Maddy. She had become inaccessible to her daughter. It was what she had feared most, and now it was happening.

When she pulled up to the school, Amber reached over and hugged her before she got out. Maddy drove off, feeling the sting of guilt. The phone rang, and it was Zep. "Maddy, that reporter for The Observer-Dispatch, Goldfarb, just called me. Somehow, he got wind of the valentine from Sarah Benning's bedroom. He's going to run a story about it on Valentine's Day. He wouldn't tell me his source, but I need to find out if there's a leaker in the department. Do you have any idea how this could have gotten out?"

"No, I don't." As soon as she hung up, she began to worry. *Does he think I might be the source?* By the time she stepped off the elevator, she had worked herself into a frenzy and bolted to his office. Zep's door was closed, and Maddy watched through the glass office walls as Sheriff Murphy and the Mayor stood by his desk, yelling. Zep sat with his arms folded and looked like a little boy who was being scolded by his parents. Maddy thought she might vomit.

Finally, the storm ended, and the two head-honchos rushed out in a huff. Maddy walked in prepared for Zep to light into her, although she knew that she hadn't done anything wrong. If she was going to catch hell, she wanted to get it over with. But Zep was not angry. He had taken the wrath of his higher-ups on the chin and didn't dump it on her. Instead, he got right down to the business of the leaker.

"So Maddy, this is what we've got. One scenario is there's a mole in the department. Another is one of our guys had a little too much to drink at Curli's Bar and blabbed his yap in earshot of someone like Goldfarb. The third, which would be a nightmare for us, is that the killer is calling the newspaper directly."

Maddy was taken aback at the prospect that the killer might be communicating directly with the media and asked, "What do we do?"

"We sit tight for a day or two and let things play out."

The next morning, while the coffee percolated, Maddy exercised her daily ritual of walking to the porch for the newspaper. The banner at the top read, "Happy Valentine's Day," and the headline was, "Cupid Leaves Sarah Benning a Valentine before Killing Her." Within minutes the phone rang. "Did you see the paper?" Zep shouted.

"Yep."

"I'm calling Harald Johnson, the Editor. I want a meeting with him, and that Goldfarb. I want you with me."

Maddy told Amber that she'd have to take the bus to school, then rushed upstairs to get dressed. She poured her coffee into a travel mug and lumbered through icy slush to her car. When she walked into Zep's office, he stood in front of his desk, glowing pink, head down and fists clenched. "Johnson said he'd meet with us as soon as we get there, come on, let's go."

Man, he's worked-up, she thought, *I've never seen him like this.* On the ride to Harald Johnson's office, Zep didn't speak. When they arrived, the secretary led them to a conference room with leather-padded chairs skillfully placed around a large cherry-wood table. Maddy and Zep sat next to each other, and within a minute or two, a tall, older man, with white, curly hair, walked in. A shorter guy with a boyish face and brush cut followed. *That's got to be Goldfarb. What a nerd.*

"Hello, Harry," Zep said. "This is Maddy Reynolds, one of the detectives working the Benning case," Harald said hello and introduced Ben Goldfarb. "Thanks for meeting so quickly," Zep said. The two newspapermen sat opposite Zep and Maddy. "I realize the importance of maintaining the confidentiality of your sources, but if there's a leaker in my department, I need you to tell me who it is. It can undermine our ability to find the murderer."

"Now Zep," Harald said in a dignified voice, "we wouldn't be in business long if we gave the police the names of our sources."

Goldfarb seemed to enjoy the tension his boss created by resisting Zep. He was in his late twenties and seemed to Maddy to be a typical go-getter type. He was dressed in a tweed sports jacket, Bostonian wingtip shoes, and a red bowtie that complemented the smartass smirk he wore on his face; Maddy had him pegged as an asshole.

"Harry, you have grandkids. What if they are next on this guy's list? How would you feel if you didn't do everything you could to stop him?"

Zep's pulling out all the stops on this one, Maddy thought.

Harald didn't seem fazed by Zep's tactic. "What I can tell you is that as far as we know, you do not have a leaker in your department."

Goldfarb gave his boss a stare as cold as steel. It was as though Johnson had given the enemy information that would help their cause over his own.

"That means the murderer, or someone close to him, has contacted you," Zep said.

"I'm not giving you anything more," Harald said sternly.

"That's all I need," Zep said. He stood up, shook Johnson's hand, and nodded to Goldfarb. Maddy smiled politely and followed Zep out.

When the elevator doors closed and the two detectives were alone, Zep said, "Our guy has contacted the paper. He's a cunning son-of-a-bitch. It's Valentine's Day, and he's going to strike. I can just feel it."

Zep's words reverberated in Maddy's head as she followed up with union leaders on the phone, trolling for information about Jenkins. The afternoon passed by slowly. Her mind drifted to Amber. She pulled a phone book from the drawer, turned to the yellow pages, and looked under 'Jewelers.'

"Jaqueline Jewelers. Jackie speaking."

"How late are you open?"

"Four thirty," the woman said.

"Great, I'll see you soon."

Maddy left work early and arrived at the jewelry store a little past four. "My daughter's birthday is in September. I want to surprise her with a necklace. It's for a dance she's going to tonight. I was thinking of something in her birthstone."

"Aha, Sapphire. I have just the thing." Jackie walked to a glass case and showed her a deep-blue stone on a delicate, white-gold chain.

"Oh, my God. This will go perfectly with her dress." Then she looked at the price tag and nearly gagged. *Holy shit, that's a week's pay. Aww, what the fuck.* "Okay, I'll take it."

When she arrived home, Amber excitedly awaited. Her new, blue gown hung in the hallway and, as Maddy promised, she started helping her get ready. "Mom, can you do my hair before I get dressed?"

"Don't you want to have dinner before you get dressed?" As she spoke, Maddy clandestinely took the white box with the necklace from her briefcase and placed it in her jacket pocket.

"I had some leftover meatloaf, and besides, they have pizza at the dance." Maddy quickly changed into something more comfortable and braided Amber's hair. When she finished, they went downstairs, where Amber carefully slipped into her new gown. Maddy gasped. *Dear God, she looks like a woman. How did she grow up so fast?*

As Amber looked in the full-length mirror, shifting the dress slightly to one side, then primping her hair a little, Maddy took the white box from her coat, walked over, and put out her hand. "This is for you because I love you so much."

Amber took the box and opened it. She looked at her mother with her mouth opened. To Maddy's surprise, she saw the pain in her daughter's eyes. Amber let the white gold chain fall between her fingers, and the blue stone lay in the palm of her hand. She looked up at her mother and burst into tears. Instinctively, Maddy held her and let Amber sob on her shoulder. "You have no idea what this means to me," Amber said. Maddy's heart ached as she realized how much pain her daughter had been holding in from the mother-daughter conflicts they had experienced in recent days. *I am so glad I decided to do this.*

It was almost five forty-five, and Jack was to arrive at six. "Come on, dear, let's clean you up. Your father will be here soon."

Jack arrived, dressed in a black suit with a blue tie that matched Amber's dress. He handed Amber a white corsage, and Maddy looked on as father and daughter admired one another. *It might look like this on her wedding day*, Maddy thought. She became filled with joy.

The plan for the evening was that after the dance, Amber would stay overnight at Jack's. While Amber was upstairs packing overnight clothes, Jack asked Maddy if he could discuss something with her. *Here we go*, Maddy thought. *Every time he uses this tone of voice, he wants to talk about taking me to dinner.* Sure enough, that's what it was.

"Let's not spoil this moment, Jack. Okay, if you insist on having dinner to talk things over, I will go, but under one condition: Amber is not to know anything about it. She's finally in a good place with our divorce, and I don't want to confuse her."

"Great," he said. "We'll do it on a night when she's at a sleepover."

Amber came back downstairs, and before she put on her coat, Maddy asked to take a picture.

"How about one with Dad and me." As Maddy snapped it, a sadness crept in. *This is how I had always wanted our family to be*, she thought, *the three of us, together, and not all crazy the way it is now.*

After they left and Maddy was finally alone, she poured a glass of wine, sat in the living room, and thought about how happy Amber had seemed. She dozed off but was awakened when the phone rang. The clock read 1:38 a.m. *Oh geez, this can't be good*. It was Zep. "Are you ready for this? He did it again. Cupid took another girl."

The room became exceedingly small, and Maddy felt it closing in on her. *I thought I was prepared for this.* She felt numb and struggled to grasp the whole of what it meant that another girl might be in the grip such a monster. Zep continued to talk, but Maddy didn't hear everything. She grabbed a pen and scribbled down some notes on a scrap of paper as he rattled off the details.

"Get there as soon as you can," he said and hung up.

For a few seconds, she couldn't move. Then she jumped up, grabbed her coat, and ran out of the house. Barely legible, her scribbled notes were difficult to read. "Female... ten years old. Went missing yesterday at three p.m.... Command center, New Hartford Municipal Building."

She tried to save time by taking the back roads to New Hartford, but the blackness of night and occasional patches of ice made her wish she hadn't. With her mind still dull from the wine, she worried that she might have missed something critical that Zep had said, so she called Al.

"What did you hear, Al?"

"They found a valentine in the kid's coat."

"So, it's the same guy," she shrieked. "Holy shit! Holy shit!"

A bolt of electricity struck her. Her thoughts scattered like bowling pins. "Fucking Myers was right. This guy is a serial killer!"

Chapter 16

By the time Maddy arrived at the makeshift command center, the night had taken on a life of its own. The clanking of tables and chairs unfolding, people scurrying around to install telephones and computers, and food supplies, pillows, blankets, and cots wheeled in from trucks created an energy that hung in the air like static electricity. Faces, fixed and purposeful, reflected the seriousness of the situation; everyone knew that a girl had gone missing.

Zep stood in front of the room and beckoned for the crowd's attention. "Come down to this end, please. Take a seat. Come on now, move along, hurry, time is short." Before the seats were full, he started in. "Thank you for getting here at this late hour. As you may know, we have a situation where every minute counts. Chief Ryan and his team from the New Hartford P. D. have been working a case of a missing ten-year-old girl. It was called in at 3:36 yesterday afternoon by the child's mother."

He paced back and forth in front of the crowd. All eyes homed in on him as he read from a clipboard. "The girl's name is Nancy Miles. When interviewing the parents at their home last night, the officers found a valentine in Nancy's blue jeans similar to the one found in Sarah Benning's bedroom."

A low rumble, like thunder before a storm, moved through the gathering. Maddy was drawn into the mood of the moment as heads turned and whispers grew into loud chatter. After Zep waited for his audience to absorb the details, he started in again. "If this is the same perpetrator as in the Benning case, and, because the valentine was in the child's possession before abduction, we think it is, he will probably keep the girl alive for forty-eight hours before raping and killing her."

His words brought the full weight of the situation into focus. Faces grew pale, and a woman in the back of the room could be heard crying. Maddy's mind raced as she tried to grasp the significance of Cupid showing himself a second time. *He intends to unleash hell on this community,* she thought. *As Myers said, he's telling us, "I am here; stop me if you can."*

"It's now almost four a.m.," Zep continued. "We have less than thirty-six hours to find Nancy alive. We know the route she walked on the way home from school. Based on that information, we have marked off areas for canvassing. You will work in teams of two. When we finish here, you'll pick up your assignments and the person who you're partnered with at the back table." He stopped pacing, turned, and looked directly at the crowd. "The clock is ticking, people. You are this girl's only hope. Now, let's move out."

Maddy waited in line at the back table and noticed that Bud Renshaw was in front of her. He turned, looked down, smirked at her, and turned back. After he opened his assignment, he turned again, and said "Whew," as though relieved that Maddy wasn't his partner. She just shook her head and said to herself, *the guy's an asshole.*

Maddy was surprised that she and Allison were partnered. *I didn't know she had started as a detective yet.* Scanning the gym, Allison was nowhere. As she headed back to see if there was a mistake, Allison burst through the front door, appearing frazzled. She walked up to Maddy and said, "I got a call from Zep a little over an hour ago. He wants me to start today, so here I am. What do I do?"

"You're partnered with me. We're assigned to the street where the victim was last seen."

"What victim?"

"Oh my God, come on, I'll tell you in the car."

Beam Street was the last place where Nancy Miles was seen. It was still dark when the two detectives arrived, and the old amber-colored streetlamps barely made a difference. A heavy mist had settled on the rundown, two-story houses, and made the street seem like it belonged in a

London murder mystery. It was just past five a.m., and, with the temperature in the forties, they pulled their heavy coats out from the back seat of the cruiser. "We won't make many friends waking people up at this hour," Maddy said.

They agreed to work opposite sides of the street and use handheld radios to communicate. Maddy knocked at the first door, and when no one answered, waited several minutes, made a note, and moved on. An older woman shuffled to the door in a walker at the next house. When Maddy asked if she'd noticed a girl who fit Nancy Miles's description, the woman said, "No. I'm hardly ever near a window. Most of my day is in a chair. But I read about it. Do you have any idea what happened to her?"

"We're working on it, ma'am." After she made an entry in her notebook, Maddy politely disengaged from the conversation. By late morning, she had finished with half the houses on her side of the street and had little to show for it. She started back to her car to check in when she noticed a white pickup parked behind her with its engine running. The driver, a man with long hair and a ski cap, seemed to be staring at her. Slowly, the truck backed up. When she got close, it made a U-turn and sped off.

Maddy jumped in her car, but in her excitement, hit the gas too hard, fishtailed, and allowed the truck to gain distance. By the time she reached the main intersection, the guy had disappeared. A bus was stopped at a red light next to her, blocking her view. She waited for it to move, ready to crawl out of her skin; the light turned green, and the bus pulled away. A white truck, off to her right, seemed too far away to catch, but she swerved into the on-coming lane and sped after it until finally, she had to pull over. "Shit. I lost him," she said out loud.

Maddy was about to turn around when a man with long hair and a ski cap walked out of a paint store only a few buildings from where she was parked. *Son-of-a-bitch, that's him!* She ran up to the guy, flashed her badge, and he stepped back, startled. "I'm Detective Reynolds from the Oneida County Sheriff's Department; I'd like a word with you."

"Are you a rozzer?"

"A what?" she asked. She didn't understand what he meant. She repeated herself.

"Oh...okay." The man looked at her, dumbfounded. "What did I do?"

"Were you just on Beam Street?"

"Ah-huh."

In addition to being slow-witted, something else seemed odd about the guy. "What's your name?" she asked.

"Mason Charles."

"Where do you live, Mr. Charles?"

"103 Beam Street."

"I knocked at your house earlier. Why didn't you answer?"

"I was probably in the basement and didn't hear you." *That's it,* she thought. *He has a slight British accent.*

"What do you do, Mr. Charles?"

"I make things."

What the hell is that supposed to mean, she wondered. Maddy got him to agree to let her follow him home and check out his house; when she walked in the front door, the smell of turpentine nearly knocked her over. Before she took two steps into the foyer, a man in his fifties, bald and rotund, came out from another room.

"How can we help you?" he asked.

She introduced herself and said she was following up with residents about the girl who went missing the day before.

"My name is Donald Charles. I'm Mason's stepbrother, and I can assure you, we had nothing to do with it."

"Oh, I'm not suggesting that you did Mr. Charles. We're talking with everyone on the block," Maddy said. "Do you remember seeing a girl around ten years old walk by your house yesterday between four o'clock and four thirty?"

"I know who you're talking about. The girl walks by here often. But yesterday, Mason and I weren't here."

He's getting pissed, Maddy thought, as Donald's face grew red. "Do you mind if I look around?" she asked.

"Is that legal?"

Maddy shrugged, "I don't have a search warrant if that's what you mean, so I can only search with your permission. It's up to you."

Donald didn't try to hide his irritation. Curtly, he said, "Go ahead."

Maddy walked through the first floor and checked out the rooms. Finding nothing, she opened the basement door and descended the stairs. Donald and Mason followed. The basement was a brightly lit workshop filled with hundreds of model airplanes that sat on shelves along its walls.

"Did you build all these?"

"Yeah, I did," Mason responded. "I build things."

"Indeed, Mason loves building his models, don't you?" Donald said, interrupting Mason as though he was trying to get him to shut up. With her suspicions heightened, Maddy scrutinized the basement. She happened to look out a window and saw a garage out back. "I'd like to take a look in that garage," she said.

As though she had stepped on Donald's toe, his eyes widened. He hesitated, then said, "Okay." Outside, Donald stood with his arms folded and said, "Help yourself, but be careful; those old doors don't work so well."

Maddy grabbed the two door handles, pulled, and then pushed several times, but they wouldn't budge. Finally, she lifted up on one with both hands and broke it free. Inside, an old, unusual car, a throwback to another era, covered with grime and surface rust, looked like it was a long time neglected. She wiped the windows and looked inside. Mason seemed unable to refrain himself and excitedly said, "It's a Rupert.... It's British."

"Hmm. Can you open it?"

"Sure." He quickly opened one of the doors.

Women's clothing—skirts, blouses, shoes, scarves, and a couple of wigs—was messily scattered around. *Maybe someone's been using these as disguises,* she thought. "Whose car?" she asked while making a note.

"It belonged to our Aunt Martha," Donald replied. "She willed it to me when she died."

Maddy looked at him with an untrusting eye, closed the door, and checked the trunk, but nothing was out of line. She stepped back into the yard, and as she made notes, asked, "So what kind of work do you do, Mr. Charles?"

"I'm a retired chef. I used to work at a fine restaurant outside of London before I had my accident. Now, I can hardly stand more than ten minutes without being in severe back pain. I am in pain as we speak."

Too fucking bad, she thought, but said, "Oh, I'm sorry to hear that. I'll just be a few more minutes. You said you weren't home yesterday. Where were you?"

"In Utica at an antique toy and model show. Mason and I didn't get home until after nine o'clock."

"Can you verify that?"

Smiling, Donald put his hand in his coat pocket, pulled out some slips of paper, shuffled through them, and held out two torn tickets to an antique show as well as a parking pass. "This parking pass shows that we were there from 9:46 a.m. to 8:36 p.m.," Donald said with a smirk that was starting to piss Maddy off.

How convenient. A ready-made alibi, she thought.

She wasn't quite ready to leave, so she eyeballed the house one more time and noticed that it had an attic. She was about to ask to see it when Allison's panicked-filled voice screeched through the radio in her pocket. "I'm in pursuit."

Maddy left the Charles brothers standing in their yard, ran to the street, and saw Allison chasing a man in a baseball hat. Since he was too far to catch on foot, she jumped in her car and rushed to where Allison had disappeared around a house. Maddy ran into the yard where she had last seen Allison and was stunned to find her on the ground holding the side of her head, her face covered with blood. "Are you all right?" she asked, as she helped her sit up.

"I think so. The guy hid behind that garage and jumped out when I got close. He knocked me down, called me a bitch, and hit me with the butt of a pistol."

"It could have been worse, Allison. He could have shot you."

"Holy shit, you're right! I could be dead."

Chapter 17

Squad cars filled Beam Street while Allison sat in the back seat of Maddy's cruiser, holding a blood-soaked towel to her head. Zep sat next to her as she explained how it happened. "I walked up to the door of 301 and this the guy bolts out, almost knocks me over, and takes off. I chased him into the yard, but he disappeared. Then, out of nowhere, he pops out from behind the garage, knocks me down, and slugs me with a pistol. He took off into those woods." She pointed to a vast forest behind the house.

"We're not equipped to go after him out there," Zep said. "There are hundreds of acres of woods that run behind these streets. We'll have to call in the K-9 unit."

Maddy sat with Allison in the car as everyone waited for the K-9 team. Finally, an ambulance arrived, and two medics examined her wound. "It's a head injury, and she really should come with us for some tests," one of the medics told Zep.

"Aww, come on," Allison protested.

"We don't take unnecessary chances, Allison," Zep said.

"Come on, I'll walk with you," Maddy said as she put her hand around Allison's shoulder and walked her to the ambulance. "I'll check in on you later." The doors closed, and the ambulance took off.

Within twenty minutes, trucks filled with people dressed in heavy gear, and barking dogs, started to arrive. The street was popping with activity, and, amid the clatter of equipment and excited dogs, Maddy heard someone shout out her name. "Hey, Maddy." She looked over and saw Trick Diaz. He came over with a big smile and hugged her. It was the first good feeling she had had the entire day. It reminded her of the previous summer when they partnered together, and all the laughs they had.

"Big-time detective now, huh Maddy?" he said through his smile. It was as though Trick couldn't help but smile. He was always upbeat, funny, and he had probably been his seventh-grade class clown.

"Yeah, and I see you got your K-9 gig too...not bad, Trick."

Diaz radiated positive energy, and Maddy loved being around him. She told a friend once that if you don't like Trick Diaz, you'll never like anybody. Although very handsome, he was a true family man, with several kids. He never flirted around with the available females in the department. Just being around him made her feel better.

Maddy watched as the K-9 team unloaded their equipment, readied the dogs, formed up, and slowly disappeared into the dreariness of the woods.

The house at 301 was surrounded by law enforcement as Zep, Maddy, and Bud Renshaw prepared to enter. With their weapons drawn, they slowly moved in. The first thing Maddy noticed was an overpowering smell of pot and incense. Dishes piled high in the kitchen sink and crumpled up sleeping bags scattered on the living room floor suggested that several people had been living there.

The upstairs revealed a more sinister aspect. On the wall of a bedroom hung clippings of child pornography, and on the floor lay scattered child porn magazines. One photo showed a man having sex with a girl about fourteen years old. *Meat!* Maddy thought. *These kids are nothing more than pieces of meat to these guys.*

"Take a look at these," Bud said as he searched a dresser drawer and found at least a dozen pairs of little girl's underwear stuffed inside. Hearts and teddy bears were on a few, and one had the name 'Dora' written on it.

"Bag those," Zep said. "We need to find out if any belong to Nancy Miles or Sarah Benning."

After they'd cleared the house, the forensics team went in, and while the K-9 unit combed the woods, there was nothing to do but wait. The scene on the street had become as dead as a wake. Cops drifted into small groups and talked among themselves as they tried to keep warm. Maddy and

Al stayed near Zep's car and listened to information as it came in on his radio.

The temperature dropped, daylight faded, and the more they learned about the guy from 301, the clearer it became how dire the situation was. His name was Benny Bowls. He was a convicted child molester hit with a recent parole violation by Fran Liberatore, his parole officer. When Zep spoke with Liberatore on the phone, she said there was an outstanding warrant for his arrest. When he asked if she'd come to the scene, she responded, "Gladly. I've been trying to track down Bowls for days. He's bad news."

Maddy overheard Zep tell the K-9 captain that he'd better bring in cadaver dogs just in case the Miles girl was buried somewhere out in the woods. The thought brought back feelings of standing before Sara Benning's body at the portable toilet, and darkness began to fill her insides.

In addition to doing time for raping a six-year-old girl, Benny Bowls had several assault charges against women. When Fran Liberatore arrived at the scene, she said Bowls, for no apparent reason, just stopped coming to his appointments. "Something was going down with him," she said, "but I had no idea what it was. He told me he'd never go back to prison again. I don't think he'll go peaceably."

By five thirty, it was pitch black, and Maddy could see her breath when she breathed. The steady drizzle and penetrating cold seemed relentless. A hand reached out to her with a hot cup of coffee, and when she looked up, it was Al. "Oh, you're an angel," she said. "Where did you get it?" She took the cup with both hands, savoring a sip, and felt its heat warm her insides as it went down.

"Never mind where I got it, just enjoy. You look like you need it." Al cradled his cup with both hands. "This day is turning into a real cluster fuck, isn't it?" he added, as he leaned back against Zep's car next to her.

"Yeah, and I have a feeling it's not over. Not by a long shot." No sooner had Maddy said the words than the sky lit up with a series of flashes. Beams of light silhouetted the trees in the direction of the K-9 team. Thunderclaps followed. "That's gunfire," Al said.

"Something's going wrong out there," Maddy said. "There are too many shots being fired."

The sounds of men yelling and dogs barking echoed through the woods. "Get a medic out here," a voice shouted from the darkness. Everyone rose to their feet. A man from the K-9 team ran out of the woods, screaming, "We've got a man down; hurry with that medic." Four guys followed, carrying a man across their clasped arms. When they passed by Maddy, a light shined on the face, and it was Trick. His head bobbled, blood flowed from his mouth, and his eyes were frozen wide.

Paralyzed, Maddy watched as they laid him on the ground. A paramedic kneeled and put his hand on Trick's neck. "He's dead." Maddy dropped her head, and her heart sank. Faces, white with shock, looked at each other, and no one knew what to do. Finally, a man from the K-9 team walked over and dropped to his knees next to the body. He bowed his head, and his comrades soon followed suit.

As Maddy thought of the joyful man, her fists clenched with rage. *This is so unfair. Just a few flashes of light, and now he's gone.* Her thoughts went to Trick's wife and kids. *Their lives will never be the same. Now those kids will be like me, growing up without a dad.*

The mood among the leadership at the scene turned to alarm. Red-faced and wet with sweat, the K-9 unit captain took off his helmet. "The guy was hiding in a thicket and opened fire when Trick got close. He didn't have a chance but was able to get off two shots as he went down." The captain wiped his face with a towel and, close to tears, continued. "The guy took off into the woods. We pursued him, but he crossed a stream, and it threw the dogs off. He managed to get over to Route 5. When we got there, a woman was standing in the road. She said a man stopped her car at gunpoint, ordered her out, and drove off."

The captain breathed heavily and stopped for a few seconds to take a swig of water. "She said the guy was limping. We found blood on the road." Before he gave Zep the description of the car and the plate number, he said, "The thing is, the guy could have made it to the road without waiting in the bushes. He had plenty of time. It's as though he wanted to kill a cop. We've got to get that son-of-a-bitch."

Zep alerted law enforcement in the area that Bowls was on the run and gave out the description of the hijacked car. Within twenty minutes, a call came in that someone sighted the vehicle in downtown Utica. Beam Street emptied like a high school parking lot after the last bell.

In the back seat of a patrol car, Maddy squeezed between Al and Bud, and she felt every bump on the pot-holed city street. Zep and another detective sat in front as sirens screamed, and lights flashed. Everyone remained silent. Maddy's thoughts were on Amber. *What will happen to her if I get killed tonight?* Trick's sudden death brought home that it could happen to her. She had always avoided dealing with her death but vowed that if she survived the night, she would make proper arrangements for her daughter, just in case.

When Al made a call to his mother, everyone in the car started to call loved ones. Maddy got ahold of Jack, explained the situation, and asked to speak with Amber. "Hi, honey. It looks like I'll have to work late, so you'll need to stay with Dad, Okay?"

"Are you all right, Mom? What's all that noise?"

"Remember when I told you there will be times that I can't talk about my work with anyone, even you?"

"This is one of them, right?"

"Yes."

"Okay, but I'll see you in the morning, right?"

"Yep, see you in the morning." *I hope so*, Maddy thought. "Love you."

"Love you too, Mom. Be careful."

The cruiser rattled and shook, and within a few blocks of the destination, Zep sent out an order for all sirens and flashing lights to be turned off. Maddy's mouth was dry, and she felt a lump in the pit of her stomach move to her throat. She reached down and felt for her father's badge in her pocket. *Be with me, Dad.*

Dozens of police vehicles converged on the stolen car. A uniformed cop ran up to Zep and said, "Someone saw a man running into that building, holding his leg." She stood gazing at a building known to be a place where lowlifes blended in among low-income families to avoid the eye of the law. A throwback to Utica's long-gone industrial heyday, it had five stories with retail stores at the street level and four floors of apartments above. The massive old edifice stood stark in the night and brought Maddy powerful feelings of dread.

She stood in the freezing rain as Zep huddled with his detectives and explained the plan. The building had two sections with separate stairwells. Teams of two assigned to each section readied themselves to enter. "Evacuate as many residents as possible, but remember, one of them is Bowls." Maddy and Bud Renshaw were assigned to the third floor.

As she ascended the stairs, the aroma of food cooking in the apartments mixed with the stink of urine in the stairwell, creating a sickly stench. Maddy's bad feelings grew with each step up, and a cruel, unforgiving doubt began to weaken her resolve. She wondered if all her hours of practice with a gun would make a difference when it counted. *Targets don't shoot back*, she thought. Again, she looked to her father for strength, reached into her pocket, and held his badge. She whispered, "Please give me courage, Dad."

The third-floor hallway was dark and dismal. Residents scattered like mice into their nests. No one answered at the first two apartments, but at the third, a woman holding a crying baby, surrounded by three kids, opened the door. "Have you seen or heard anyone in the hallway within the last hour?" Maddy asked. Barely able to speak English, the woman became distracted by a weak voice in another room calling for her. "I'll be right back," she said and walked away.

While Maddy and Bud waited at the door, a girl about four stayed behind and stared at them. She was in pink pajamas, held a stuffed kitty-cat, and sucked her thumb. When Maddy smiled at her, she took her thumb from her mouth and pointed her index finger at the apartment across the hall, two doors down. Maddy knelt. "Did a man run into that door tonight?" The girl slowly nodded her head. "Alright, sweetie, now go back in with your mommy and don't open this door, okay?" The child put her thumb back in her mouth, turned and shut the door.

Any fear or doubt that Maddy felt washed away. She knew what had to be done, having practiced it at least a hundred times. She whispered to Bud, "I'm going in low; you cover me."

Bud looked at her as if she had lost her mind. "Are you crazy? What about a search warrant?"

"Fuck a search warrant," she said as she pointed at the blood on the doorknob. "That's probable cause. On the count of three, kick the door in. I'll go in low while you stay back and cover me." Bud gave a reluctant nod. Maddy counted with her fingers. Her thoughts were on Trick and as the count reached "three," her last thought was, *I want that bastard.*

The door blew open. Maddy slid to the floor, and saw Bowls waiting with both hands on his gun. He fired. She heard the bullet whiz overhead as she shot three times. A gaping hole opened around his heart. Bowls stood frozen, still holding his gun, trying to get off another shot. Maddy fired before he did and popped a hole in his forehead. He dropped with a loud, slapping sound to the floor. Bowls lay on his back, blood gurgling from his mouth. Maddy sat with one leg extended, her ears ringing and surrounded by a cloud of smoke. *I just killed a man.*

Throbbing pain in her left knee demanded her attention, and she grabbed it with both hands. After Bud checked out the rest of the apartment, he came over and put his hand on Maddy's shoulder. She snapped around. "Are you okay," he asked.

"I think so, but I smacked my knee, and it's killing me."

The sounds of feet pounding on the stairway shook the walls. Zep, Al, and another detective ran into the room. "Did you do this?" Zep asked Renshaw. Bud shook his head and pointed to Maddy. "She's not shot, but her knee is banged up pretty good."

Zep knelt next to her and asked if she could stand, as Al went over to Bowls and confirmed that he was dead.

"I think so, but I need help."

Maddy felt the throbbing in her knee begin to radiate up her leg as Zep and Bud each took an arm and helped her up. Her arms around their shoulders, Maddy moved with the men into the hallway. Al cleared a path through the crowd of gathering residents.

"How did you learn to shoot like that?" Zep asked as they carefully descended the stairs.

"Lots of practice."

When they reached the street, Al brought a squad car to the front of the building. Together, Zep and Bud lifted Maddy into the front seat. As Al drove to the hospital, Maddy lay back, hands lightly rubbing the banged-up knee and her mind reeling from what she had done to Bowls. A sickening feeling, spurred on by the image of his lifeless body as it hit the floor, began welling up inside her. She became aware of the power she possessed. It was a power that she'd worked hard to attain through years of practice with a gun, and it had served her well when she was young. It had allowed her to ward off the dread of the man who killed her father; the man she feared would come back to kill her. *I have the power to take life*, she thought, and at that moment, wished she did not. *Only God has that right.* She knew such thoughts could get her killed against someone out to destroy her, so she pushed them from her mind.

Late that night, she returned home from the E.R. with an ice pack, ace bandage, some pain pills, and a monster swollen knee.

Chapter 18

Nigel, 1955, Chicago, Illinois

Nigel's father was loud, boisterous, and a braggart, but he made Nigel feel welcome, and that was all that mattered. Although the neighborhood was like a war zone and the apartment a mess, he was free from Mother's wrath and felt a deep sense of gratitude to his dad.

"Chumps, most people are chumps," his dad would say, and "School? Don't talk to me about school. You don't have to go to school as long as you live with me, kid. I'll teach you everything you need to know. You're going to learn ways to hustle a buck, and believe me when I tell you, brother: I know 'em all."

Nigel loved living with his father. Every day was a new adventure. *Sleep 'til noon, meet up with Dad's friends at Lucky's Coffee Shop and laugh at all those goodie-two-shoes assholes out there stuck in their grinds. I wouldn't trade this for anything.* He particularly liked afternoons at the pool hall. That was when the day began. One at a time, guys would stroll in and tell tales of adventures from the night before. The energy slowly grew until the evening, and then the fireworks would happen.

By dark, everyone knew what they wanted to do that night. Some guys quietly disappeared to pull off a caper. A trip to a whorehouse was a staple if there wasn't anything better in the offing. Some, though, and it was always the same ones, couldn't get enough of crashing high stakes card games. Then, the next morning, like déjà vu, the whole damn thing started over again. It was a glorious time, and Nigel wanted it to go on forever.

To make matters even better, Nigel's father was a master thief. He knew every con game imaginable. He loved to say, "I can swindle an old lady out of her false teeth." He'd laugh hard, smile, and his gold tooth would shine. His friends called him Louie the Lob. He was a large man, like Nigel, about six feet tall, well over two-fifty, and was a beast in the streets. No one messed with Louie the Lob.

They lived in an apartment downtown in a crime-ridden neighborhood where few cops came around. "You can go weeks without seeing a Dick among these rat traps," Louie would boast.

As Nigel sat with his father in Jimmy's Billiard one afternoon watching a couple of guys shoot a game of straight pool, Louie put his arm around his son and said, "My favorite caper for quick money is churches. If you need a fast buck, it's the only way to go. Those Catholics are dumb. They light candles and put money in metal boxes with locks that are a piece of cake to pick. On a good day, I can hit eight churches and make over a hundred and fifty bucks."

Life was like strawberry shortcake every day compared to the fish guts with Mother and Gertie. *And to think, my favorite thing back then was to play with those stupid rocks,* he thought, although he kept Jade for good luck.

"I'm proud of you, son," Louie told him the day he raked in over three hundred bucks after rummaging through the clothes of basketball players while they were out on the court. "That's my boy. He's going to make it big someday," he bragged to his friends.

On Nigel's fifteenth birthday, Louie took him to Lady Lila's Men's Club, which he said was the cleanest whorehouse in Chicago. When they walked in the vestibule, the light was low, and a dizzying scent of sandalwood struck Nigel. He wasn't sure if it was the pint of brandy he had drunk or the opium he had smoked an hour earlier, but the flowers on the wallpaper danced like the babes at Alfie's strip joint.

A middle-aged woman came out from behind a beaded curtain and greeted them. Dressed in a low-cut burgundy gown, Nigel was barely able to keep his eyes off her huge boobs. *How does she keep those things from falling out?*

"My name's Lila. You must be Nigel. Your father tells me you're ready to become a man. I have just the girl for you. Her name is Tamatha, and she is waiting upstairs." Louie put his hand on Nigel's shoulder and said, "You're going to like this, boy."

Lila took his arm and began walking him up the stairs. He looked back and saw his father's head bob up and down as he chuckled to himself as though he knew something that Nigel didn't. When Lila opened the bedroom door, he understood his father's smile. A tender young girl lay on her side in a nearly transparent silk nightgown. Her milky white skin revealed her age, which was not much older than Nigel's, although she had the body of a woman. Her hair was jet black, and her smile was broad and sweet.

Lila left them alone. He walked to the bed, and Tamatha put out her hand, gently pulling him close, then kissed his lips. His heart pounded, and blood rush to his groin. Without saying a word, Tamatha undid the buttons and zipper on his pants, slid them off, and encouraged him to lie on his back next to her.

One button at a time and in no rush, she unbuttoned his shirt as she kissed his chest and stomach. When she put him in her mouth, an unexpected force took over. "You fucking pig!" He jumped up, slapped her, and had a powerful urge to snap her neck like a pretzel. It took all his effort to restrain himself. Tamatha crawled to her knees, face red and swollen; tears ran down her face, but she did not make a sound. It was as if she had experienced such assaults before and knew better than to make a scene.

Filled with confusion, Nigel pulled up his pants, and a sense of repulsion raced around his brain. *What's wrong with me*, he wondered. The heat of humiliation pressed against his face as he passed his father on the way out the door. *I can never face him again.*

Nails gnawed at Nigel's insides. He walked the streets in a cold drizzle wishing he were dead. *Who am I? What am I? Why did I do that? What will he think of me?* He walked for a long time and finally entered a café where he sat near a window, drank coffee, and watched cars creep up and down the street in the rain. He wished he were anyone but himself.

Hours passed, closing time neared, and finally, Nigel caught a cab home. When he walked into the apartment, his father was watching television with a Bud in his hand. Nigel looked at him and waited for his Dad to denigrate him like Mother used to do. But to his surprise, he simply said, "Don't worry, son, it happens to all of us." And that was it. Nothing more was ever said about the incident, yet Nigel remained haunted by the rage inside that made him want to snap Tamatha's neck.

Chapter 19

Nigel, 1957, Chicago, Illinois

"Wake up, Nigel, Johnny Nero's here." Nigel rolled out of bed, got dressed, and went to the next room, where Louie talked with a tall, lanky man. Louie introduced the two, and they shook his hands. *This guy looks like a pimp.* Dressed in black, with a gold chain dangling a black swastika around his neck, Johnny sat in the big chair like he owned the place. He lifted what seemed to be a size fourteen boot up onto the coffee table and glanced around the apartment as though he was casing the joint.

He's not here to visit. He looks like a man on a mission, Nigel thought. After some chitchat, Johnny got down to his real purpose. "I have a big job in mind, and I'm thinking about letting you guys in on it." He lit up a cigarette, took a drag, and seemed to be looking for Louie's reaction. "Liquor stores used to be easy pickings, but now everybody's got a gun. Shit, you never know what you're gonna run into. The way I figure it, if you're going to take a risk, you may as well go big."

Louie sat at the edge of his seat and nodded at everything Johnny said. He seemed impressed by the guy, but Nigel regarded him with a cautious eye. There was something about Johnny that didn't feel right. *He reminds me of a used car salesman.* But when he said, "Bigger than the Lampert Jewelry robbery," Nigel sat up straight and listened. Everyone knew about the Lampert heist. The guys who pulled it off left town with a boatload of money and were living the life in Miami, or so everyone said.

Boy, Dad's bought this guy's line of shit. Although his instincts told him Johnny couldn't be trusted, he wasn't about to leave his father alone to deal with Johnny's powers of persuasion, so he decided to remain silent. "There's going to be a truck full of cash headed to a department store vault.

Are you interested?" He smiled, and his huge eyeteeth reminded Nigel of a snake.

"Definitely!" Louie said.

"Good! I got it all figured out, and I know the information is reliable. If we play our cards right, it'll be a piece of cake."

A piece of cake, my ass, Nigel thought.

"It'll only be the three of us...less to split up. Nigel, you'll be the lookout. Louie, you and me will go in and get the money. I got it all figured out, and it came from a guy who used to work there, so I know it's reliable."

Each morning the three partners met at Lucky's for breakfast and sat at the same corner table, where no one could hear them talk. "Me and Louie will take care of the truck driver, and Nigel will be the lookout. You'll stand in front of the cigar store across the street. If someone comes, Nigel, walk to the alley and start whistling Camp Town Races."

"I don't know Camp Town Races."

"He don't know Camp Town Races," Johnny said as he turned to Louie, laughing. "What the fuck do you know?"

"Take Me Out to the Ball Game."

"Okay, sing fucking Take Me Out to the Ball Game." Johnny shook his head as though he was talking to an idiot.

Nigel didn't like being laughed at and looked over at his father to see if he was laughing too, but he wasn't. Louie glared at Johnny in his son's defense, and it made Nigel's heart soar. At that moment, Nigel felt more warmth inside than ever before. Despite Louie being taken in by Johnny's bullshit, Nigel realized how much he genuinely loved his dad.

After a week of breakfast meetings, their plan became as smooth as custard, as Johnny liked to say, and the heist was all set for the following Friday. They met at Louie's place early Friday morning and stepped through their scheme one more time. When they had finished, Johnny smiled, his fangs protruding, and said, "Are you boys ready to get rich?"

It was a typical summer morning in Chicago: blue sky, comfortably warm, and a refreshing breeze blowing in off the lake. On the way to the caper, Nigel's stomach churned, and when Johnny stopped the car in front of the Cigar Store, he thought he might have to hurl. Johnny turned to Louie and Nigel. "We're not fucking around here, right?" *What's he getting at,* Nigel wondered.

Johnny slid two pistols out from under his shirt and handed one to Louie. "Take this, and I'll keep one. We don't use these on the guy in the truck. We need to take care of him quiet-like," he said as he pulled out a knife and held it in his hand. "We only use the guns if a cop sticks his nose where it ain't supposed to be. Got it?" Louie nodded.

"This isn't what we planned," Nigel protested.

"Never mind what we planned." Johnny scowled at him. "These are our insurance policies."

Nigel didn't like dealing with the unexpected, and the guns showing up at the last second were unexpected. His anxiety grew, and he wanted to back out, but it was too late. Nigel knew he'd be labeled a pussy and he couldn't live with that. So, he took his place in front of Benny's, leaned on a mailbox, and acted as casually as he could, pretending to read a newspaper. Johnny and Louie walked across the street and entered the alley next to the department store.

According to Johnny's information, the truck with the money was to arrive at 9:17. By 9:16, Nigel felt so conspicuous that he thought every passerby was looking at him. At 9:20, he nearly bolted, and by 9:30, with great relief, he believed the information was wrong, and it was time to pull the plug. As he started across the street to the alley, he heard the rumbling of an engine, turned, and saw the money truck rolling toward him. *Holy shit!* he said and scurried back to his position.

As the truck pulled into the alley, Nigel noticed two men inside, not one. *What the fuck. That's not what we planned for!* He was anxiously waiting for something to happen when a string of pops, like firecrackers, echoed out of the alley "Nigel, Nigel, help." It was Louie calling out to him. He ran across the street and into the alley. Two uniformed men lay on the ground. One was face down with a hat a few feet away and blood running out of his ears. The other was on his back, eyes opened, jaw wide, and looking up at the sky. Both were dead. Louie sat with his legs outstretched, pants blood-soaked at the hip, and clasping his hands over his wound. His gun lay next to him on the pavement.

"The vault in the truck is locked," Johnny shouted. Blood dripped down one hand as he held his gun with the other. "Fuck the money," he said. "Let's get out of here."

Nigel helped his father stand. Together they started for the street. Johnny walked slightly ahead of them. When an unmarked police vehicle pulled into the alley, Johnny lifted his weapon, unloaded its magazine, and blew out the windshield. Louie raised his gun and shot three times.

The detective had taken cover behind the opened car door. He rose, fired four times, and hit both Johnny and Louie twice in the chest. Johnny fell on his back. The clang of his big swastika echoed in the alley when it hit the pavement. Johnny was dead.

The thud of Louie's body when it landed sent an ache through Nigel's heart. His eyes called to his son for help, but there was nothing Nigel could do except watch his father moan and squirm. Louie grabbed Nigel's arm, pulled him close, and uttered something, but Nigel only heard the sound of blood gurgling in his throat. "Father, what did you say?" Louie looked up, tears on his face, mumbling unintelligibly. His eyes rolled back, and his body went limp.

Nigel was stunned with disbelief. He looked over at the detective and screamed, "You son-of-a-bitch, you killed my father, and I'm going to kill you." He charged, but the taller, stronger man quickly pinned him down.

Police began to swarm the area like buzzards on roadkill. Two uniformed cops ran over to assist in handcuffing Nigel. They pushed his face against the hot pavement. Nigel, filled with rage, fought to get free. "We're going to have to medicate this guy. Get a medic over here," one of the cops yelled out.

Four men held him down as a fifth man injected him. A tingling sensation began to spread throughout his body, and all strength drained from his limbs, yet he was conscious. His mind still churned, just more slowly. They lifted him to a gurney, and as they rolled him through a crowd of cops, Nigel caught a glimpse of the man who shot his father. He heard someone say to him, "Good job, Jimbo." Nigel repeated the name over and over and burned the name "Jimbo" into his brain.

Chapter 20

Maddy, 1979, Utica, New York

A loud bang on the front door startled Maddy awake. "That damn paperboy." She tried to get off the couch, but a stabbing pain in her knee sent shock waves up and down her leg. "Shit, that hurt!" *The pain medication from the E.R. must have worn off.*

She edged her hips sideways, and sat up, grabbed her jacket from the floor, and took another pill. She lay back, waiting for it to work, and tried to piece together the events of the night before. *I killed Benny Bowls! I feel like the morning after I lost my virginity. There's no going back now.* Years of practice with a gun didn't prepare her for how she would feel if she killed someone. There were no words to describe it.

When the pill kicked in, she limped to the door and got the paper. The headline read, "Cop Kills Suspect—Can Nancy Miles Be Saved?" Ben Goldfarb wrote the article. It insinuated, without coming right out and saying it, that by killing Bowls, Maddy had doomed the Miles girl.

"What? This is bullshit." Helpless to defend herself against the public attack, she gimped around the room, agitated, while she read the article aloud. Before she had finished, the phone rang; it was Jack.

"Are you okay, Maddy? The paper says you killed a guy last night."

"Yeah, but they got it all wrong."

"They always do. They always do."

Maddy wasn't in the mood to have a conversation with Jack at that moment, anticipating it would lead to a litany of gripes about journalists dumping on cops. "I appreciate that you called, Jack, but I need to get some coffee in me right now. Can we talk later?"

She made the coffee extra strong, sat at the kitchen table, and looked outside at the gloomy morning, dark, wet, and dank. Despite the pain medication she'd taken, she felt a pressure building in her head from the newspaper's account of what had happened. She dialed Zep at home, and a woman answered.

"This is Susan, Zep's wife. He's asleep, but I can wake him if you'd like."

"No, please don't do that," Maddy said.

Then, in a motherly tone, Susan asked, "How are you doing with what happened last night, Maddy?"

"I'm not sure. It hasn't hit me yet."

"You know, Zep had a real hard time when he killed a man. He talked about it for months."

Maddy felt a sudden pang of envy. She, too, had someone to share her troubles with once, but after Jack's affair, all trust went out the window, and she couldn't confide in him anymore. "I think I'll be dealing with it for a long time as well," she said.

"You can call me anytime, dear. I mean it."

After she hung up, Maddy managed her way upstairs, showered, and got dressed. Her knee was double its normal size and throbbing. When the bottle of pain pills fell on the floor, she picked it up and thought how easy it would be to numb not only the pain in her knee but all the pain she was feeling. *I better ditch these*, she thought, and flushed them down the toilet. She hobbled to the car, awkwardly worked her way inside, and thought how lucky it was that her left knee was damaged and not her right. *At least I can still drive.*

On the way to New Hartford, she wondered if the cadaver dogs were still searching the woods for Nancy Miles's body. *Maybe Goldfarb is right. Did killing Bowls hurt the chances of finding the girl alive?* Ultimately, however, she rejected the notion and concluded that Goldfarb was simply a jerk trying to make a name for himself by being overly dramatic.

The morning rain had stopped by the time she arrived at the Command Center, but piercing dampness ran through her body like radiation as she hobbled across the parking lot. The bells of St. Michael's Church rang for nine o'clock mass, and the sound brought into focus the strange dichotomy of what was taking place in the church versus the high school gym.

Zep called together a small group of detectives, including Maddy, to meet at his makeshift office. They pulled steel folding chairs around a card table that he used as a desk and began brainstorming possibilities regarding Nancy's whereabouts.

"Bowls could have buried her in the woods, and we just haven't found her yet," someone suggested. "He could have her hidden at another location, and she's still alive," was another idea. Al said, "It's possible that Bowls isn't the perp at all, and it was just a coincidence that we came across another child molester the way we did."

As the team worked on a game plan, an administrative assistant put a note in front of Zep. "I'm going to have to take this, folks. Let's regroup in ten. Al and Maddy, stick around." When the crowd broke up, a call came through, and Zep put it on speaker.

"This is Harry, Zep."

"Hi Harry," Zep said coolly. "I'm guessing you're calling to apologize for the distorted article you let Goldfarb print in this morning's paper."

"No, that's not it. Ben wrote it as he sees it. I'm calling about something a little more serious."

"I'm listening."

"Just before I made this call, I spoke with Ben. Cupid called him this morning."

Maddy could see Zep's jugular vein puff up.

"Zep," Harry said with a hint of what Maddy thought was fear in his voice, "he told Goldfarb where Nancy Miles's body was."

Oh my God, Maddy thought.

Zep sat up in his chair. "Harry, before you say another word, send that son-of-bitch out to New Harford right now, or I am going to have his ass dragged downtown for questioning."

"Calm down, Zep. I'll send him out."

No sooner had he hung up than another call came through. This time he didn't put it on speaker. Maddy watched as he sat in silence. His face changed from tomato red to plum purple. Finally, he said, "There's something else you need to know, sir. Cupid called the newspaper and told Goldfarb where Nancy Miles's body is." He winced, and during the period of silence that followed, all color drained from his face. "Okay," he said, finally, and hung up. "That was the Sheriff."

Zep turned to Maddy. "When Goldfarb gets here, you and I will talk with him out in a car. There is no privacy in this damn place. It's just our luck someone will overhear the location of the body, alert the press, and they'll be waiting at the scene when we arrive. Wouldn't that look great on the front page? Al, start alerting law enforcement in the area that we may have the location of the body shortly." He paused, shook his head, and said, "I feel another shitstorm coming down."

When Goldfarb arrived, Maddy noticed he had lost his swagger. *Maybe he doesn't like being used by a madman*, she speculated. They went out to a large police van, and Zep started right in. "I need to know every detail of what Cupid said to you." Maddy had her notebook opened, ready to take it all down.

"Well, he called me at about eight fifteen this morning at my home and was using some sort of filter to distort his voice. He started by saying that the police have made a mess of things and killed the wrong guy last night. He said he could prove it. I asked him how. That's when he told me where the body was." Goldfarb paused, put a white handkerchief up to his mouth like he was trying not to barf. "He said the girl is in a sewer on the corner of Genesee and First Streets. That was it. He hung up."

"In a sewer?" Zep roared, putting his hands on his head. "Oh, sweet Jesus."

Maddy looked down, shook her head, and felt prickles moving up her arms.

"Who else did you tell about this? Zep asked.

"Just Harry."

Zep turned to Maddy. "Tell Al to inform the Utica Police and ask them to cordon off the area." Then to Goldfarb, he said, "You can be at the scene, but absolutely no pictures. Those parents don't need to see their little girl pulled out of a sewer on the six o'clock news."

By the time they arrived at Genesee and First, the drizzle had turned to ice and raw darkness shrouded the area. A tent covered the sewer to keep the public from looking on. The forensics trucks arrived at almost the same time as Zep, Al, Maddy, and Goldfarb, who stood inside the tented area to watch Forensics work.

Maddy held her breath as one of the men used a long steel hook to pull up the sewer grate. Another took a flashlight, knelt, and shined it inside the hole. His face told the story. Expressionless, he looked at Zep, nodded, then looked down at his feet, shaking his head.

Maddy walked up to the sewer and looked in and saw the white skin of a girl's naked body covered with thick black sludge. She was face down, and her blond hair floated in the sewage. It was a most unholy sight, and feelings of finding Sarah Benning in the portable toilet came rushing back. *How can anyone do such a thing to a child? He's a fucking monster, a motherfucking monster.* She couldn't look any longer and had to walk away.

People working the scene looked lifeless. Each person seemed to be in their own hellish solitude, as though it was one of their kids in the hole. Even Goldfarb appeared white after looking in, and seemed to have lost his eagerness for the story.

"Who is going to tell the parents?" Maddy asked.

"I'll do it. I'll tell the parents," Zep said. Maddy stayed at the scene long after the body had been removed, waiting for forensics to finish their work. Snow began to fall, and the crowd thinned out. It was almost five p.m. when she finally returned to the command center.

She looked at the empty gym. Abandoned, with half-filled cups of coffee strewn on tables, papers scattered on the floor, and all but emergency lights turned off. She thought *That's it. The search for Nancy*

Miles is over. It was as though law enforcement had been puppets on strings held by a crazed puppeteer. She was thoroughly depressed as she drove home. Zep called on the way. "Meet me at the office; we need to talk."

What now? She made a U-turn, got on the expressway, and headed into the city. When she walked into his office, she knew something terrible was coming down. She could tell by the way Zep gazed off to the side and didn't make eye contact. *This is not going to be good.*

"Have a seat, Maddy." Hesitantly, she sat down. "It's time to take a look at where we are now. Two girls are dead, and thanks to our friends at the paper, the public believes we're incompetent. They've lost all confidence in us. The murderer is in complete control and playing a very public game. To make things worse, the Mayor and Sheriff were just here." Zep stopped, unfolded his arms, put his hands on his desk, and took a deep breath. *Here it comes*, Maddy thought.

"They're starting to micromanage us and have ordered me to do something you're not going to like." Maddy's stomach was in her throat, and she sat up to brace herself. "They want me to put Hawk Jenkins's composite picture in the paper as a suspect to make the public feel we're homing in on the murderer."

Maddy stood and screamed, "What! That's bullshit! It'll fuck up everything."

"Maddy, sometimes things are taken out of our hands, and we have to roll with the punches."

"But it will drive him deeper underground and make him harder to find. We're going to be flooded with calls from hysterical people, and they'll suck up all our resources." As she spoke, Maddy was barely aware that she was moving toward the door. "You know there's no direct evidence tying Jenkins to Nancy's murder. Why would you do that?"

"Everything you're saying is true. But they'll be bringing in other agencies now, the State Troopers, the Utica P.D., and we have to face it, we're not in complete control anymore. How do you think I feel?"

Maddy couldn't listen to what Zep was saying. She shouted, "Did we do something wrong? Did we? If we did, tell me, because I don't know what it was."

"You're taking this way too personally. It's political now. Nancy Miles's uncle is a political bigwig, and he called the mayor. There's an election coming up this fall, and the Mayor's intimidated."

"But there are so many things that can go wrong by doing this," she said, shaking her head.

"I know, but maybe it'll buy us some time."

"I just can't believe this," she said, facing away from Zep. She waited a moment, then gimped out of the room, bad knee throbbing.

The next morning, plastered on the front page of the Dispatch, was Hawk Jenkins's face. The headline read, *'Missing Girl Found Dead. Police Identify Suspect in Murder.'* A sting of betrayal ripped through Maddy, and she tossed the paper in the wastebasket. *Politics, fucking politics*, she thought. *We risk our lives, do all this work, just to have the mayor waltz in and undermine everything for his gain. It's just not right.* At that moment, she lost all enthusiasm for her work.

Before going to the office the next day, she stopped at the Friendly Bean, sat hidden in a corner booth, and sipped her coffee while looking out at the street. Goldfarb was at the counter, chatting it up with Rusty. "Hey, Maddy, you look like you just lost your best friend," Rusty called over when he saw her sitting alone.

"I'm fine," she said, feigning a perky tone, then quickly got up to leave.

The hours passed slowly during the day, and she had to push herself through the motions of her job. She filled her time with meaningless busywork generated by countless calls from people who thought they'd seen Jenkins. She made a point of avoiding Zep whenever possible. That evening, at home after work, Samantha complained that her mother was so scared that she wouldn't let her do anything. "How soon do you think it'll be before you catch that guy so I can have my life back?"

"There are a lot of good people working on it," Maddy said. "We'll get him." *That's what I'm supposed to say, isn't it?* she thought. *The truth is, we're lost, and Cupid is in complete control.*

Like everything else in her day, dinner was a halfhearted effort. She fried up a few hot dogs and threw frozen French fries into the oven. As she and Amber ate at the kitchen table, her mind still reeling about the bullshit situation at work, Amber asked if she could go to her girlfriend Abby's house for a sleepover Thursday night. "There's no school Friday, and Abby's Mom doesn't mind." Maddy hesitated for a moment as she entertained the same fear about Cupid being on the loose that Samantha had complained about earlier. Finally, she said, "Probably," which Amber took to mean "Yes."

Later that evening, Maddy became suspicious when she overheard Amber on the phone talking about the sleepover with her father. "How did Dad get involved in your sleepover plans?" she asked when Amber hung up.

"It was his idea, and he asked me to let him know if you were okay with it."

That asshole. Maddy seethed inside. Her stomach twisted while she tried to act unbothered. "Are you finished with your homework?"

"I just have some math to do."

"You can finish it in your room if you want."

Once Amber was out of earshot, Maddy called Jack. "I just found out that you put Amber up to arranging a sleepover at Abby's. I know why you did it, and I'm so pissed I can spit."

"Come on, Maddy, all I wanted to do is take you to dinner."

"It's not what you wanted to do that I'm reacting to, Jack. It's how you did it. You manipulated Amber and me. Don't you realize that's the kind of shit that drove me away when we were married?"

"So, what did you want me to do?"

I can't believe he just asked me that question, she thought. "You could have called me and said there's a day off from school on Friday; if Amber goes on a sleepover Thursday night, would you like to do dinner."

"I don't feel I can do anything right in your eyes. I'm sorry," Jack said with a sigh.

Although his frustration seemed genuine, it bewildered Maddy that even though Jack had stopped drinking, he still thought like an alcoholic and manipulated people even when he didn't have to. "Look, Jack, I'm spent emotionally with all that's going on at work. Why don't we just bag the dinner thing for now and try another time?"

There was a brief silence on Jack's end, and Maddy knew she'd hurt him. Finally, she heard him say, "Okay," and hang up. The pain she felt at that moment was reminiscent of a long history of similar incidents while they were married. The way they interacted was like a record that played over and over. She wondered if going to marriage counseling when she had asked him to years earlier would have made a difference. *But it's too late now,* she thought to herself, *that train has left the station.*

Chapter 21

Another day in paradise, Maddy sarcastically thought as she pulled her chair up to her desk to start another day. She ripped a hole in the plastic cover of her coffee cup, took a sip, and scanned her desk, looking for a place to start, when the phone rang. Lucy at the switchboard said she had a call from Chicago. Maddy told her to put it through.

"Is this Maddy Reynolds?"

"Yes, who is this?"

"Joyce Bennett, Bob Bennett's wife."

"Oh, hi. It's been so long."

"I'm at the hospital with Bob. He had a heart attack, but he's going to be all right. The thing is, he insists on speaking with you. I've tried to convince him not to call, but he won't take no for an answer. You know how stubborn he can be."

A gruff voice came on the line. "Maddy. It's me, Bob."

"Bob. What's going on with this heart attack thing?"

"Ahh, these damn doctors won't let me go home. But I'm not calling about me. I've been having the weirdest dreams since I've been here, and you're in every one of them. Is everything all right with you?"

I can't believe he's asking me this. I haven't spoken to him for over a year. How can he possibly know that I'm in the middle of a storm?

"I'm fine," she said, not wanting him to worry him in his frail health. She loved the old man, but he'd be worried sick if he knew what was happening.

"Oh, okay, good," Bob said. He seemed surprised. "We haven't talked in so long. I guess I was worried. You know, because of the dreams and all."

"I'm sure there's a lot we can catch up on, but why don't we wait until you're back on your feet."

"Sure, sure," he said. "And don't go worrying about me, I'm going to be okay." As she was about to hang up, Bob said, "And Maddy."

"Yeah."

"Are you sure everything's okay?"

"I'm sure, Bob." Bob was as real a friend as she'd ever had, and Maddy hated fibbing to him. *I'll tell him everything as soon as he's better.*

When she hung up, her eyes landed on a pile of mail. She grabbed a letter on top, from the legal department, that caught her attention.

"Finally, we caught a break."

The letter was from the department's attorneys and said they were able to broker an arrangement with the V. A. Hospital in Albany to gain limited access to Jenkins's medical information. "Although you are not allowed to obtain any of Mr. Hawk Jenkins's physical records, you can interview his psychotherapist, Dr. Julie DiMartino."

Maddy immediately called DiMartino and set up a meeting for one o'clock that afternoon. She swung by Zep's office on her way out, still pissed at him over the whole Jenkins's-sketch-in-the-paper thing, and was relieved to find that he wasn't there. She left a message with his secretary and headed out.

Road construction made the normally two-hour trip to Albany take closer to three hours, and Maddy's stress level was redlined the entire way. *I can't miss this appointment,* she thought, half tempted to get out of the car when traffic was at a standstill and force the workers to let her through. When she pulled into the V. A. parking lot, she was so flustered that she hurried out of her car and ran to the meeting.

"I'm sorry I'm late," she said when shook DiMartino's hand. The young, attractive psychologist seemed unbothered. Maddy sat across from her, and after introducing herself, explained the murders of the two girls. "Hawk Jenkins is a chief suspect," Maddy told her.

"Yes, I remember reading about what happened," DiMartino said; she clasped her hands together on her desk, as though prepared to be as open as possible. "I saw Mr. Jenkins for about eight months. He's a Vietnam veteran and came to me because he was suffering from depression, anxiety, and sometimes anger issues. He had bouts of suicidal thoughts as well. Explosive episodes caused him to lose several close relationships, which added to his depression. During his time here, he seemed to make significant progress, but a little over a year ago, he suddenly stopped coming. I haven't seen him since."

Maddy looked up from her notebook. "Do you have any idea why he stopped coming?"

"It may have been because we were beginning to touch on subject matter he found too disturbing."

"Can you tell me what that was?"

"He came from an extremely dysfunctional family, was often beaten and once almost died. He was very conflicted about it, but we never got to the root cause of why."

"We have reason to believe he's a heavy drinker and into child pornography," Maddy said. "Did he discuss any of that with you?"

DiMartino tilted her head thoughtfully and said, "Yes, excessive drinking was a means of self-medicating when he was depressed."

"And child pornography?" Maddy prodded.

"Near the end of our time together, he shared his difficulty with women and said he read pornographic magazines. But he did not mention child pornography."

Maddy decided to go for the jugular. "Dr. DiMartino, I witnessed the discovery of the two girls. They were brutally raped, sodomized, strangled, and dumped in the filthiest of places. Do you think Mr. Jenkins is capable of that?"

Doctor DiMartino looked at her clear-eyed and said without hesitation, "No." She put her hand up to her chin and stroked it as she said, "That's just my opinion, of course, but Mr. Jenkins's problem involves reacting in anger to situations where he feels slighted. He might lash out at a woman whom he perceives has rejected him, but not at a child. I just did not see that in him."

Maddy thanked Julie and took Jenkins's last known address from her secretary before she left. The neighborhood where he lived looked a war zone. Kids played wildly in the street lined with small, run-down houses. An old man sat clutching a bottle, and a young girl pushed a baby carriage, with a toddler at her side. Maddy pulled over in front of the house, and before she left the car, she unsnapped the holster.

As she approached the house, she noticed one of the curtains move back, as though someone was watching her. When she knocked, no one answered. After a second try, the door unlatched, slowly opened, and a woman spoke through the cracked door.

"How can I help you?" she said cautiously.

Maddy introduced herself and said she'd like to speak with Hawk Jenkins.

"He doesn't live here anymore."

"Can I come in?"

"Do you have a search warrant?"

"No, I just want to talk."

After a moment's hesitation, the door slowly swung open, and Maddy stepped in. The smell of chicken soup simmering on a stove somewhere, a playpen with a child about two who stood staring, and an old man with an oxygen mask asleep in a recliner gave Maddy the impression that the woman was holding her family together quite well, although meagerly. The place was small, untidy, but clean.

The woman moved a stuffed giraffe from a chair, asked Maddy to sit, and introduced herself. "I'm Nicki, Harold's wife. And by the way, his name is not Hawk Jenkins; it's Harold Hawkins. He uses Hawk Jenkins so people like you won't come creeping around here, but somehow you managed to find this address anyway."

"When was he here last?" Maddy asked.

"It's been over a year. But now that the newspapers have covered their front pages with his picture, I'll probably never see him again."

"Do you have any idea where he is?"

"If I did, why would I tell you?"

"Well, it might save his life. Coming with me is the safest thing he can do."

"You know, he didn't do those awful things to those little girls."

"How do you know that?"

"We have three daughters, and he would never harm a child," Nicki said as she ran a hand over her eyes.

"They say your husband has an explosive temper."

"There's a big difference between having a temper and killing children."

Maddy paused at Nicki's words, which were consistent with Dr. DiMartino's sentiments. "I hope you're right," she said.

"Whether I'm right or wrong, he's still a marked man now."

"What do you mean?"

"In case you haven't noticed, child killers don't live too long, whether in jail or out," Nicki said, glaring at Maddy, as though looking right through her. The penetrating words brought back Maddy's anger at the mayor and chief for forcing Jenkins's sketch to be published. She felt a pang of shame. As she got up to leave, she looked at the woman and could only say, "Thanks for your time."

As she drove home, the notion that Jenkins might be innocent hit Maddy hard, and she called Zep. "I think we've gone down the wrong rabbit hole with Jenkins," she said. "I interviewed his psychologist and his wife, and neither thinks he's capable of killing a kid. They both seem like straight shooters, and they might be right. If they are, we've signed the wrong guy's death warrant."

"I started thinking that Jenkins might not be our man recently too," Zep said, with a hint of guilt in his voice. "If it's true, not only have we put his life in jeopardy, but we've got a serial killer on the loose and no clue about who the guy is."

Maddy thought the conversation with Zep was over, when he said, "Maddy, don't hang up. I know you've been pissed at me for not putting up a fight about Jenkins, but I want you to know that I felt I had no choice but to do what I did. I was in a battle with the mayor and chief that I couldn't win. All I could do was retreat to fight another day. If they had taken us off the case and brought in an outside agency to run the show, where would we have been then?"

She heard humility in Zep's voice and knew it must have been hard for him to speak those words. His authenticity was the quality she most admired about him, and at that moment, she forgave him. "I guess you did what you had to do," she said softly.

"See you tomorrow, Maddy."

That evening Maddy sulked as she wrestled with her belief that Jenkins wasn't Cupid. After Amber had gone to bed, she sat downstairs in the dark with a bottle of wine and listened over and over to "I Wish It Would Rain" by The Temptations. The bottle slowly emptied, and she had begun to nod off, when the phone rang.

"Turn on Channel 3," Al said excitedly. "Something is coming on about Jenkins."

When the TV lit up, an announcer from a Binghamton news outlet was on a live feed to a local station. He stood at a barricade of cop cars, and in the background, a spotlight shined on a small white house.

"About an hour ago, police got a tip that a man wanted for the murder of two Utica girls is in that house," a passionate announcer said. "Earlier, when police approached, shots rang out. Thankfully, no one was hurt."

In the background, a heavily armed group of men dressed in military gear slowly walked in a formation behind an armored vehicle. "Jesus, what the hell are they going to do?" Maddy said out loud.

"I see canisters of tear gas being hurled into the windows," the announcer said, barely able to control his excitement. After a long pause, he continued. "I can see snipers on rooftops, and police behind that armored vehicle that is nearing the house."

In her inebriated state, Maddy began talking to the television. "Why the fuck are you people doing that?"

"The vehicle is getting very close to the house now," the announcer said. Suddenly, repetitive popping sounds of automatic weapons rang out, and the nearly hysterical announcer bellowed, "The police are unleashing a hail of bullets. I can see holes in the door and walls, and the windows are all shattered." When the barrage had stopped, there was only the night, an eerie silence, and a cloud of smoke. Then a man dressed in fatigues, who had apparently entered the rear of the house, came out waving his hands. The announcer said that the shooter had been neutralized.

Slurring her words, Maddy cried out, "They just executed the poor bastard!" With the last of the wine on the bottom of her glass, she stood before the TV, and mockingly, held the glass high as though saluting and said, "Here's to you, Sheriff and Mr. Mayor. You just killed the wrong fucking guy." She slugged down the wine, and the negative thoughts that followed edged her closer to despair.

Chapter 22

After the Jenkins sacrifice, the investigation faltered, and Maddy fell into a funk. Winter entered its fiercest months, and by the end of February, the smallest of tasks felt like a heavy burden. Her liquor store stops increased, and by March became a nightly ritual. She was in sweatpants and a sweater by five thirty, made a quick dinner for Amber and herself, and after Amber was asleep, grabbed a good Merlot or Cab for her rendezvous with *Tempest on the Sea*. Her rut deepened, and she wondered why she even bothered to try anymore.

Late one Friday night, as she worked on *Tempest*, and after she'd killed a bottle of wine, Maddy thought she heard a tapping on the front window. It was a windy night, and she attributed the sound to the rhododendron in the front yard. But when the tapping grew louder and took on a rhythmic beat, it struck her that only a human could make the cadence. "What the hell," she thought, stopped what she was doing, and tried to grasp what it might be. *It's Cupid!*

With her mind in disarray from the wine, a shot of adrenaline forced her to the floor. She reached for the light switch, turned it off, and wondered where she had put her gun. *Shit, it's in the car*. She crawled to the window, peeked out, and saw the figure of a man ducking behind a bush. Fear as cold as ice chilled her as she ducked down low. Dizzy, she lost track of what was happening for a moment. *Too much wine,* she thought, then regained her bearings. She ran upstairs, grabbed the Beretta from her nightstand, and, in a matter of seconds, was on the front porch, again ducking low, gun in hand, looking for the man, but saw nothing.

She sat at the edge of a wicker chair with her eyes glued to the street until daylight. By the time the wine had worn off, she had begun to question herself and wondered if it was just the wine; *Maybe I didn't see anyone after all.*

The next morning, as she nursed a splitting headache with black coffee, Jack came by to pick up Amber for the weekend. "You look terrible," he said. "I see you're getting back into the red wine."

"Please, save the sermon for another time." It dawned on her that the shoe was on the other foot. Jack was sober, and here she was, teetering on the brink of a drinking problem.

When Maddy was finally alone, she went back to bed, where she spent her entire Saturday. It wasn't until after ten a.m. on Sunday when her feet hit the floor. She slipped on a pair of sweatpants and a sweater, went down to the porch for the paper, and glanced at the bush where she thought she had seen a man. *A drunkard's folly,* she said to herself, shaking her head in self-disgust. *I've got to slow down.*

After her third cup of coffee, the caffeine finally kicked in, and Maddy felt a desire to pamper herself. She vowed to stay away from the pantry. *No wine today*, she told herself, then went upstairs and took a long bath while listening to a Rickie Lee Jones album. She got dressed, tidied up the bedrooms, and changed the sheets on her and Amber's beds. She did her nails in the comfort of her favorite bedroom chair and, although it was chilly outside, opened the windows to let in the fresh air.

She grew tired, and she curled up under a throw blanket on her bed and started a Stephen King book. A peacefulness grew inside her in the quiet of the afternoon. It felt good to be in the comfort of her room. By the time Jack dropped Amber off late that afternoon, she was looking forward to seeing both of them.

"What smells so good, Mom?" Amber asked when she walked in.

"I made your favorite: turkey with stuffing, mashed potatoes, and gravy."

"Wow, this is great. What's the occasion?"

"No occasion. Just felt like cooking today."

After the kitchen clean-up, Amber and Maddy talked in the living room until bedtime, mostly about Amber's friends, school, and her new boyfriend. When Amber went up to bed, so did Maddy, and before turning out the light, she pulled out her journal and wrote: "Dad, I'm sure you know what it's like to have an investigation go bad. I am trying not to let it drag me down. Today was a good day, got lots of rest. I took care of myself, the home front, and your precious granddaughter. I'll try to keep it up, promise. Love, Maddy."

The next day was the first workday of the week, and Maddy looked forward to starting it out with her new attitude. *I'll simply do the best I can with what I've got.*

It felt strange to stop by Zep's office after she had put him on ice for so long. They made small talk without diving too deep into the case, and, as she was about to leave, he said, "Oh, by the way, a call came in from Artie over at the Friendly Bean. A woman who lives upstairs keeps calling Rusty, complaining about some kind of noise. According to Artie, Rusty is at his wit's end and wants someone to talk to her. Our police counterparts are short-staffed today, and I told them we'd handle it. Since you seem to know the Bean pretty well, I thought you'd be the person to calm things down."

It had been awhile since Maddy had had a cupcake assignment, and it felt good to get her mind on something other than the Cupid investigation. When she arrived at the Bean, Rusty wasn't in, but Artie filled her ear with snippets of frequent phone calls from the old woman upstairs. "Frankly, I think she's nuts," he said.

Maddy wrote it all down and started up a flight of stairs to the woman's apartment. Tonya Petrov was a short woman, about eighty. When she came to the door, she was as sweet as strawberry shortcake. After Maddy introduced herself, Tonya led her inside and gestured for her to sit.

"I'm Tonya Petrov. I'm so glad you're here, dear. I assume it's about the noise, is it not?"

"Yes, the proprietor of the Friendly Bean says you call several times a day, and he would like you to stop. Can you please explain what it's all about?"

"I will dear, but first, can I get you some tea?"

"No thanks," Maddy said, as she pulled out her notebook and began to write. Tonya had grayish-yellow hair wound tightly in a perfect bun that sat on top of her head. She had an ear-to-ear smile and perfect teeth. *Russian.* Maddy said to herself. *I think she's Russian,* as she tried to distinguish the nature of Tonya's accent.

"Before I begin, let me say that I am glad that you're involved. I hate to bother the people downstairs, and, until now, I had nowhere else to turn."

Oh great, Maddy thought, *now I'm going to get all the calls.*

"To understand the problem I'm facing, you'll need to know a little about my background."

Oh boy, here we go, the lady's a looney tune.

"I was a violinist with the New York Philharmonic but had to stop performing ten years ago because arthritis in my hands would not allow it. But my ear is still good. It's always been extremely sensitive; in fact, I have perfect pitch," she said proudly. "Although my hearing was of great benefit in the Philharmonic, it causes me problems now. Certain sounds I find very bothersome.

"Recently, a sound that seems to be coming from the restaurant below causes me great distress. It is high pitched, piercing, and gives me a headache. I've talked to the proprietor, and he said he has no idea what I'm talking about. It's intermittent and occurs only in the morning. I began to notice it about a month ago. I am sure that you, with your detective, problem-solving skills, will be able to figure it out and make it stop."

"So, you live here alone?" Maddy asked as she tried to understand more about Tonya.

"I do now," she said. "I used to have a nice apartment in Manhattan and many friends. But when I left my position, my son, Arnold, made me move here to Utica. He felt it would be safer for me to be close to him."

"Why didn't you just move in with him?"

"With Arnold? Oh, goodness, no. He lives by himself. He's always been a loner and prefers it that way. But he's a good boy. He's taken over my finances for me, pays the rent every month, and makes sure I have enough money to do the things I enjoy."

"And what are they?"

"Well, I subscribe to several journals and periodicals in my field and, from time to time, make contributions to charities that I believe represent worthy causes. Why, just yesterday I sent twenty-five dollars to the local animal shelter."

Maddy was beginning to suspect that her son wasn't the angel Tonya was making him out to be. "How often do you see Arnold?"

"He stops by every week or so. He's a particularly good boy."

"What does he do for a living?"

Tonya hesitated, looked down and to the side, then said, "I'm not sure."

Maddy wanted to say, *your son sounds like an asshole and a parasite*, but restrained herself. Although Tonya's story about the noise sounded bizarre and she seemed eccentric, Maddy felt sorry for her. In some ways, she reminded her of her grandmother: lovingly gullible. "Okay, Ms. Petrov. I'll try to swing back here and speak with the owner of the restaurant over the next few days. But, please, if you feel the need to call someone, call me and not him."

Maddy gave Tonya her card, and as she got up to walk out, Tonya said, "Would you like to stay for lunch?"

"I have much to do today, but thank you anyway."

"Oh, of course, dear."

It was approaching noon when Maddy left Tonya Petrov's, and instead of going directly back to the office, she found herself driving onto the expressway. A gnawing feeling of being adrift had been growing in her gut all day, and instead of hiding in paperwork, she just wanted to drive. She felt lost in a desert without a fixed point on the horizon to guide her. Her mind turned to the most reliable guide she knew, Mary Thompson, and as if on autopilot, the car headed to Mary's house.

On her knees, planting seeds in a newly tilled garden, Mary smiled when she saw Maddy pull in the driveway.

"Hello there, fine lady," Maddy said when she got out of the car.

"Old Man Winter sure didn't want to give up the ghost this year, now did he?" Mary said. "Here it is June, hot as blazes and I'm rushing to get my tomatoes planted. How are you, Maddy Reynolds?"

"Always better when I see you."

"Come on, let's have some lemonade." Mary got up off the ground slowly, her age seeming to fight against her, and together they walked to the house. Three red padded chairs around an enameled metal table in the kitchen overlooked an alfalfa field, green and lush. Maddy sat as Mary took a pitcher of lemonade out of the fridge and poured two glasses. Caught up in the splendor of an intoxicating citrus fragrance, Maddy asked, "What is that scent?"

"Mock orange," Mary said, pointing to a vase of small white flowers by the window. "Beautiful, aren't they? I wait all year for them."

A hummingbird darted to a red feeder strategically placed outside the window that was visible from all chairs at the table. It dashed away when a sudden strong wind blew the feeder sideways. A gust entered the window. "Oh, dear. It looks like a storm's brewing," Mary said, gazing out at a few dark clouds in the distance.

Mary carried a tray with the two glasses of lemonade, spoons, and extra sugar to the table. "I saw you in the paper. You killed a man." She said it in an empathetic way, as though she knew it must have been traumatic. Maddy looked down silently.

"Pretty scary, isn't it?" Mary said. "You know, walking up to the gates of hell the way you did and looking in?"

"Indeed, it is," Maddy whispered. "Indeed, it is."

"Talk to me, Child. There's more going on here, isn't there?"

"How did you know?"

"I'm not sure."

"Everyone thinks the man who was killed in Binghamton last week was Cupid and that the danger is over."

"But you don't, do you?"

"No. I know the killer is still at large."

"I know it too," Mary said. "I can feel his presence. He's very evil and exceedingly dangerous." Mary reached out and put her hand on Maddy's. The two friends sat quietly, looking out at the field, watching life come forth, and enjoying one another's presence. A soft knock at the front door broke the silence. "I wonder who that could be?" Mary got up, and when she returned, a tall, slender girl about fourteen was with her.

"Let me introduce the two of you," Mary said. "Maddy Reynolds, this is Jodi Novak. Jodi, this is Maddy. She's a detective."

"Oh, hi," the girl said and put her hand out to shake Maddy's.

Wow, she's beautiful, Maddy thought as she shook the girl's hand. Jodi had Asian features: straight, jet-black shoulder-length hair, high cheekbones, a sharp jaw, and milky smooth, dark skin. Yet her eyes were as blue as sapphires, and the freckles on her face made her seem of Irish descent.

"Come sit with us," Mary said. "I just made some lemonade; would you like some?"

Jodi nodded as she sat. Maddy mused at the girl's quiet confidence. *There's a grace about her, and she seems to smile with her eyes,* Maddy thought.

"Jodi and I have been friends for a long time," Mary said, placing a glass of lemonade on the table. "We met at the Holy Ghost Baptist Church. But I don't see her there nowadays."

"We moved out to Forestport," Jodi said softly. "I had my mother drop me off on her way into Utica today." Jodi sipped her lemonade then said to Mary, "I miss our talks," and looked up with a smile.

Mary became distracted when a fly buzzed around her head. She tried to swat it away, but it kept coming back. In a flash, Jodi's hand snatched it out of midair, placed it in a napkin, and crumpled it up.

"How did you do that?" Maddy asked.

"Oh, Jodi has a lot of interesting abilities," Mary said with a smile. "But you don't get to see them until you've known her for a while."

Jodi seemed embarrassed, smiled timidly, and took another sip of her lemonade. Maddy's curiosity ran rampant, and she wanted to know more about the strange girl but didn't want to embarrass her with questions. Seeming to know what Maddy was thinking, Mary said, "Jodi has an interesting background. Tell Maddy a little," she prodded the girl.

"Am I a suspect?" Jodi said with a giggle and looked at Maddy, her blue eyes all lit up. "I'm just kidding," she said. "I don't mind. I was born in Vietnam. My mother is Vietnamese, and my father was an American Marine, or so I'm told. I never knew him." She paused to drink. "In Vietnam, they called kids like me Children of the Dust, because our fathers were American soldiers, and they considered us as insignificant as dust." Maddy thought she detected a sadness in the girl's voice as she said this.

"When I was ten my mother gave me to a family who ran a work camp because she couldn't find enough food for both of us. People in our village wouldn't swap or give us work because of who my father was. There were lots of kids like me at the camp. We worked in rice paddies, and as long as we did our work, we were fed and had a place to sleep. One night there was trouble, and I escaped with the help of another kid. Eventually, I was taken in by nuns and then adopted by an American family."

When she'd finished her story, Jodi looked at Maddy and inquisitively asked, "What about you, where did you grow up?"

"I was raised in Chicago."

"Why did you come here?"

"My parents died when I was young. I moved here to live with my grandma."

"So, we have something in common."

"What's that?" Maddy asked.

"We both got off to a rough start."

Much intrigued, Maddy looked at the girl and smiled. Jodi seemed like a lake, calm on the surface, but very deep. Though Maddy wanted to know her better, the day was getting away from her. "Indeed," Maddy said, "We both got off to a rough start."

Maddy thanked Mary for the lemonade, turned to the unusual girl, and said that she hoped to see her again.

Jodi just smiled.

When Maddy was about to leave Mary's, a strong wind nearly blew the door out of her hand. "It looks like all heck is about to break loose," she said, as Mary and Jodi stood behind her. No sooner had the words come out of her mouth than a flash of light lit up the sky. Thunder rumbled through the ground and shook the walls. The rain came down in buckets and peppered the windows. It became dark as night.

"Come on back in here," Mary said. "You can't go out in this." Maddy stepped back into the house and shut the door. "Now you two go in the living room and relax until this blows over. Jodi, why don't you tell Maddy more about your story? Believe me, Maddy, it's well worth hearing. I'll go tidy up in the kitchen."

Maddy and Jodi sat across from each other in soft leather-covered cushioned furniture that, though worn, were wonderfully comfortable. Jodi slipped off her shoes and sat with her legs tucked under her, and Maddy crossed her legs.

"So, do you have any kids?" Jodi asked, nervously.

"I have one. Her name's Amber."

"She's lucky," Jodi said. Maddy looked at her and wondered what she meant, then noticed how the girl seemed to be reading her expression. "I mean, to have you as a mother," Jodi said. Maddy noticed Jodi's forehead wrinkle as if an unspoken thought had caused her pain.

"What about your mother?"

After a long moment, Jodi said, "All I remember is the day she left me at the work camp. The rest I must have pushed out of my mind. I was ten. She said she'd come back, but she never did. I waited every day for her; every day." Jodi looked down, sighed, and shook her head, as if she were shaking off an unpleasant memory, then looked back over to Maddy and asked, "How did your parents die?"

Maddy put her feet on the floor and leaned toward Jodi. "My mom was killed in a car accident when I was ten. When I was twelve, my dad was murdered. He was a Chicago Police detective.

"Did God send you someone special?"

Again, Maddy wasn't sure what she meant and noticed how Jodi seemed to read her uncertainty. "You know, to help you through that sad time?"

"Oh, my grandma raised me, and yes, she helped me get through it."

"I had someone special sent to me, too," Jodi said. "His name was Cais, and he saved me."

Mary walked in carrying a tray of chocolate chip cookies and a pitcher, refreshed their glasses with lemonade, set the tray down, then quietly left the room.

Jodi continued. "Cais was sixteen and was like a brother to me. One night another older boy crawled in my bed while I was sleeping. I felt his hands all over my body. He covered my mouth, and I tried to fight back, but he was powerful." Maddy watched Jodi clutch the cushion of the couch, and the veins of her hands swelled as she squeezed tightly. Her face twisted with what appeared to be fear, hatred, and rage.

"You don't need to continue if you don't want to," Maddy said.

"I want to. I do. It helps me each time I tell my story, and there are so few people who I can share it with." Jodi took a deep breath, reached for a cookie, and began to nibble at it. Outside, the rain had settled into a steady downpour, although the thunder seemed to have moved on.

"It was so dark in that room," Jodi said, "I could hardly see anything. Then, suddenly, I felt the boy lifted off of me. I heard scuffling and fighting, and there was a loud thud. Something substantial had hit the floor and shook the hut. All the kids woke up, and somebody turned on the light. Cais stood next to me, bloodied around his neck, and on the floor, a boy lay with eyes opened. He didn't move, and someone said he was dead.

Maddy couldn't believe what she was hearing. Considering how Jodi had carried herself with such grace and confidence just a short while earlier, it was hard to believe she had experienced such trauma as a child. Outside, the deluge had quieted to heavy rain. Maddy's stomach was tied in knots, and she wrapped her arms around herself as if trying to comfort it. Jodi changed positions, reached for her lemonade, and took a gulp.

"It was the beginning of the most frightening night of my life," Jodi said. "We ran out of the hut and into a marsh that spread out for miles behind the camp. It was dark, and men with dogs chased us. They got close, and I couldn't breathe. I froze. Cais had to force me into a stream, and we hid beneath the surface. I could see flashlights above. I thought for sure they'd see us. We lifted our faces just enough to get air and went back down several times before the men moved on. Cais said that if they had caught us, we'd be dead. They had killed other kids for trying to run away."

Jodi paused, held her fingers to her forehead, elbow on a knee, as if in reflection, while simultaneously holding a cookie in her other hand. The rain had started to let up. *I could probably make it to my car without getting too wet,* Maddy thought, *but I'll be damned if I'm going to leave now.* Jodi reminded Maddy of herself, and she needed to hear her story out.

Jodi put the cookie back on the plate, rested her arms at her sides, and started up again. "When the night had passed, the men were gone. We followed the stream to a road that led to Saigon. Once in the city, Cais immediately began to teach me how to survive on the streets. 'Everything matters,' he said, 'who to talk to; who not to talk to; how to be light-fingered and snatch food, and how to fight.' He even taught me Sa Long Cuong, a martial art. I got to be rather good at it too. Eventually, we got jobs and rented a room above a little store. It was the happiest time of my life."

"Enough about me." Jodi seemed self-conscious, as though she had been hogging the conversation. "Let's talk about you now."

"Oh no, you don't," Maddy said. "You need to finish. How did you get to the United States?" Jodi's story was like a magnet that drew Maddy in further and further, and in many ways, it was Maddy's story too.

Looking at her hands folded on her lap, Jodi hesitated, and Maddy wasn't sure if the girl was willing to continue. Then she nodded, as if to say, "Okay, you asked for it," and started in again.

"One morning, while we slept, we were awakened by a loud banging at the door. Cais opened up, and it was the man who owned the building. He was frantic, and we could hardly understand him. When he calmed down, he said that the North Vietnamese Army had entered the city; he was taking his family, locking up the place, and we had to leave."

"We grabbed some clothes, and just like that, the dream was over."

"That must have been devastating," Maddy said as she sat on the couch. Her elbows rested on her folded knees and hands propped up her chin as the wind blew rain against the window.

"It was. We stepped out into insanity. People crowded the streets, pushed and shoved, argued, and fought. It was pure chaos. We knew we had to leave the city. Cais was able to retrace the way we had come months earlier, and by late afternoon we had made our way out. We even found the stream that we traveled before we first came to the city and followed it to a place where we thought we'd be safe.

The road was visible from where we rested, and all afternoon we watched masses of bodies flooding out of Saigon. Every once and a while, a truck of NVA barreled toward the city, people screamed, and some were killed. I'll never forget the horrified looks of the little kids as their parents threw them in the ditches to keep them from being run over."

Suddenly distracted when she looked at a brass clock on a table next to her, Jodi said, "Aren't you worried about getting in trouble with your boss?" obviously referring to Maddy not being at work.

"No, I have lots of time coming. They can do without me for a few hours."

Mary popped in from the kitchen. "The rain is slowing down. I'll be out checking on my plants. You two stay right where you are for as long as you'd like."

When Mary left the room, Jodi stood up, walked to the front window, and looked out. "You know, people in this country don't know what they have." A glint of sunlight broke through a few scattered clouds, and a deep blue sky was beginning to show itself. Then she took her place back on the couch, and said, "That night, when darkness came, an oddly shaped moon hung in the sky and gave off a dim light. The sound of machine-gun fire in the city was constant, and I knew people were dying. Flashes of light and the rumbling of heavy artillery made everything seem unreal, like in the movies, but it wasn't. It was all happening. The night was alive with death."

As though the hardest part was about to come, Jodi took a deep breath. "Are you sure you're okay?" Maddy asked.

"Yes, I'm okay," Jodi said with a faraway look in her eyes. She put her feet on the floor and wrapped her hands around her stomach as though she were holding back a powerful feeling, then continued.

"Cais had fallen asleep first, then I found some soft grass and lay down. I looked up at the night sky and listened to the sounds of death around me. I felt safe where I was and fell asleep but then was awakened by the sound of feet crashing through the water. I couldn't tell where it was coming from and didn't know where to run." Maddy watched Jodi's forehead wrinkle as fear seemed to grip her.

"I couldn't move," she said, then, like a child, she repeated it in a whimper, "I couldn't move." She breathed heavily, and Maddy had an impulse to hold and comfort her. But something told her not to, and she stayed put.

"I felt hands wrap around my neck from behind and squeeze me like a vice. I couldn't breathe." Her voice quivered. "I started to black out, but the hands let go, and I fell to the ground. I saw Cais fighting a man.

He used his skills to knock him down, then shouted for me to run." With her eyes wide and face flushed, Jodi said, "I found a place in the tall grass where I could see Cais. A second man appeared and had a gun. The guy on the ground got up, grabbed the gun, took a bottle from his jacket, drank, then shot Cais in the head. A flash of light broke the darkness and Cais drifted to the ground like a leaf."

Jodi looked at the floor and softly said, "The men went through our things, took what they wanted, and disappeared into the marsh. I stayed where I was, afraid they might find me. I watched Cais's body all night, hoping it might move, but it didn't."

As she sat, a calm came over her, and she appeared serene. "At daylight, a gust of wind shook the reeds around me, and I heard a whisper, 'Go now Jodi, be brave and live.' I knew it was Cais speaking to me. I went back into the city, found the sisters of St. Michael's Missionary, and they took me in. When Saigon fell, we were able to escape on a helicopter to Cambodia, and eventually, I was adopted by the Novaks."

As Jodi leaned against the arm of the couch, her hand on her forehead and body limp, she seemed emotionally depleted. Maddy fought an urge to comfort her and instinctively knew that as a self-contained person, Jodi drew strength from her self-reliance. "That's quite a story, Jodi."

"Yes, and it's all mine," she said.

Maddy was searching for the right words to say when a car horn beeped, and Jodi's head turned toward the door. "That's my Mom." She stood up, stretched her back, and said, "I guess I got to go."

The two walked to the front door. The storm had left the air clean and crisp. Before Jodi stepped outside, Maddy detected a look of embarrassment in her face. "Thanks for letting me bend your ear," Jodi said meekly, as though concerned that she had shared too much of herself.

When Maddy gestured to her with slightly opened arms, Jodi fell into her embrace and put her head on Maddy's shoulder. Maddy felt the warmth of the girl's body. *The poor thing feels like she's just run a marathon.* "You are quite a person, Jodi Novak," she said. Jodi turned to leave, and Maddy added, "Let's be sure to have Mary get us together again soon."

"Yes, and next time, I want to hear your story," Jodi said. She smiled, turned, and walked to the car.

After Maddy said goodbye to Mary, she headed back to the office. Even though it was late and there wasn't much she could accomplish, she thought she should at least show her face. She felt uplifted as she drove. It was as though Jodi's story had forced her out of her shell and helped her see things from a different perspective. The similarities between Jodi's life experience and her own didn't escape her, and Maddy believed it was no co-incidence that it was through Mary that the two had met. She was beginning to see the old woman as a very spiritual person.

Chapter 23

Nigel, 1957-1961, Chicago, Illinois

After Nigel was sentenced, Greenville Juvenile Detention Facility became his new home, and on his very first day, he feared he might never walk out. A home for the mentally retarded years earlier, the building had been converted into a prison for troubled kids. Although no bars were on the windows, there was a feeling of confinement just the same. None of the residents were older than sixteen, but many looked over twenty-five, proudly displaying long hair, goatees, tattoos, scars, and bulging biceps beneath rolled-up sleeves. The heavy scent of ammonia on newly mopped floors and echoes of basketballs dribbling in the gym made Nigel realize he had entered a world that he knew nothing about. *I hate this fucking place.*

As Nigel's world slowly darkened, he felt lost. He withdrew by staying to himself, and he distrusted everyone, especially the counselors. They were known for ratting out kids who were stupid enough to confide in them. He learned to deal with each day as it came, followed orders, and did what was necessary to stay out of trouble. When he was alone, he would think about life with his father. *No more sleeping until noon, no more adventures with the guys, and no more late-night talks over a beer with Dad. And all because of that fucking Jimbo rozzer.*

Things didn't change much as time passed; each day seemed like an eternity. At night he was tortured by his father's face looking up at him, begging for help as he lay dying. His mind, body, and spirit ached, and in time, all he wanted out of life was for it to end. *If this is all there is, I'd rather be dead, but killing yourself is easier said than done.*

As he sat in the game room one morning, staring at the walls as other kids played cards and ping pong, one kid thundered out, "Hey, check it out." Nigel looked outside, where the kid was pointing, and saw a laundry truck with its engine running. "How much would you give me if I walk out of here, hop in, and take off?"

"You are an idiot," another kid said. "If you took off, how could we give you any money?"

Everyone in the room laughed, except Nigel. Instead, he was preoccupied with the exhaust pipe pumping carbon monoxide into the air. *That's it. That's how I'm going to do it.*

Like all vendors that delivered to Greenville, the laundry truck had scheduled times to arrive each week and a designated time frame to exit the facility. Laundry deliveries were Mondays, Wednesdays, and Fridays, and for the following week, Nigel tried to calculate the amount of time the truck was unattended. He determined that the driver was in the building for a little over twenty minutes, but according to what he could research, dying from asphyxiation in a space the size of the truck would take more time than that. To accelerate the process, he came up with the idea of placing a plastic bag over his head and holding a hose attached to the exhaust pipe beneath it.

On a Tuesday, after shop class, Nigel secured a length of hose from the scrap heap and, after dinner, stole a plastic bag from the kitchen. That night before he was to execute his plan, he lay in bed, and he reflected on his life. Nigel thought about the abuse endured from Mother and Gertie and how he'd freed himself by killing his sister. *It was the best thing that ever happened to me. Until I went to live with Dad, that is,* he thought. He recalled the good times he'd had with his father and how he wanted them to never end. But his death at the hands of Jimbo was the cruelest of all wounds. *Nothing in life matters,* he lamented. *There is only pleasure and pain, and when the joy is gone, all that's left is pain. I hate everybody,* he thought. *If I don't kill myself, I will make their lives miserable.*

Usually, when Nigel didn't sleep well, he would be short-tempered the next day. But Wednesday morning, he felt good. *Only a few more hours and all this will be over.* He watched the parking lot from the game room and waited for the laundry truck to appear. As it did every Wednesday, it pulled in right on time. He watched until the driver had wheeled his last load into the building, then resolutely walked to the restroom, grabbed the hose and plastic bag he'd hidden in the trash basket, and strolled to the loading dock. Crouching next to the truck to stay out of view, he shoved the hose over the hot exhaust pipe. He looked around carefully to be sure no one could see him, hopped in the back with the other end of the hose, and shut the door.

"All right, all right, almost there," Nigel said out loud to himself. He lay on his side, slipped the bag over his head, and jammed the carbon monoxide-spewing hose underneath it. He took his first breath, gagged, and his eyes burned. He had to cross his arms over the tube to hold it in place. A piercing pain ripped through his head as he forced himself to breathe the poison gas.

Nigel entered a dreamy place and found himself back in the alley with his father while he died. He looked at his dad's twisted face, eyes filled with pain, begging Nigel for help. Unlike before, Nigel was able to understand the words his father mumbled: "Destroy that motherfucker." He looked over and saw Jimbo looking on, laughing, and felt an overwhelming rage. Before he could charge the shooter, Jimbo's voice changed to a woman's voice. *Fuck, that's Mother*, he realized as panic ran through him. Finally, Jimbo's face transformed into Gertie's face, and the voice became Gertie's cackle. She screamed at him, "You killed me, Nigel." Terrified, Nigel shook with fear. Suddenly, a bright light shocked him out of his dream.

"I've got a pulse here," a voice said. "He's coming out of it." Nigel saw a hand through a plastic mask that was being held over his face, and the air he breathed was like pure spring water, crisp and clean. He heard a siren, saw faces looking down, and a light shined brightly above him.

Oh, I fucked up. It didn't work. A parched throat, eyes burning, and esophagus raw, yet he was alive. Nigel couldn't open his eyes without the inside of the ambulance spinning around and making him nauseated. His body shook as the medics held him down. His mind was in a haze, but he remembered the vision of his father and the words that he spoke: "Destroy that motherfucker." At last, he had a purpose in life.

After a week in a hospital bed, Nigel felt the rawness in his lungs start to subside. His x-rays looked good and, most importantly, to his therapist his mood showed no signs of depression.

The psychiatric unit had a locked door, and patients were under constant surveillance by the staff, but to Nigel, it seemed more like a hotel than a hospital. Individual and group psychotherapy sessions were a requirement, but he didn't mind because he found himself feeling much more sociable.

Befuddled by how the mood of someone who had only recently tried to kill himself appeared so healthy, his therapist commented in a session that the staff was amazed at his progress. Nigel smiled as though he was grateful for the help he'd received, but deep down, he knew it wasn't the therapy that put the bounce back in his step, but the new sense of purpose he was given by his father. With lots of time to contemplate his mission to find and kill Jimbo, he realized that time was his biggest ally, and patience, combined with strategy, as they are in chess, would be the tools by which he'd accomplish his goal.

And to think, I almost killed the wrong guy—me. He made peace with himself and decided not to hide from the person he was, the one whom he once considered his dark side. His father's words changed all that, and he vowed to never again doubt what his inner self told him to do.

He carefully scrutinized words from his vision, and it dawned on him his father didn't say, "Kill that motherfucker," but instead, "Destroy that motherfucker." Nigel decided that "to destroy" was higher than "to kill," and that he not only needed to kill Jimbo but his entire family, wiping his seed from the face of the earth. *This is going to be the longest chess match ever*, he thought, realizing the enormity of the task. *This might go on for years, even decades. But so what. There's a lot I can do in the meantime.*

After his nineteenth birthday, and a long stint of doing and saying all the right things, Nigel finally was moved to a half-way house. He was on probation and quickly established himself in good stead with his PO by securing a job and showing up with a paystub, on time, to his weekly meetings. Within six months, he was released. He lived on his own and enjoyed the sweet smell of freedom. *Finally*, he said to himself when he walked out of his last visit at the probation office, *fuck all those assholes*. He felt like a bird let out of a cage, and not a parakeet either, but a vulture.

A cheap apartment near where he and his father used to live, and a job as a fry-cook-in-training at the Jolly Roger greasy spoon, and Nigel was ready to start his new life. About his apartment, he would say, *hot in the summer, cold in the winter, and always smells like rat shit*, then he'd laugh. But the apartment and job were only temporary, *no fuss, no muss, and off the radar. Perfect.*

I work with a bunch of morons, Nigel laughed to himself one afternoon as he tossed a couple of burgers in the hot, smoky kitchen, listening to his co-workers' senseless chitchat. "Hey, check it out," one of them nudged him and said. A beautiful girl about fourteen had walked in with a woman that looked to be her mother. She had long, brown hair, skin as smooth as a baby's, and a smile that lit up the greasy hole. Her clean, pure presence, pink dress, and knee-high socks that went halfway to heaven froze Nigel in place.

"Your burger's burning, man." Nigel quickly snatched the burgers from the griddle and looked back at the girl's long neck, smooth skin, and a smile that drove him absolutely crazy. He popped a rod just looking at her. When she got up to leave, Nigel ran to the window. He wanted to see the silhouette of her body through her dress in the sunlight. *What a babe,* he thought. *Perfection on two feet.*

The very next week, the girl and her mother walked in and sat at the same table. For weeks, the routine repeated itself until one afternoon, the girl's mother left her alone and walked across the street to the department store. Although Nigel hadn't planned on it, he walked by the table, and when the girl looked up and smiled, he instinctively said, "Hi. I see you in here every week. My name is Mark." *Mark? Why the hell did I say that?*

"My name is Patty Bronson," she said warmly, forcing Nigel to quickly sit down to hide the bulge in his pants.

"Oh look," he said, nodding toward the window as a fat lady walked by with a small bulldog on a leash. The woman looked as though she had been inflated with helium. Her flesh bulged out around her bra like the innertube of an overinflated tire, and the bulldog wore a pink collar that matched her dress.

"They go together well, don't you think?" Nigel said dryly.

Patty broke out laughing, put her hands to her face, and blushed. *I think she likes me,* Nigel marveled.

"Well, I have to go, but maybe I'll see you here next week," he said.

"You will. I come here every week after my piano lesson."

When he walked away, the same strange ambivalence he experienced with Tamatha overwhelmed him. It was arousal yet hostility, a powerful attraction, and a loathing. It bothered him, and he could make no sense of it, so he decided to put it out of his mind.

Over the next several weeks, when Patty's mother left her alone Nigel came by the table to chat. Finally, he got up the nerve to take the next step. He asked where she lived and when she said near Ashton Park, Nigel asked if she'd like to meet there Saturday and take a walk.

"Okay," Patty said with a smile.

Elated, Nigel floated home from work with Patty on his mind. Yet deep down inside, a battle raged between his feelings of titillation and his rage. As he lay in bed that night, he wanted her more than he hated her and imagined that she was lying next to him, with his hand inside her underpants. He ejaculated without even touching himself, and in an instant, a dark and little-known part of him reared its head. He filled with rage. It bothered him that another person had the power to make him lose control like that. Perplexed, he rolled over and ruminated about what might be wrong with him until he finally fell asleep.

The next morning while at work, Nigel tried to think of things to do with Patty when they met. By ten a.m., he decided to call the whole thing off. *I have a lot of other things to do tomorrow.* He felt a sense of relief the remainder of the morning, but by early afternoon, second thoughts began to boomerang around in his head. *Shit. If I don't show up, I'll have blown it with her.* That night, he put the whole damn mess out of his head and slept like the dead.

When he woke up Saturday morning, he rolled over and fixed his gaze on his greasy work clothes that hung on a chair next to his bed. *If I don't go*, he said to himself, *then all I am is a fry cook. I have to go.*

An unexpected excitement, warmth, and even tenderness welled up within him as the morning went on. He decided he wanted to do something beautiful for Patty. Inside his dresser was a box of vintage valentine cards that he had stolen from his mother's room long ago. Handmade and pretty, they always made him think of life the way he wished it would be. He went to the drawer, picked out his favorite, and signed it "Mark."

Ashton Park was small but very pretty. At a glance, Nigel could see several lawns, park benches, clumps of trees and bushes, some footpaths, and in the center, a pond with swans floating in the middle. Patty sat on a bench wearing a blue dress and a ribbon in her hair. "This is a beautiful place," he said when he walked up to her. She turned and smiled the same way as she had at the Jolly Roger, arousing him as she had before. As he tried to think of something to say, he glanced at the pond. "Aren't those swans beautiful?"

"Oh my, yes, they are."

"Would you like to walk over?"

"Sure."

They strolled together along a path that led to the pond, Patty put her arm through his, and a warm feeling filled Nigel that was like nothing he'd experienced before. Further along the path, she laid her head on his shoulder, and rockets ignited from his feet up through to his head. In front of them, the trail wound into a wooded area that was thick with bushes on both sides before it reached the pond.

He heard a whisper within him say, "She really wants it, Nigel. Now's your chance. Don't be a pussy." As they entered the bush-covered area, he felt his heart pound, stopped, turned, and slipped the valentine out from under his shirt. He handed it to Patty. "This is for you."

"Oh, how sweet," she said. As she opened the envelope, Nigel looked around to see if anyone was nearby. There wasn't. He grabbed her by the shoulders, pulled her close, and kissed her hard on the lips. His teeth bumped hers, and Patty appeared stunned. She pulled back and looked at him, face filled with confusion and anger. The heat of humiliation warmed Nigel's face, and he tried to kiss her again, even harder this time. "No, stop!" He put his hand over Patty's mouth, dragged her into the bushes, and threw her down.

The thud of Patty's body when it hit the ground, and the look of shock in her eyes, frightened him for a moment. It was as though he was watching himself from above. *Don't stop. You can't stop now,* he heard himself say, or maybe it was that other voice, he wasn't sure. He forced his way on top of her. Patty fought back and started to scream. He put one hand over her mouth and the other up under her dress, ripped off her underpants, and felt all the places he had fantasized about, but they didn't the same feel as he imagined.

Nigel unzipped his pants and penetrated the girl violently as his lust turned to rage. When Gertie's face flashed before him, he thrust himself into Patty even harder. His erection had become a weapon, and the more he rammed it, the clearer Mother and Gertie's faces became. Patty squirmed, and she found a way to bite his hand. He pulled it away, and she screamed a high-pitched scream. Panicked, he grabbed her neck with both hands and squeezed it tighter and tighter, trying to shut her up. Suddenly her body began to twitch violently and then went limp. The look on Patty's face reminded him of Gertie's when she lay on the kitchen floor.

Nigel stood up and looked around. He didn't see anyone and didn't think anyone saw him. He zipped up his pants and looked down at Patty's half-naked body. Blood oozed onto her dress. Somehow her death did not seem real to him. He turned his attention to what he had to do next, which was to get out of the park, but he needed to wait for an opportunity.

The sky had become dark, and rumblings of thunder were getting close. Nigel crouched down next to Patty's body and waited for the storm to come. Lightning hit a tree across the pond, and a loud clap of thunder shook the ground. A steady rain fell, and within minutes, people began to exit the park. *Now is the time.*

Before he left Patty, Nigel took the valentine from the mud, wiped it on her dress, and placed it on her stomach. He picked up her torn underpants, and he tucked them in his pocket as a souvenir. He was one of several people who covered their faces as they scurried out of the park in the downpour that afternoon. No one seemed to notice him as he walked home and, for the rest of the day, he listened to the radio for news, but there wasn't any.

The incident did appear in the newspaper the next day, but with no mention of immediate suspects. It was business as usual for the rest of the week, but he was on pins and needles. As the days passed, according to articles in the newspapers, the police had become more and more perplexed. One morning, however, a breakthrough came over the radio. Nigel was eating breakfast when an announcer said that Ramon Sanchez, a maintenance man at Ashton Park, was charged with the murder of Patty Bronson. He had apparently been working the afternoon of the crime and had a prior sexual assault conviction. "Police have reason to believe he entrapped the girl during a rainstorm, raped her, then strangled her to death," the announcer said.

Poor chap, Nigel thought, *he's being used, I'd say. The cops have gotten pretty desperate.*

After several months of legal mumbo jumbo, Sanchez's case was thrown out of court when it was established that he was with several co-workers in a car waiting out the storm at the time of the murder. By that time, the story had become old news, and from time to time, only a small article about it would appear on the back pages. Nigel's confidence grew that he was in the clear, and he put the whole incident out of his mind.

Chapter 24

Maddy, 1979, Utica, New York

The worst part about doing laundry is chasing down stray socks, Maddy thought after she lugged up a basket from the basement. She tried to set Saturdays aside for housework unless she could find something better to do. Maddy sat in the kitchen, turned on an oldies station, and began folding clothes. She was singing *My Girl* out loud when the phone rang. "Mom, can I stay at Abby's one more night?"

Once again, Maddy found herself hesitant to agree. "But, Amber, that's two nights in a row. I don't think that's fair to Abby's mom. And besides, you don't have clean clothes for tomorrow."

"Abby's Mom said it's okay with her, and Abby has extra stuff I can wear."

The kid should become an attorney, she thought. "Oh, okay." After she hung up, she looked at the basket of unfolded clothes, peeked out the window at the sunny afternoon, and decided to take a break. She grabbed a glass of lemonade from the fridge and went out to the front porch.

Aww, that feels good, she thought as she plopped into a soft-cushioned wicker rocking chair. *It's a beautiful day in the neighborhood, as Mr. Rogers says*, Maddy chuckled to herself looking out at the blue sky. She watched two boys play catch out front. The intoxicating scent of a Linden tree filled the porch and raised the spirit of springtime within her.

Her troubles drifted away as she closed her eyes for a moment, and when she opened them again, the boys were walking away. *Lost in little boy conversation, probably talking baseball.* The phone rang, and thinking it was Amber, she got up to answer. "Hello." Silence. "Hello." Still nothing, then Maddy hung up. When she returned to the porch, just inside the door a rolled-up newspaper lay on the floor. "What's this?" As she picked it up, a small, white, and fluffy ball fell to the floor. Confused, she picked it up, and it was a dead kitten. The headline in the newspaper read, *Cupid One-Ups Cops Again*.

She stood in disbelief, and realizing Cupid had to be watching her, she ducked behind the door. She peeked over the windowsill but saw no one. The phone rang again. Staying low, practically crawling, she reached the phone and picked it up. She heard only breathing. Then a distorted voice said, "Check Amber's backpack."

Rattled, Maddy dropped the phone and frantically looked for the backpack. "Where the hell is the damn thing?" she yelled as she ran through the downstairs. Her hands were shaking, and her knees felt weak. She vaulted the stairs to Amber's room and on the floor of her closet, she found it. She emptied the backpack on the bed, praying there was no valentine inside because if there was, Amber was already dead.

Folders, books, papers, pencils, gum wrappers, and lip gloss were scattered across the bedspread, but no valentine. In one of the side pockets, she saw a white envelope. *Oh, my God.* Lightheaded, she reluctantly lifted the envelope from the pocket. On the outside was written *To Detective Reynolds*. She ripped open an end and slipped out a plain sheet of paper with a typed note that read: *Unbeknownst to you sweet dear, I am always near.* It was signed, "Cupid."

A tingling sensation spread from the nape of her neck to her face and sweat beaded up on her forehead. She had to force herself to breathe.

Maddy had always felt that an invisible shield protected her home from the bad guys. It was as if her house was a safe zone insulating her and Amber from the cruel happenings of her job. She had been more than willing to blame the tapping-at-the-window incident the night before on drinking too much wine, because she needed to believe her home was her sanctuary. It was a place where she did normal things with her daughter and where the cherished memories of growing up with her grandmother still lived. But at that moment, as she sat on Amber's bed, her safe haven was obliterated, violated. It was as if Cupid wanted Maddy's full attention and used Amber to get it.

The ringing phone dragged Maddy out of shock, she ran downstairs to answer it, and her terror turned to rage. "Listen, motherfucker, if you touch my daughter, I'll make you suffer before I kill you," she screamed.

"Maddy, what's going on!" When she heard Zep's voice, she leaned against the wall and slid to the floor with the phone still in her hand. Barely able to catch her breath, she eked out two words: "Cupid...Amber."

"I'm on my way."

As she sat on the floor, forehead resting on folded arms propped up by her knees, she tried to collect her thoughts. In an instant, it hit her. "Amber, I've got to call Amber."

"Mom...what's going on?"

Maddy stammered as she tried to come up with a reason for her call. "Are you sure you don't want me to bring you some clothes?"

"No, really, Mom, I'm fine."

"Okay, just checking. Love you."

"Love you too," Amber said.

She hung up with a sigh of relief and began to rehash what had happened. *Cupid's trying to fuck with my head*, she thought as she went to the front porch with her Beretta. It was a perfect late spring afternoon, and the street was quiet. *Why me? Why is he doing this to me?*

An unmarked car pulled in front of the house. Zep and Al jumped out and ran up to the porch. "Working Saturdays, boys?" Maddy said with half a smile. Zep and Al didn't smile. They listened as Maddy explained what had happened and gave an occasional glance to the street.

Al slipped on a pair of plastic gloves and placed the dead kitten and newspaper into evidence bags. Zep dialed a number to check on arrangements he had already set in motion for Maddy's protective surveillance.

"What's that all about?" she asked.

"You have to be under protective surveillance now, Maddy. There's no way around it. You've been targeted by a killer. Amber too, where is she now?"

When Maddy had given Zep the address where Amber was sleeping over, she angrily said, "Great, now I won't be able to make a move without someone in my back pocket."

"You'll have another cop near you at all times. You can work, but not alone. That's the way I want it. No arguments. Amber will have someone assigned to her at all times as well."

"You mean like that?" she asked as she pointed to another unmarked car that was just pulling up in front of the house.

"Yep, just like that," Zep said.

"Who's in the car?" she asked.

"Bud Renshaw," Al said. Zep looked up at Al, then over to Maddy, and the three started to laugh.

"Bud Renshaw! How did that happen?" Maddy asked.

"He heard about what was going on and volunteered," Zep said.

"I guess I should feel honored."

"Actually, ever since the Bowls situation, he's been a different guy," Al said. "I suppose we have you to thank for that."

Al and Zep were taking time away from their families to help Maddy feel safe, and although she hated to burden them, she was still shaken by the close call with Cupid and wasn't ready to let them leave. "Would you guys like something to drink? I've got Coke, beer, coffee." When she said "coffee," their eyes lit up. She went to the kitchen, started a pot, and brought back a tray with three cups, silverware, milk, and sugar.

"Why did you call me earlier?" Maddy asked Zep as she set the tray down.

"To tell you that you were right about Jenkins. We were able to get into his medical record. Over the years he had become impotent and the medical experts say there was no way he could have raped those girls." Zep

160

turned his face away sheepishly and, not being one to rub it in, Maddy said nothing. She did, however, feel a sense of relief, knowing she'd been vindicated for her insistence that the Jenkins situation had been handled wrong.

Al broke the uncomfortable silence. "So, what happens now?"

With an expression as serious as death, Zep said, "He's about to strike again."

Maddy and Al looked at one another in bewilderment. "Why do you say that?" Al asked.

"Cupid doesn't do anything without a purpose. I think what he did here today is to send a message that he intends to strike soon. But I don't understand why he's focused on Maddy. For some reason, he's inviting you into his world."

"Maybe he wants to torture me before he kills me," Maddy said, semi-jokingly. Zep and Al glanced at each other, but not jokingly.

"I think it's because she's a woman," Al said. "He hates women."

It was getting dark, and her stomach was still churning. "I can't believe that Cupid got close enough to Amber to put an envelope in her backpack," she said. The thought made her tremble inside, and she was tempted to drive to Abby's house and bring her daughter home, but she realized that she'd be panicking her unnecessarily. She turned her attention to Zep and Al.

"You guys have been great, but I'll be okay now; I have Bud Renshaw in front of my house and Mr. Beretta at my side," she said, forcing a smile.

Before they left, Zep and Al smiled and told her to call either of them if she needed anything. As soon as they walked out the door, she phoned Jack and explained what had happened. His ordinarily calm demeanor exploded into a panic. "I'm bringing Amber to my house tonight."

"Think about what you're doing, Jack. She's safe at Abby's. Zep is assigning a unit to that house; it's probably already out front. All you're going to do is alarm her. Do you really want to do that?"

Jack sighed. "Okay...okay. But I'm going to stay in my car where I can keep an eye on that house tonight, unit or no unit." Maddy knew she couldn't stop him and, deep down inside, was glad he was doing it. *He drives me crazy, but he's a good dad*, she thought.

Before she crawled into bed for the night, Maddy glanced out at the street and saw Bud in his car eating a sandwich. *How the worm turns*, she thought. She covered up, pulled out her journal, and wrote, *Dad, a serial killer is targeting me, and I have no idea why. Please watch my back. Maddy.*

Chapter 25

Nigel, 1964, Chicago, Illinois

On days off, Nigel liked to eat breakfast at the Fiddle De Dee greasy spoon just down the street from his apartment. As he was about to dig into the Hungry Man's Flapjack Special, he glanced over at a newspaper lying on the counter, and a headline caught his eye. "Renowned Detective to Head Bronson Rape-Murder Investigation. In the following article it talked about James Reynolds, nicknamed Jimbo, and his long history with the Chicago police."

Oh my, what do we have here? Jimbo is coming for me, how convenient. Nigel felt he was on a lucky streak. He was off probation, the Bronson investigation was going nowhere, and he'd just made big bucks selling off parts from cars he had boosted. *Now even Jimbo is at my doorstep. I'll be damned.*

With the pressure off, Nigel's cravings for new love interests came back stronger than ever. Through trial and error, he had perfected his approach to wooing young ladies. He'd bring them to an abandoned shack in the woods, where screams could only be heard by trees and rabbits. Jojo, his new assistant, was stupid but loyal and aspired to be just like Nigel someday.

Nigel had discovered that his exploits were managed more effectively when he had someone he could command. Some people, he learned, had malleable minds, and with them, he was able to establish himself as an idol and persuade them to do whatever he wanted. JoJo was a person like that. From the first moment Nigel met him in a bar, he knew JoJo was the perfect partner. It was something in JoJo's eyes that conveyed a desperate need for approval. Nigel used this need with crumbs of approval off his table to train JoJo, like a dog.

When the next two "romances" ended up like Patty's, he wasn't bothered, for he had entirely accepted what he had once thought of as an alien force within himself. *Hey, some guys are fags, and some guys, like me, prefer them young, so big fucking deal.* The only problem was that the incidents brought down a lot of heat.

When Jimbo was seen interviewing people in his neighborhood, Nigel knew it was time to make his move. With his business interests dissolved, Nigel purchased a ticket to London and started training JoJo for his role in the Jimbo operation. Unbeknownst to JoJo, however, his survival was not part of the plan.

Bob Bennett was a fly in the ointment, Nigel thought. *He's experienced, tough, old school—with a moron like JoJo as a partner, I'm at a disadvantage. I've got to get Bennett out of the picture.*

Nigel wrote a letter to the chief of police, pretending to be a journalist working a story on crime in the city, and the chief took the bait. Bennett was ordered to meet a fictitious journalist at the Grand Hotel at eleven a.m., about the same time Jimbo was to receive an anonymous tip. Nigel's plan went down like ice cream.

It was a bleak, overcast morning outside the shack in the woods north of Chicago. JoJo played solitaire and talked to himself as Nigel stared out the window at the road. Every time JoJo made a play, he'd laugh to himself and make a snorting sound that bugged Nigel. "You're driving me nuts with that noise. You sound like a pig inhaling slop. Knock it off." When he turned back to the window, a glimmer of a reflection caught his eye. "Shit, was that a car? See what you made me do." Sure enough, a car pulled into the front yard. "JoJo. Get in place. The cops are here."

JoJo had instructions that if two men showed up, he would shoot the shorter of them. Jimbo was six-foot-five, and Nigel wanted him all to himself.

From inside the front closet, Nigel heard a car door clunk shut, then another. *There are two of them. I hope JoJo don't fuck this up.* Through the slightly opened closet door, he saw Jimbo and a young detective walk up to the house, hands covering their weapons. After three knocks with no answer, the two walked in with guns drawn. Nigel watched as Jimbo went to the left and the other cop to the right, where JoJo waited. A loud bang rang out. Jimbo darted past the closet toward the sound. Nigel snuck out and tiptoed behind him. The young detective was spread out on the floor. JoJo aimed at Jimbo, but the detective was too fast, put two slugs in his chest, and dropped him with a crash.

Kneeling next to his comrade, Jimbo felt for a pulse. Nigel came up from behind and plunged a knife into the back of Jimbo's neck. The big man stood, winced, arched his back, and stiffened. Nigel twisted the blade to the left and right, enjoying the crunching of steel against vertebrae and bone. The detective finally fell forward to the floor. Blood pooled up around the man who had killed his father. He watched the body twitch. He put his face close to Jimbo's and said, "Fuck you, Reynolds. That's for killing my father. I want you to know that I'll be coming back to kill your daughter too."

Like he was deadlifting five hundred pounds, Jimbo made a straining sound. His face elongated as he struggled to get up, but his body gave way, and his head flopped to the floor. Nigel took out a valentine that he had already signed 'Mark' and placed it on Jimbo's back.

Shit, I've got to get moving, he thought, realizing Jimbo's backup might be on the way. Nigel grabbed his bag, ran to the back of the shack. He hopped in a car that he had stolen the day before and drove to O'Hare International Airport. A sense of satisfaction filled him, knowing that a big part of his assignment had been accomplished, although the task was not yet complete.

Chapter 26

Maddy, 1979, Utica, New York

Rolling with the punches was never easy for Maddy, and protective surveillance put her to the test. Each morning a squad car waited to drive her to work, and in the evening, someone drove her home. Detectives alternated, and although no one complained, the process made her feel like an invalid.

"I guess you're my babysitter this morning," Maddy said to Allison when she walked out of her house to the car that morning.

"Come on, don't make it bigger than it is. Do you want to drive together or separate?"

"Why don't you follow me. I want to stop by the Bean and pick up cinnamon rolls for everyone at the office. It's the least I can do for all my taxi-driver comrades. Do you mind?"

"Cinnamon rolls? Don't mind at all."

They pulled up in front of the Friendly Bean. Maddy walked over and said, "I want to check in on the old woman upstairs while I'm here. Okay with you?"

"No problemo," Allison said.

Maddy came out, laid a box of cinnamon rolls on her passenger seat, and headed upstairs to check on Tonya.

"Oh, what a nice surprise. I am so glad it's you," Tonya said when she saw Maddy. "Won't you come in and sit?"

"Not today. I just want to see how you're doing."

"I am just grand. Haven't heard that awful sound in a week."

Tonya started chatting about her trips to the doctor's for various ailments and then mentioned how her son had taken her to see a symphony in

Syracuse. "I hardly ever get to see him lately. He seems to disappear for weeks at a time, but last Saturday, he was at my door with the tickets. It turned out to be a most enjoyable evening."

"Wonderful," Maddy said. "If you need me, you know where I am."

Shortly after she got to her desk, Al stuck his head around the corner of her cubicle. "Guess who wants to meet with us in his office."

Maddy laughed, and the two walked to Zep's office. He stood with his arms folded, face muscles bulging, and looking like he was about to explode. "I want to get my head wrapped around where we are with the Cupid investigation," he said, obviously agitated.

"I got a call from a big wig at the State Troopers. The mayor requested that they send in an 'experienced' detective to help with the case. The Utica police will be getting more involved now too." Zep paced back and forth as he spoke. "My full-time job now is going to be coordinating information for these other agencies." He sat in his chair and took a deep breath, as though he was resigning himself to being micromanaged.

Lost in reflection, Zep suddenly sat up and said, "Before we have outsiders crawling around, second-guessing everything we're doing, let's take a look at where we are right now." He stood up, leaned back on his desk, and said, "We've been chasing the wrong rabbit. Jenkins led us down a hole that's gone nowhere, and we've lost the scent of the real killer. Let's face it, we're back at square one." Scratching his head like he was trying to jog loose a good idea, he said, "We need to go back to the beginning and start over. Al, you know what you've got to do."

"Yep, the basement record room."

"Maddy, why don't you go through the notes of everyone who has worked the case. Look at the interview affidavits and try to find gaps. You know, things that didn't get followed up on; anything. There's got to be something we've missed."

Maddy carried an armful of folders to her desk, plopped them down, and spent the remainder of the day culling through them. It was tiresome work, and she took several breaks to keep from falling asleep. She drank a lot of coffee and, at lunchtime, grabbed a tuna fish sandwich to eat at her desk. By four o'clock, her eyes were falling out of her head. As she sat back in her chair and yawned, Zep burst in wide-eyed. "We got a call on a missing girl in Oriskany. Al's gone to City Hall to chase down some documents. You and Allison need to handle it."

Like ice water had been poured over her head, Maddy was shocked awake. She became super-hyper and tried to talk herself down. *Calm down, Maddy,* she told herself. *Chances are this is not the work of Cupid.*

She met Allison in the parking lot where the sun was so hot it made the car feel like a sauna. She cracked open a window, and as she drove, Allison read Zep's notes aloud.

"The girl's name is Candice Bishop. She's ten years old. At about 2:40 this afternoon, she left her mother's house on her bicycle to visit a friend who lives about five hundred yards down the road. After thirty minutes, the mother got a call from the friend's mother asking where Candice was. Mrs. Bishop drove up and down the road looking for her daughter, but there was no sign of her. I know the road," Allison said. "There's not much on it. She could have been hit by a car and be lying in a ditch."

"I don't know, Allison," Maddy said. "A kid goes missing on a lonely country road; it sounds all too familiar."

"Are you thinking of the Sarah Benning case?" Allison asked. Maddy nodded her head.

When they arrived at the Bishops' house, they walked across the lawn to the porch. A late afternoon breeze was blowing across an open field, and the sound of half a dozen high-pitched wind chimes clamored loudly. Next to the house, a swing tied to the limb of a tree twisted and turned. It was as though the chimes and swing were crying out for someone dear to return.

A tall, lean man in his thirties opened the door. "Come in." Calm and in a stoic manner, he couldn't entirely hide the fear in his eyes. He said his name was Tom Bishop, Candy's father. He led them to a family room adorned with photos from Christmas mornings, birthdays, and vacations.

Somewhat out of place was an unusually well done, highly detailed pencil drawing of a dog.

"Who is the artist?" Maddy asked.

"Candice is gifted," Tom said. Maddy made a note.

A frail-looking woman with long black hair sat looking out a window at a vacant field behind the house. She twisted a handkerchief with both hands and looked like a bomb ready to go off.

"Judy, this is Madison Reynolds and Allison Abbott from the Oneida County Sheriff's Department."

The woman got up and gingerly walked to the detectives. "Please find my daughter," she begged. Her eyes were half-closed, and her head was cocked back. "She's only ten and has never been away from us...never." Tom put his arm around his wife and tried to console her.

"We'll do everything possible to find her," Maddy said. "Right now, while it's still light, we need to check the road between your house and your neighbors. We'll be back."

Maddy and Allison walked on opposite sides of the five-hundred-yard span of road between the houses. The sun glowed a pinkish-red as it began to set on huge fields of corn. Halfway between the houses, on Maddy's side, stood a single tall tree with branches that extended over the road. Maddy and Allison walked slowly, inspecting bushes, tall grass, and anything that obscured their view. On Maddy's side, near the mid-way point, a culvert had standing water and white patches that surrounded the tree. As she moved nearer, she realized the white spots were water lilies.

Fully leafed tree branches blocked the sun, making it challenging to examine the ground cover. Maddy stopped and looked carefully at each segment of the lily patch. She noticed a small disturbance where the lilies seemed uneven. "Allison, do you see that?" she said, pointing.

"I think so."

Maddy slid down the side of the embankment. Cold, muddy water seeped into her shoes from the muck below. As she sloshed toward the disrupted lilies, a glint of light seemed to reflect off something beneath the surface. She passed her hand along the bottom, and it hit something hard. She pushed at it, but it wouldn't move, then grabbed what felt like a steel bar and yanked hard. With the suction-sound of mud releasing, the object broke free, and up from the depths of a parent's worst nightmare came a little girl's bicycle.

"Aww, Jesus," Maddy moaned, as she held up the pink, mud-covered bike, its streamers dripping with silt. Allison, on one knee, shook her head, looking to the side, as if unwilling to accept what the object meant. Maddy waded toward her and handed up the bike, then climbed back onto the road.

"She must have been hit by a car," Maddy said. "Her body has to be out here somewhere. We should probably start looking for it."

"Maybe we should let Forensics do that," Allison suggested.

"You're right. Of course."

They leaned the bicycle against the tree and returned to the car to call in. Maddy explained what they found and that it was a possible hit and run. "Maybe so," Zep said. "But proceed to investigate as though it might be an abduction."

They decided it would be best for only one of them to communicate with the Bishops. Allison waited by the car while Maddy trudged up to the house. Tom opened the front door and came out to the porch. After a few deep breaths, Maddy said, "Mr. Bishop, we found a child's bicycle by the oak tree." Tom turned his head and looked off into the direction of a field across the road where a burgundy streaked sky marked the end of the day. When Maddy described the bike, he looked back and nodded his head, confirming it belonged to his daughter, then looked away again.

Judy had been listening from the front room and screamed, "Oh my God, oh my God, my poor baby."

Tom rushed to her as Maddy patiently waited for Judy to calm herself. "It's important that I gather more information to cover all possibilities," she said. "Would you like me to wait outside for awhile?"

Judy, still crying, pulled away from Tom, shook her head, and said, "No." As she wiped her eyes and nose with a handkerchief, Maddy stepped inside, and they sat down together. She asked the Bishops questions about the names of Candy's friends, recent happenings in her life, and any new people that she may have met. Maddy wrote it all down, then asked to see Candy's bedroom. Tom led the way. The room was painted pastel pink and blue with posters of dogs, cats, and rabbits. A funny picture of a raccoon with sunglasses reading a book hung over a neatly made bed.

"Does Candy have a special place where she keeps things?" Maddy asked.

When Tom said he didn't think so, Judy interrupted, "Check the pink box on the closet shelf."

Maddy pulled a large box from the closet and set it on the desk. She slipped the lid off and began lifting items out, one by one. A green cloth banner read, "The World's Friendliest Girl Scout." Beneath the flag, a stack of greeting cards was held together with a rubber band. She inspected each, but nothing was amiss. When Maddy pulled out a bag of small seashells and emptied it out onto the bed, Judy burst into tears.

"Those are from our vacation last summer," Tom said.

At the very bottom of the box lay a pink envelope. Maddy's stomach sank. She picked it up and slid out a valentine onto the bed. It looked vintage. On the outside was the image of a little girl walking on a country road carrying a hand basket filled with vegetables. She flipped the card open, and it was signed, 'Mark.'

Eyes wide, Tom said, "Is that what I think it is?" Judy, whose head had been buried in her husband's embrace, snapped it around, locked her eyes on the valentine, and, like she'd seen a vision of hell itself, wailed frantically.

"I thought he was dead?" Tom shouted at Maddy, obviously referring to Cupid, whom everyone thought was killed the night Hawk Jenkins was slaughtered.

"Jenkins is dead," Maddy replied, holding herself in check, "but we think Cupid might still be alive."

Tom struggled to keep Judy from collapsing while he stared at Maddy with a horrified expression. Maddy turned her head and felt the shame of being associated with an organization that had intentionally misled people into thinking their children were safe from a crazed child killer. As Tom attended to his wife, Maddy signaled to him that she was going outside and would be back.

"What's going on?" Allison asked when she came out to the car.

"Cupid has the girl."

Chapter 27

Maddy and Allison waited by the oak tree for Zep and the troops to arrive. Darkness had fallen, and a slight, warm breeze had picked up again. They leaned back against the car next to each other, arms folded, and gazed down the road, watching for friendly headlights to appear.

"I'm not sure I'm cut out for this job," Allison said, eyes fixed straight ahead. "I mean, I just started, and it's already pulling me into a dark place. It's scaring the shit out of me. How do I even begin to explain any of this to my daughter? Or do I even try?"

"How old is she?"

"Eight."

"I wouldn't try," Maddy said. "She's too young. All you'll do is make her world dark too."

"But I feel like I'm lying to her. I've always tried to tell her things as they are."

"I know how you feel. It's like we live in two different worlds; one with our work, which is dangerous, and death is everywhere, and the other with our innocent daughters, filled with hope and beaming with life. Maybe you shouldn't listen to me, though. I'm not sure I'm doing it right. I just remember how hard it was for me growing up, always being afraid. Maybe I shouldn't try to protect Amber so much. I know one thing for sure, I've grown a much harder shell since I've started this job. I worry I'm becoming too insensitive."

"How do you mean?" Allison asked.

Maddy took a few steps away from the car and put her hands on her hips, still looking at the road. "It's like when Amber needed a new dress for a dance before Valentine's Day. She asked me to take her shopping. I blew up at her. I said she should have told me sooner and she started to cry. The thing is, I wasn't available sooner either. I was so wrapped up in the Sarah Benning case, I couldn't focus on anything else." Maddy sighed and shook her head.

"I think you're a good mom," Allison said as she reached out and put her hand on Maddy's shoulder.

Maddy turned and gave her a half-smile. "Thank you."

In the distance, the road lit up. Tiny lights glowed in the blackness. "Here comes the cavalry," Maddy said. In a few minutes, cars and trucks drove up and pulled over.

Zep got out and looked up and down the road as though he was inspecting lawn damage after the winter snow had melted away. "There is nowhere to hide," he said.

Maddy wasn't sure what he was talking about. "What was that, Zep?"

"There's nowhere for anyone to hide. If you're going to abduct someone who doesn't know who you are, you would expect resistance and pick a place where there's lots of cover. But here, except for that tree, there's nothing. I think the kid knew her abductor." At that moment, a technician walked by with Candy's bicycle in hand. Zep looked at it and said, "My kid has one just like it." He then turned to Maddy. "Have you interviewed the Bishops yet?"

"I started to, but the wife lost it when we found the valentine. I'm headed back up there now."

Maddy could see Tom's silhouette on the porch as she walked back up the road. She approached the house and asked him how Judy was doing.

"She's sleeping now," he said. "Our doctor's a friend. He came by and gave her a sedative."

"Would you mind a few more questions?" Maddy asked.

"Come up and have a seat."

They sat across from one another in Adirondack chairs on the porch. It was dark, and with only the pale light from inside the house to write by, Maddy pulled out her notebook. "Can you try to reconstruct Candy's whereabouts over the last few weeks?"

Tom leaned over, propped his elbows on his knees, held his head in his hands, and seemed to be concentrating. He then pulled out a small calendar from his wallet, and he began to rattle off Candy's activities—Scout meetings, math club, religious education, art lessons, a field trip to the museum with her class, and playdates with her friends. The one that stood out to Maddy was the art lesson because it was the only event Tom mentioned where she might have been alone with an adult.

"Tell me about her art lessons."

"She takes them from Dr. Albright. He's an art professor at Syracuse University and Candy's in his workshop for gifted children. I normally take her on Saturday mornings at ten o'clock."

"How many kids are in the class?

"About ten, but recently she started seeing him individually for an additional hour."

Maddy sat up and moved to the edge of her chair. "Explain that."

"Dr. Albright said Candy is particularly gifted, and he wanted to work with her one-on-one for no additional cost."

No additional cost? That sounds fishy, Maddy thought to herself. "When was the last time she saw him?"

"Two weeks ago, Saturday."

When she finished writing, Maddy asked if they could look in Candy's room for anything that might give a clue to her recent whereabouts. Tom led her back through the house, and together they pulled clothes out of a hamper and checked the pockets. Other than gum and candy wrappers, some loose change, and two one-dollar bills, there was nothing.

Maddy lifted the top off a toy chest filled with stuffed animals, picked up each one, inspected it, and tossed it on the bed. "Nothing here." She looked through the clothes hanging in the closet as well, then he leaned over and slid a large cardboard box out from under the bed. It was filled with drawings.

"That's some of Candy's work," Tom said as he gently picked up each one by its edges to show Maddy.

The first sketch was done with colored pencils. It was a magnificent autumn scene of the outside of their house. Fallen leaves gathered around the foundation of the porch, and sunbeams streaming through scattered clouds made perfect shadows of tree limbs on the ground. The sketch seemed like something that might be found in a museum.

"I can't believe a child her age is capable of such a creation. How did she learn to do this?"

"It's a gift. The people at the university said she'll be famous someday."

A sketch of the inside of a restaurant struck Maddy hard and gave her a feeling of déjà vu. People sat talking at tables as coffee steamed from cups. Half-eaten pastries resting on plates looked familiar, and she began to smell cinnamon rolls. "Is that the Friendly Bean?" When Tom said that it was, she examined the drawing more closely and noticed the back of Rusty's head as he sat talking with a group of smiling customers. "Do you go there often?"

"Sometimes when I run errands Candy waits there for me. She'll do homework, read, or draw. Rusty, the owner, is a nice guy and keeps an eye on her while I'm gone."

"When was the last time Candy was there?"

"A week ago."

"Do you mind if I take this with me?"

"Only if you promise to return it in the condition it's in." Tom handed her a special plastic cover, and she slid the drawing inside. As she was about to leave, Tom stopped at the door and asked, "What are the chances of getting my baby back alive?"

An honest answer was less than ten percent, but she saw no sense in causing more anxiety than he was already feeling. "I can't answer that, Mr. Bishop. All I can say is that we have everyone working to find your daughter."

As she left the house and walked back to the oak tree where Allison and Zep waited, she felt an uneasy, weighty feeling growing inside of her. She thought of what Sarah Benning's and Nancy Miles's families had to endure when their daughters were found gruesomely murdered, and feared that Tom and Judy were next.

"Any luck?" Zep asked when she reached the tree.

"I have some new information."

"Tell us about it in the car," he said.

They piled into Maddy's car and headed to the old Forestport Fire Department, which was being converted into a command center for the operation.

"So, what do you have?" Zep asked.

"Candy is an unusually talented artist, and one of her drawings is of the Friendly Bean. It was made a week ago while her father ran errands."

Zep turned to the back seat and said to Allison with a chuckle, "It seems everyone goes to that place except me."

"I have the names of two of Candy's friends from school, Kat Banes and Carol Corella. They might know something. She's also taking drawing lessons from a guy named Albright, who she met with alone, two weeks ago."

"Well, it's a place to start," Zep said.

When they arrived at the old brick firehouse, Al, who had been assigned to oversee the setup, walked over. They grabbed folding chairs and sat around a card table.

"Let's see the drawing," Zep said. Maddy gently placed the plastic cover on the table and slid out the picture.

"Holy shit! A ten-year-old drew this?" Zep asked.

"Yep, and that's the Bean," Allison said.

"It's perfect," Al chimed in.

"Okay, we have four sources of new information," Zep said. "It's after nine o'clock. Let's try to get to one of the kids tonight. Al, I need you here, so Maddy and Allison, pick a kid and do an interview before it gets too late."

Although Maddy was under protective surveillance, considering the urgency of the situation, she thought she could get Zep to be flexible. "Allison and I can cover both kids tonight if we separate. Time is of the essence, Zep."

He looked at her, squinted his eyes as though trying to decide whether to call or fold in a poker game, then shook his head and said, "Okay."

Allison took the Banes girl and Maddy, Carol Corella.

Chapter 28

It was just past nine fifteen when Allison and Maddy left the command center and went off in different directions to interview Candy's friends. On the way, Maddy's phone rang and a woman said she had information about the missing girl. Unsure how she got her phone number, Maddy asked what the information was. "I overheard something, and I'm scared. I want to report it, but I don't want to do it on the phone. I heard you're one of the main detectives. Can we meet at Bernie's All-Night Doughnuts on Wolf Road at about ten thirty?"

"What's your name?"

"I'm not giving it. If you want me to tell you what I heard, I'll be in a blue Honda at Bernie's at ten thirty. I really have to go." Maddy called Zep when the woman hung up and told him about the call.

"Allison's interview crapped out," he said. "No one was home. I'll have her handle it."

When Maddy arrived at the Corella house, the place immediately gave her the creeps. A broken chair was on the front lawn, a car stood on blocks in the driveway, and two shutters hung crooked. She decided to park down the street and approach the house from the sidewalk. *I hope these people take better care of their kid than they do their house*, she thought as she walked up onto the porch.

Several of the downstairs lights that had been on suddenly went dark. When Maddy knocked on the glass front door, she saw a woman slowly coming to answer, while a large bearded man stood close behind her. The door opened only slightly, just enough to talk through. After introducing herself, Maddy said she needed to speak with Carol. "Her friend, Candy Bishop, has been abducted, and we need her help." The woman stood expressionless. Maddy had to repeat herself. "Candy Bishop has been abducted by a killer and her life is in danger. Can I speak with Carol?" she said forcefully.

The man behind the door suddenly pulled the woman away, stepped in front, and said, "It's late. Come back tomorrow."

"Tomorrow might be too late."

"Carol's sleeping, come back tomorrow."

Maddy caught a glimpse of a young girl sitting halfway down the living room stairway. "I'm not sleeping," she said.

The guy turned and shouted, "Get in bed...I'll be right up."

There's more going on here than meets the eye, Maddy thought. "Are you Mr. Corella?" she asked.

"No, I'm Mr. Jones; there is no Mr. Corella," he said sarcastically.

The woman stood nearby, arms folded, not seeming to like what she heard. The more the guy talked, the tighter the skin around her jaw stretched. Maddy directed a question directly to her. "Would you be able to answer a few questions, ma'am?"

She nodded and smiled, but immediately the guy cut her off. "Not tonight, damn it," he grunted and slammed the door.

That son-of-a-bitch. Maddy wanted to force him to let her talk with Carol but knew she didn't have the grounds to do so. She was determined to speak to the child, so she walked over to the pickup in the driveway and wrote down the plate number. *Let's see what happens when we call this in.* When she requested information on the owner of the truck, she had a pleasant surprise. *What do we have here; it looks like Mr. Nice Guy is on parole.* That was all she needed. His name was Charles Munns, and after a few phone calls, she was talking with Hector Sanchez, his parole officer. It took little convincing to get Sanchez to come to the Corella house, and when he pulled up, Maddy explained the situation. "Is that guy the girl's father?" she asked Sanchez.

"No, he's not even the husband. He is a freeloader who found himself a cozy little situation here with this mother and her kid."

Hector suggested a plan that would allow Maddy a chance to interview Carol. "I'll have Munns come out to the porch to give me an update on what he's been doing. I have a right to do that. Then you can go in and talk with the mother and girl."

"Sounds like a plan," Maddy said.

When Munns opened the door, he snarled at the sight of Maddy and his PO together.

"I'd like to speak with you alone, Charlie," Sanchez said. "Let's go out on the porch."

Maddy could feel hateful vibes as Munns walked by. The woman, still with her arms crossed, seemed relieved. "Let's start all over. I'm Maddy Reynolds."

"I'm Joan Corella," she said, extending a hand. Maddy shook it, and Joan asked her to come in and sit. The two women went to the dining room table. "How long have you been living here?" Maddy asked as she pulled out her notebook.

"Three years."

"Do I hear a little Texas in your accent?"

"Very good. Yes, I was born in San Antonio. My husband was with the 10th Mountain Division up at Fort Drum. When he died, Carol and I moved here to be close to my sister."

"What about Charlie?"

"I met him when I moved here. He's nice to me most of the time."

Maddy wanted to ask her about the rest of the time but held her tongue. She shifted the subject to Carol. "Candy Bishop's life is in jeopardy. I really need to speak to your daughter."

Joan went upstairs and, after a few minutes, returned with a black-haired girl with lots of freckles. "This is Detective Reynolds. You're not in any trouble, she just wants to ask you some questions." The phone rang, and Joan said it was probably her mother and left the two alone.

Maddy showed Carol a picture of the valentine. "Have you seen this before?"

"Yes. One day when we were in the schoolyard at playtime, Candy put her jacket on a bench. When she came back for it, the valentine was on top. We kidded her that Mark Talbert had a crush on her."

"Did you notice any adults around school that day?"

"A lady was walking up and down the street in front of the school. I remember because we kind of made fun of her. She was dressed weird, had a skirt on, and wore stockings in the heat. She was big and walked wobbly in high heels."

Maddy wrote so fast the pen slipped out of her hand and fell to the floor. Carol bent down to get it, and her pajama top rode up, revealing black and blue stripes on her back.

"What happened to your back?" Carol clammed up. She looked away, and her face turned bright red.

"Charlie did this to you, didn't he?"

"Please don't say that I told. Please," Carol begged.

"Don't worry, honey, he'll never touch you again."

When Joan came back, Maddy glared at her. "Stand up, Carol." Maddy pulled up the back of Carol's pajama top and exposed the welts. Joan hung her head and began to sob.

"I'm so sorry," she said.

"Take your daughter upstairs and put something on these wounds. I'm going outside and will be back." When she went to the porch, snarky-faced Munns seemed to be having fun dodging Sanchez's questions, and when he saw Maddy, he smirked.

"Charles Munns, you're under arrest for child abuse," Maddy said as she moved in and handcuffed him before he could respond. Munns looked as if he'd been coldcocked and stood frozen as Maddy read him his Miranda Rights.

"I'll help you secure this piece of shit in your vehicle," Maddy said to Hector. "The child is covered with whip marks from this asshole."

After Sanchez had left with Munns, Maddy went back inside and called upstairs for Joan to come down. "Charlie's gone and won't be back.

I doubt the court will ever let him come back here again. Carol is going to need a lot of help healing from whatever he's done to her. You will too. Tomorrow social services will be out here. Cooperate with them, or you'll run the risk of losing your daughter."

As Maddy left the Corella house and started back to the command center, she saw Carol standing on the porch, watching her part, and she felt a pang of sadness. Just then, the phone rang. "Maddy, what's going on?" It was Jack. "You didn't call Amber tonight, and she's worried sick about you," he said with more anger than worry in his voice.

Aww shit! Maddy thought. "There's been another abduction, Jack. Can you keep her for the next few nights?"

"Yes, but I think you need to break away at some point to see your daughter."

"I'll do what I can. I miss her too. I'm just running on empty."

"I told you it was going to be like this."

When Jack started pontificating about the trials and tribulations of being a detective, it would always lead to a pity party, and Maddy hated it. She wasn't in the mood to listen to his sob story at that moment.

"Look what it did to me," he continued. Maddy wanted to end the conversation, but Jack hit a nerve when he said, "The fucking job cost me my marriage."

That was it. Maddy, still reeling from seeing the whip marks on Carol Corella's back, knew it was the wrong time to dig up the cesspool of shit that preceded their divorce, but there was something about Jack feasting at the table of his self-imposed woes that made her want to reach through the phone and slap him.

"What cost you your marriage wasn't the job, Jack. It was the blonde you were fucking while I was at home thinking you were working late. It was the DWI and the small fortune we spent so you could save your job with the State Troopers, only to have you lose it anyway by going into work drunk and blowing an investigation. It was the lies and manipulation and the poor-me bullshit you're running to me right now. That's what cost you your marriage."

"But I've been sober now for two years, and it's still not good enough to get you back, is it?"

This night is turning into a real cluster-fuck, Maddy thought, as she tried to fend off Jack's guilt trip. The clock was ticking out Candy Bishop's life, and she had to end the conversation. She took a few deep breaths, and as empathetic as she could be, she said, "Jack, you are doing better now, I'll give you that. You've stopped drinking, and I'm happy for you. But you have to understand, other people are still recovering from the damage you did when you were out of control."

A long pause was followed by Jack's deep sigh, and Maddy calmly said, "Let's not do this now. You've been wonderful lately, and I truly appreciate all your help with Amber since this Cupid stuff's been going on. But I have to get back to the command center, so please tell Amber I'll call her tomorrow. Good night, Jack."

"Okay, 'night Maddy."

When she hung up, a tidal wave of guilt about not calling her daughter washed over her. Despite her best intentions, there didn't seem to be a way to balance Amber's needs with the requirements of her job, and as far as her own needs were concerned, they didn't even enter into the equation. There was no time for herself whatsoever. At that moment, she did the only thing she knew how to do: push it all out of her mind.

She called Zep at the command center, but there was no answer. *That's weird,* she thought. After she tried several times, she finally resorted to tracking down a temporary command center phone number. It put her through to an unfamiliar female voice. "Who is this?" Maddy asked.

"Marcia Dunham. I'm the new assistant. Is this Detective Reynolds?"

"Yes."

"Captain Zepatello said you'd be calling. He wants you to meet him at Bernie's All-Night Doughnuts."

"What's going on?"

The woman reluctantly said there had been some sort of incident but didn't elaborate. Aggravated by her double talk, Maddy demanded to know what was going on. In a frightened tone, Marcia said, "Something happened to Detective Abbott, but that's all I know. I'm the only one here; everyone's gone to Bernie's."

"Everyone is gone?" Maddy felt her heart skip a few beats. She made a U-turn and bolted toward Wolf Road. *I was supposed to be at Bernie's, not Allison.*

When she turned onto Wolf Road, Bernie's was lit up like a Christmas tree with flashing lights. A crowd gathered around an ambulance and blocked her view. She got out and ran through the maze of people to see who was injured. Zep stepped in front of her. Maddy looked over his shoulder and saw a blood-soaked bandage wrapped around someone's head.

"Who is that?" she screamed.

"It's Allison."

"Allison!" she wailed. Allison was on a gurney rolling by. Maddy stretched out her hand and placed it on her leg, trying to follow into the ambulance. Zep pulled her away. "This should have been me!" she cried.

Zep put his hands on Maddy's shoulders and looked directly into her face. "There's no way you could have known Cupid was waiting here." Maddy wasn't listening and kept turning her eyes toward Allison.

"How did it happen?" she asked.

"Ambushed, shot in the face with buckshot," Zep said.

"Is she alive?" Maddy weakly asked the medical tech standing nearby.

"Barely," the guy said.

"I'm going with her," Maddy demanded.

"You're not allowed to."

Zep shouted at the med-tech, "Let her go, it's important."

The tech relented, and she climbed in. A bright light shined down on Allison. Maddy found a small, out of the way space to kneel. Each moan from Allison was like a knife penetrating Maddy's gut. "Can she hear us?" Maddy asked.

"I think so. Put your finger in the palm of her hand and ask her to squeeze if she can hear you."

"Allison, it's me, Maddy. I am here with you and won't leave you alone. Squeeze my finger if you can hear me." Allison squeezed.

"Squeeze once for 'no' and twice for 'yes.' Did you get a look at the guy?" Allison squeezed twice. "Did you recognize him?" Allison tightened her grasp once, then tried to raise her head as though she wanted to say something, but no words came out, only a raspy-wheezing sound. She began to shake, then convulsed violently. With an arch of her back and loud painful whine, she suddenly dropped to the gurney, and her grip loosened around Maddy's finger. She exhaled a whispered breath.

"She's gone," said one of the techs.

Maddy blinked as though she did not believe her eyes. It was as though she were watching a movie, and nothing seemed real. She leaned back against the hard wall of the cramped ambulance as a numbness crawled through her face and spread to her chest and limbs. She felt nothing. It was like an emotional spigot somewhere in her brain had been turned off and stopped the flow of feelings to her body. Only a heavy deadness remained.

One of the techs removed the bandage from Allison's once-beautiful face, now grotesquely distorted by puffy red holes, each the size of a pea. Maddy had become a lifeless shell, and though she could not feel, she could think, and her only thought was to get out of the tiny space that reeked of betadine and blood.

Finally, the back doors opened in the emergency room parking area. No sooner had the fresh air begun to pour in than the press swarmed like flies around the ambulance. Questions, photos, pushing and shoving; the scene was chaotic. Maddy stepped out and hid behind two uniformed cops who pushed the crowd back. When she was finally able to shoulder her way through the throng to the street, she heard a clock on top of an old building ring four times.

Once on the street, separated from the bedlam inside the E.R., she became overwhelmed by an intense sense of loneliness. A young man's voice broke through to her. "Would you like a ride home, detective?" It was the voice of a uniformed cop who had been assigned to escort her home.

"Oh, yes, thank you." She stared out the window as they drove. The streets were as empty as she felt inside. It was as if she was twelve again, on the night her father died, but this time, it was Allison whom she grieved.

Chapter 29

Maddy lay on the living room couch, where she'd plopped herself at 4:37 a.m. She was unable to sleep, and her mind raced. It was as if a bomb had gone off in her world. Fragments of life as she had known it lay scattered all about in her mind. *How can I possibly go on from here?* Her heart ached every time she thought of Allison.

As the sun rose above the neighborhood, her eyes blurred from daylight that beamed through the windows. The clock on the mantel read 9:36, then it struck her, *Candy Bishop!* The fiasco at Bernie's had derailed the investigation. She sat up, rested her head in her hands for a moment, went to the window, and saw a patrol car planted in front of her house.

She walked to the kitchen and stopped to gaze at *The Tempest on the Sea*. The man in the window of the ship, shrouded in darkness, surrounded by pandemonium, had become Cupid. "Why have you come to kill me?" There was no doubt in her mind now that Cupid wanted her dead.

After she made coffee, Maddy sat at the kitchen table reflecting on the night before. Two new pieces of information pertinent to the case had emerged: Candy Bishop had been at the Friendly Bean before she went missing, and an art instructor had met with her alone. Both situations needed to be assessed immediately. Zep called when she was on her third cup. "How are you hanging in, Maddy?"

"Just putting one step in front of the other."

"I know. Losing Allison like that...it just doesn't seem real." He paused as though he were giving Maddy a chance to say something, but she didn't. "For what it's worth, our people are in contact with her daughter's father and her parents. They'll stay involved with the family from now on. It's something we've always done when things like this happen."

"That's good to know," she said.

An awkward silence set in as Zep seemed to struggle for words. He finally said, "I know it's hard to get back up on the horse at times like this, but there's a ten-year-old girl out there who still needs us."

"I know," she said.

They started talking about the case. "If you're up to it, I'd like you and Al to handle following up on Candy's sketch and her meetings with the art teacher."

"I'll make myself be up to it," she said. Again, there was silence. Then she added, "Who's that in the car in front of my house this morning?"

"Al," Zep said with a snicker.

Maddy smiled, shook her head, and mused to herself how Zep was a captain through and through. She remained in the kitchen after they hung up, and before turning her attention to Candy Bishop, her thoughts returned to Allison. For the first time since the breath of life had left her friend's body, Maddy felt the full thrust of her loss. She bellowed out loud, "I'm so sorry, I'm so sorry," and dropped her head onto her arms as they lay on the table. Maddy had not wailed as hard since the night of her father's death. When she stopped weeping, face and shirt wet with tears, she forced herself to stand, leave her grief behind and resume the battle against time to save Candy Bishop.

Under the circumstances, Maddy was as ready as she could be to jump back into the case, although she knew she wasn't a hundred percent. She walked up to the driver's side window of the car, where Al waited. "Looks like it's you and me this morning."

"Yeah, I talked with Zep. It sounds like we have some follow-up to do." Al spoke with about as much enthusiasm as Maddy felt. Few words were uttered in the car as they drove.

When they walked into the Bean, Rusty came out from behind the counter to greet them. "I can't tell you how sorry I am to hear about Allison," he said.

They both nodded. Maddy asked if there was somewhere they could speak with him alone.

"Why certainly. Let's go to the kitchen."

They entered a brightly lit room where food was being prepared. "Is there a place I can lay this?" Maddy asked, holding up Candy's drawing, still in its cover. Rusty moved two half-made sandwiches from a table and wiped it clean with a rag. She slid the sketch from its cover and laid it down. "Recognize it?"

"Oh my, yes. It's like a photograph."

"It was drawn right here at The Friendly Bean by a ten-year-old girl just two weeks ago," Maddy said. "Her name is Candy Bishop."

Rusty's eyes lit up. "The girl that was just abducted?"

"That's the one," Al said.

Rusty looked confused and seemed hurt, as though he was pained to think Maddy suspected him. He stood looking dumbfounded, then his eyes opened wide. "That was about the time that guy was hanging around here. You know, the one we made a sketch of. He always sat over by the window near where the girl would sit."

As though Maddy and Al's brains were operating on the same frequency, their eyes met. They turned toward the door, and before they bolted to the car, Maddy blurted to Rusty, "Don't discuss this with anyone, especially the press."

Back in the car, Al said, "We're running out of time. We should tell Zep that the guy's sketch should go into the paper tonight."

I hate doing that shit, she thought, remembering what happened to Jenkins. But she knew Al was right and when they called Zep, he agreed. "I don't think we have any choice. Shit, we'll be lucky if the kid's not dead already." Everyone knew they had lost valuable time dealing with the calamity the night before at Bernie's. "I'll take care of it. In the meantime, keep me posted on that Albright guy."

As they headed to Syracuse to interview the art professor, Maddy asked Al what he was able to find out about the professor.

"He's a renowned artist, but quite controversial. He's British, working here as a visiting professor."

"What's controversial about him?"

"He specializes in photographing nudes of young girls."

"What?"

"Grab that folder on the back seat and take a look at some of his work."

Maddy opened the folder. "You got to be shitting me." She was looking at a photo of a girl, about thirteen, lying on a couch with her legs partially open. Every aspect of her blooming womanhood was visible.

"This isn't art. This is child pornography."

"That's exactly what the courts are trying to figure out," Al said.

She shook her head and was predisposed not to like the guy by the time they arrived at his office. When his secretary sent them in, Albright was standing behind his desk. He was a tall man in his mid-fifties with a full head of brown hair that he wore combed back. He had a partially gray goatee that made him appear distinguished, and when he spoke, he sounded sophisticated. "Please sit. How can I help you?"

He sat back in a large leather chair. Behind him hung an abstract painting of a nude woman and across the room, terracotta wall hangings that depicted men and women having sex. Beneath them, different colored rocks, shaped like male and female genitals, sat on glass shelves.

"We understand Candice Bishop is one of your students," Maddy said.

"Yes, she is in the Advanced Childhood Development Program."

"Have you heard what happened to her?" Al asked.

Albright said that he hadn't heard and asked if she was all right.

"She was abducted yesterday by a person who we believe killed two other girls," Maddy said.

"You mean Cupid." His eyebrows rose.

"We're here because Candy had a private lesson with you two weeks ago. Can you tell us about it?"

Albright glared at her. "I have a few specially gifted students whom I give one-on-one instructions to," he said, sounding irritated.

"Pardon me for saying it," Maddy said, "but I find your preoccupation with photographing young girls nude troublesome."

Unflinchingly, Albright responded. "The female body is a thing of great beauty. There have been many artists like me who have made it a major part of their work. That I focus on girls who are on the brink of womanhood would not trouble you if you understood this genre."

"Have you photographed any nudes since you've been in Syracuse?" Al asked.

"One."

"How old was she?" Al continued.

"Sixteen, and I have all the parental consent forms if you care to see them."

Maddy chimed in. "Have you approached any other subjects since you've been here?"

"Yes," he snapped at her.

"Was Candice one of them?"

"Absolutely not."

"Dr. Albright, can you provide us with documentation of your whereabouts since your last appointment with Candy?" Al asked.

"Do you have a subpoena?"

"No, but we can get one in about fifteen minutes," Maddy sneered.

Albright stiffened and sat straight up in his chair. "I would like to consult with my attorney before I give you anything."

Al and Maddy looked at each other. "We don't have much time," Maddy said. "How long will it take?"

"If you wait outside, I'll make some phone calls."

When they left the room, Maddy told Al she couldn't understand why anyone would let their kid have private lessons with Albright. "He's a freaking sicko."

"Maybe they didn't know enough about the guy," he said.

When the door opened, Albright came out and said his secretary would fax over the information. They handed him their cards and left quickly. Maddy and Al were barely back in the car when the phone rang; it was Zep. "Ready for this?" he said. They looked at each other with raised eyebrows, as if to say, *Now what?*

"Before Allison was killed, a large woman was seen in the area carrying a box. I think Cupid is using disguises."

A giant piece of the puzzle from the night before flashed back to Maddy. "Carol Corella said a large woman was hanging around the school about the time Candy found the valentine." As she spoke, something else tugged at her memory, but she couldn't pinpoint what it was.

"That's one more device in Cupid's bag of tricks," Zep said. "What did you two find out about the good professor?"

"We found out that he's not too good," Al said. "He has a preoccupation with girls around Candy's age, and he's into photographing them nude. We think we should put a tail on him."

"I'll reach out to the Syracuse police for that," Zep said.

Maddy had to find time to visit her daughter and thought now was as good a time as any to ask her boss. Resources were thin, and she knew he couldn't afford to tie up another detective, so she just came out and asked. "I really need to spend a few hours with Amber. How about easing up on the surveillance thing for a little while?"

After a long pause, Zep sighed and said okay. "But make sure you check in with me every hour or so."

When she hung up, she felt a sense of relief. But other concerns were eating at her, and she decided to confide in Al. "Cupid got Allison last night but was trying to get me. I'm worried because if he succeeds, I've made no arrangements for Amber."

"I had to do that for my mother," he said. "It hit home for me a while back when I was stabbed in a domestic violence case. While I was laid up in the hospital, all I could think about was what would happen to her if the knife had entered above where it did. You should take care of it," he said. "It'll make you feel better. It did me."

Maddy sighed. "I'll do it. But I need to start by talking to my ex." She had become wonderfully comfortable sharing her concerns with Al, and decided to ask him a question that had been on her mind. "Something else that I don't understand is why Cupid's preoccupied with killing me. I realize he hates women, but he's singled me out. Why? There has to be more to it. There's a missing piece to this puzzle, and I'd like to know what it is."

"Cupid is crazy. What more do you need to know?"

"I just feel there's something else at work here."

When they arrived at the command center, Al walked in the building as Maddy got in her car and headed to Jack's. She was determined to make her wishes for Amber known in case she ended up like Allison.

Chapter 30

This was all mine. Maddy's thoughts wandered as she drove to Jack's on a perfect summer afternoon. Although unsure of what the thought meant, it seemed to be something a dying person might think when they realized all the fascinating aspects of life that they had taken for granted. She couldn't help but be aware that, just like Allison, her life could be snuffed out in an instant too. The knowledge made the sun, the sky, and the clouds seem different somehow.

She pulled into Jack's driveway and saw him on his front porch, swinging in a chair with headphones over his ears. When she walked up and sat next to him, he took the headphones off and laid them on his lap.

"What's wrong, Maddy?" he asked, as though he could read her thoughts.

"I need to know what will happen to our daughter if I don't make it through this Cupid nightmare." She looked down and sensed that Jack was taken aback by her solemn mood. "He's obsessed with killing me, and I'm not sure I'm going to make it."

"What do you want to happen?" Jack said in a soft, understanding voice. He seemed to be feeling genuine compassion, and she thought that for the first time in a long while, he was where she needed him to be.

She was looking at the world without herself in it, and said, "I want Amber to stay in the same school she's in now. She's happy there. She has friends and is well-liked. That means you'll have to move. I want her to go to college. You'll need to stay on her about her grades the way I do. And most of all, I don't want her to go into law enforcement."

Jack said, "I will do these things."

She nodded her head, looked down into her lap as a wave of sadness washed up onto the shore of her soul, and she began to weep. Wiping tears from her eyes, she asked where Amber was. "I'd like to speak with her."

"I'll get her." While Jack was gone, Maddy realized she wanted to make things right with him as well. *Ours may not have been the most successful family, but we are the only family we have,* she thought. When Amber came out to the porch, she sat across from her mother, and Jack left them alone. Amber pushed her hair from her face, bit her lower lip, and seemed to know something important was coming her way.

"There are some things I need to explain to you: adult things that I haven't talked about because I didn't want to worry you."

"You mean about Cupid?"

"Yes, about Cupid."

"I hear kids talking in school. They say you're one of the important detectives trying to catch him. Is it true?"

"Yes, but it's extremely dangerous. I can get hurt...even die."

Amber looked at her mother, eyes squinting, like she was looking into the sun, and said nothing for a moment. Finally, she asked, "What will happen to me if you die?"

"Dad will take care of you."

Amber looked down in silence. She got up, went over to Maddy, knelt next to her, laid her head on her mom's lap, and began to cry. As they held each other, Maddy cried too, gently rocking back and forth as she did when Amber was little.

There was a long silence before Amber asked, "Why does he do it... why does he hurt girls?"

"I don't know," Maddy said with one side of her face buried in Amber's hair as she rocked her.

"And why does he give them a valentine?"

"I don't know that either."

"Does that always happen? I mean, do bad men always give people they hurt valentines?"

"No, Amber, it's very unusual."

"Then why did it happen when Grandpa was alive?"

"It didn't, honey."

"Yes, it did. I saw pictures of valentines in Grandpa's green metal box in the basement."

A bolt of lightning struck Maddy. She pushed Amber away, looked directly in her eyes, and said, "What do you mean?"

"Remember the night you read me the letter Grandpa left you? I asked if there was anything else he left behind, and you said, just an old green metal box in the basement with a bunch of work stuff. One day when Melissa was over, we were playing in the basement, and I saw the green box, so I opened it. Inside were lots of envelopes and some had awful scary pictures. I didn't tell you because I thought you'd be mad at me. A few had old-fashioned valentines like the ones I saw in the newspaper."

"Oh, my God!"

"What does it mean, Mom?"

Not wanting to alarm her, Maddy took a deep breath and tried to compose herself. "I am not sure. I'll have to check into it." Her mind began to race. *Can it be? Can Cupid be a copycat of the guy my father was after?"* She was able to get Amber's attention off the green box by telling her that when the Cupid case was over, they would go on a vacation together somewhere fun.

"Can we go to New York City and see *Annie*?"

"It's a date," Maddy said with a smile.

I can't wait to tell my friends." Amber gave Maddy a hug, and excitedly ran inside. She seemed to have pushed the discussion about her mother's death out of her mind.

"What's that all about?" Jack asked as he came back outside.

"I told her I'd take her to see *Annie* when this is over."

As she started to walk to her car with Jack, Maddy returned to the subject of their previous discussion. "If something happens to me, remember, keep Amber's life as stable as you can. I don't want her to go through what I did when my father died."

"I promise," Jack said as he opened the car door for her. Before she got in, she turned and said, "I know things haven't worked out the way we had hoped, but I think we've done something wonderful with our daughter. Thank you for that." Maddy put her arms around him. Jack seemed stunned at first but then hugged her. When the embrace ended, Maddy noticed tears welling up in his eyes.

As she drove away, her mind returned to the metal box. She started to think of what it might mean when the phone rang. Zep yelled, "Where the hell are you?"

"I'm sorry I didn't call when I was supposed to. I just left Jack's. Zep, I need to stop by my house for a few minutes before I come back to the command center."

"Maddy!" he said sternly. "This is a matter of life and death."

"I'll be okay. I promise I'll be back in an hour."

It was almost six p.m. when she pulled into her driveway. She ran inside, leaped down the cellar stairs into the messy basement, and started looking for the box. As she shuffled through a pile of old board games, something green caught her eye. Beneath a wooden checkerboard, the green metal box containing items from her father's office sat slightly covered with rust. She carried it up to the kitchen where the light was brighter, placed it on the table, and before opening it, she thought, *This could change everything.*

She began to pull out envelopes of different sizes from the box. Some were small and white, others large and brown, and all contained case notes related to various crimes. At the bottom of the box, she grabbed a package, more substantial than the rest, and emptied it on the table. Black and white glossy photos of crime scenes involving young girls, all dated between 1960 and 1961, slid out. Written on the back of each was the name of the case.

One by one, Maddy examined each photo, scrutinized it, and read the penciled writing on the back. They were glimpses into her father's world. She saw a picture of a girl around fourteen, lying partially naked in the mud, dress torn and bloodied with a valentine on her stomach. The name 'Patty Bronson' was written on the back. A second photo showed the inside of the card. It was signed, *Mark*. Maddy cringed and cried out, "Holy shit! Holy shit!"

She sat frozen and confused, unable to connect the dots from her current nightmare to the photo. Two other sets of similar images were also signed, "Mark." *How can this be? Cupid has to be a copycat.* The more she learned, the less she understood. *I have to find out what happened back then.* The only person that she trusted to tell her the truth was Bob Bennett. She hadn't spoken with him since he was in the hospital, and though she didn't know how he was faring physically, she called him anyway. Bob answered right away.

"Bob, it's Maddy." She was unable to stop her voice from quivering.

"Talk to me, Maddy. What's wrong?" There was a tone of anticipation, almost like he was expecting her to call.

She explained that two girls, ages ten and eleven, were found raped and strangled in Utica. She told him that a third girl was missing and that a vintage valentine signed *Mark* was found in possession of each one. "The killer has been harassing me personally and killed another detective, thinking it was me." Maddy heard a low, barely detectable groan on the other end of the line.

"Bob, I just found out that the murders in Chicago involved similar valentines. How can this be? Do you think this new killer is a copycat?" She walked out to the living room with the phone, sat down, and waited for Bob to give her missing pieces to the bizarre puzzle.

She heard him take a deep breath before he began to speak and did so in a deadly serious tone. Slow and deliberate, as though he was about to reveal a long-held secret, he said, "Shit, Maddy. I should have told you this a long time ago. I meant to when the time was right, but a lot of time passed, and eventually, I thought maybe I wouldn't have to say anything." Maddy prepared herself for whatever he might say.

"It's not a copycat. It's the same fucking guy." *That*, she was not prepared for. Bob continued. "His M.O. was to take kids to an isolated place in the woods, like an abandoned house, or a cabin, where he'd rape and kill them. A valentine signed *Mark* was always found in their possession, sometimes on the body. And Maddy, one was found on your dad, too."

A spear pierced Maddy's heart. Unable to speak, she watched her hands shake as she struggled to catch her breath. Her voice cracked as she asked, "What makes you think it's the same man?"

"I know it is," Bob said emphatically.

"But you told me Dad's murderer died in prison!"

"That's what we were ordered to tell everyone. I wanted to tell you the truth, but you were just a kid. After your father was killed, the city went ballistic. People wanted the heads of the mayor and chief of police. The press was merciless, and there were no clues. The guy vanished like spit in the ocean. All the cops wanted revenge; we loved your dad. That's when things got out of control."

"What do you mean 'out of control'?"

"False arrests, harassment...we came down hard on any low-life we thought might have information. Then one day, we came down too hard. A guy died, and the whole department started falling apart. Higher-ups tried to hold it together. That's when word came down about this guy in Detroit named Rico Neselli. He had just started a ten-year hitch for Grand Larceny and had bragged to his cellmate that he was the Chicago Child Killer. That was it. He was a marked man and dead within a month, killed at the hands of other inmates. They hate guys who target kids."

Bob was becoming emotional, and Maddy heard his voice tighten. "Then, fucking politics took over. It had been ten months after Jimbo was murdered when the Neselli thing came out, and there hadn't been a peep from the killer in all that time. He must have split town, but the public still wouldn't rest easy. The mayor and chief wanted it to be over, so they grasped onto the Neselli story and pushed it with the press. They ate it up. Everyone wanted to believe the guy was dead, so they convinced themselves he was. There were serious consequences for any of us who disputed the party line. We weren't even allowed to work the case anymore."

"How do you know that Neselli wasn't really the murderer?"

"He couldn't have been. One person got a good look at the killer. It was from the back and a short distance away. She was certain the guy was large, over six feet tall. Neselli was a runt."

Bob's voice was cracking. "I never could accept it. I retired the next year. Your dad was a great man and my best friend. He deserved to have his killer brought to justice, but it never happened, and now the lunatic is back in action."

After a long silence on both ends of the phone, Maddy said, "So why do you think he is in Utica?"

"There is only one explanation. The guy's there to kill you!"

"But why?"

"I don't know. Because he's insane. Because he's connected you with your father somehow. Because of any one of a hundred reasons why maniacal killers do the crazy shit they do. We may never know. But rest assured, Maddy, he's there to kill you. Killing those girls...that's just an appetizer. You're the main course. You're up against one of the most twisted, cunning, and intelligent killers ever. I knew there was something bad going on with you when I had those dreams in the hospital. They all involved you and that fucking maniac. I wish I could be there to help you, but I'm worthless nowadays."

"You have helped more than you know," Maddy said, her mind still reeling from Bob's revelations.

As they were about to hang up, Bob said, "You know, not a day goes by that I don't think about that Halloween night. And now I realize it's still not over for you. I am so sorry. But listen carefully to what I'm going to say. If you do come across that bastard, don't give him any chances. Kill him at your first opportunity. When it comes to this guy, fuck the law; the law failed with him. Now it's time to think of yourself and your family."

Maddy hung up. From the time that she picked up the phone to call Bob to the moment the receiver clunked back down, her life as she understood it had changed. *I feel like I've been on a railroad track oblivious to a train charging at me, and now it's here.* Everything she'd understood about her father's death and the man who killed him was false. She couldn't move from her chair. She sat, wondering what to do next. When she thought about telling Zep, something told her not to. Maybe it was what Bob said to her, "Kill him at your first opportunity. When it comes to this guy, fuck the law." She wasn't sure why, but for the time being, she would keep it all to herself.

Chapter 31

Maddy ran out of the house and raced back to Forestport. Her mind was in a haze, and fragments of new information floated around in her head: Cupid had killed her father, Allison was dead, and the murderer had come to kill her. It was as though she had entered an alternate reality where anything was possible, and she was waiting for the next dragon to manifest.

It was 9:09 p.m. when she reached the fire station. Zep was waiting when she walked into the building and looked more worried than pissed. "Oh my God, are you...all right?" he asked.

"What do you mean?"

"There's no color in your face. You're as white as a ghost. Are you sick?"

"No, just tired, like everyone else."

"There's a bunch of cots in the far corner," he said. "I want you to get some rest. That's an order." He was clearly concerned that the strain she'd been under might be making her sick. Maddy found a cot, and within minutes she was asleep.

Loud guffaws from two young cops joking around woke her up. For a moment, she couldn't remember where she was. Her eyes were blurred by daylight pouring through a window. She rubbed her eyelids, lifted up her head, and checked her watch. *Eight thirty? Damn. Why didn't someone wake me up?* She dragged herself to her feet and went to the coffee table, combing her hair with her fingers. The first sip of high-test coffee gave her a jolt and helped her shake out the cobwebs. She saw Al standing nearby with a grim expression, so she walked over and asked him what was going on. "It appears our Dr. Albright has disappeared," he said.

"What happened?"

"The Syracuse police were tailing him last night, and he just vanished. That's not all. I found out he raped a ten-year-old girl in the U.K. The guy is more than just a quirky artist. He's a pedophile."

Zep walked over to where they stood. "Did you tell her about Albright?" he said to Al. Al nodded. "Apparently he has friends in Buffalo. According to his secretary, he spends a lot of time there, and the telephone logs show a bunch of calls just before he disappeared. I'm about to send two of our people out to work with the Buffalo P.D."

"So, when do we leave?" Maddy asked, assuming she and Al would be going.

Zep turned to Al and said, "You better get moving and make the arrangements. You and Renshaw should leave as soon as possible."

"But Zep..." Maddy said, taken aback. "What the hell?" Zep gestured to Al to leave Maddy and him alone.

When Al was gone, Zep turned to Maddy. "I'm concerned for your safety, Maddy. There's a lot that needs to be done right here. Check the Call Center to see if we got any bites on the sketch." He turned and walked away.

Maddy felt as if someone had punched her in the solar plexus and knocked the wind out of her. She went outside, pacing around, trying to make sense of what had just happened. Zep's sudden change of heart felt like he'd lost confidence in her. Al rushed out the door toward his car, and when he passed Maddy, stopped, and asked what was wrong.

"Zep's got me under lock and key. I can't believe he's sending Renshaw to Buffalo instead of me."

Al dipped his shoulder to one side and sighed. "He's lost Allison, Maddy. He knows Cupid has it in for you, and he doesn't want to lose you too. Come on, cut him some slack." Al put his hand on her shoulder, looked her in the eyes, and said, "Everyone knows all that you've done on the case. But we have to count on Zep to keep us from making mistakes and getting ourselves killed. That's all that's going on here. Don't take it personally."

Al had a knack for getting to the heart of things in a few words, and what he said helped her put the situation in perspective. She nodded her head somewhat reluctantly, as Al smiled, turned away, and headed for his car. "Be careful, Al," she said, as she watched him walk away.

Back inside, she followed up with the Call Center, as Zep had asked. The attendant who answered the phone said no calls on the sketch had come in, but there was a message for her from a woman named Tonya Petrov. "She was agitated and wanted to be sure you knew that it was happening again. She said you'd know what that meant."

Oh shit, Maddy thought. Tonya's noise was the last thing Maddy wanted to deal with at that moment. "All right, I'll handle it." She tracked down Zep and told him there were no bites on the sketch, but the noise lady had called in and was apparently losing it. "Do you want me to go over and calm her down?"

"You may as well," he said, seeming preoccupied with more important matters. "When you're done with her, why don't you stop out to the Bishops. They've been calling all morning looking for an update."

"What do I tell them?"

"Tell them the truth. We think we have the guy in our sights and are zeroing in on him. Don't give them any more than that."

Zep seemed to have forgotten about surveillance, and Maddy didn't bring it up. She thought that he was probably less concerned now that the threat from Cupid had shifted two hundred miles west to Buffalo.

When she arrived at Tonya's apartment, the door was unlocked, and she heard weeping inside. She walked in and saw the poor woman sitting at the edge of the couch, hands clasped over her ears and rocking back and forth. She looked up at Maddy, her face twisted, as if in despair. "It's back... it's back. Can you hear it?"

Maddy heard a barely detectable humming sound and thought, *That's it?*

"Do you hear it?" Tonya asked again, almost pleading.

"I think so. It's extremely high pitched." She stood in the middle of the room, slowly turning in a circle, trying to locate the direction of the sound. It seemed to be coming from the left, and she opened a closet door. "It's in here. That's strange." Numerous coats and jackets hung on hangers. Boxes of wrapping paper and sewing supplies were piled up behind them. *How many coats does one woman need?*

One at a time, she checked each item for anything that might be making the sound, then, when she finished, placed the thing on the couch. When the closet was empty, she stepped inside, and to her amazement, still heard the vibration.

"What the hell." She placed her ear to the wall on her left and then the right, but nothing. When she got down on her knees and put her ear to the floor, she still heard no sound. Finally, she tried the back wall and listened to a faint sound. *Son of a bitch, there it is.* She scrutinized the wall and noticed four screws, in each corner of a wooden board that covered the back of the closet. "Tonya, do you have a Philips head screwdriver?"

Tonya had moved to the hallway and shouted back, "Under the kitchen sink." Maddy grabbed several screwdrivers buried beneath a bunch of tools in a bucket and started back to the closet. It had been a long time since she had immersed herself in something other than the Cupid drama and she was eager to tackle the wooden board.

The first screw took a good deal of strength to break free from dried paint that had caked up around it, but the rest came out without effort. On her knees, Maddy finished the last screw, and thought, *I wouldn't want to do this for a living, but then again, it's better than chasing a crazy killer around town.*

Once freed from the screws, the board remained wedged in too tight to pull out, so she tapped a flathead screwdriver into the crack at the edge near the wall, pried the board loose, and pulled it out. Behind it, four pipes ran parallel from floor to ceiling. She placed her hand on each pipe and felt a slight vibration on one. *There's the sucker. Now to find where it leads.*

"Tonya, I'm going downstairs and will be back." Maddy tried to approximate the location of the closet relative to the rest of the building and determined that the pipe went down into The Friendly Bean's kitchen. When she walked into the restaurant, Artie said Rusty wasn't there, but that he'd be glad to help. He led her to the kitchen and showed her a nook where the pipes came down through the ceiling.

The pipes ran behind a small table, where a portable oven and a large coffee grinder rested. She asked Artie to help her move the still-running grinder away from the pipes. The grinder was made especially for restaurants. It was large and cumbersome. Artie squeezed his body awkwardly into the cramped area, and on the count of three, they slid the grinder out about eight inches from the pipes. Immediately, the humming sound stopped.

"Ah-ha!" Feeling a sense of accomplishment, Maddy scooched around the side, stuck her hand behind the grinder, and fished out a pencil. "There's the culprit. How do you suppose it got back there?"

"It must have happened when the grinder was out for repairs a few months ago," Artie said. "Every few days I grind up a lot of coffee. It must have been vibrating between the coffee grinder and the pipe, making that noise.

"Well, Tonya upstairs will be one happy old lady. Do you mind if I take it?"

"It's yours. We've got lots of pencils."

As she walked up the stairs, Maddy noticed that the lead in the pencil was a unique shade of purple-red. Stamped on the side of the pencil was a company's name—Faber-Castell—and the name of the color: Falu. When she opened the apartment door, a smiling Tonya awaited. "You stopped it. Oh, thank you," she said as she threw her arms around Maddy.

"This was the source of all your troubles," Maddy said, holding out the pencil.

"Something so small, yet it was driving me mad. Please don't leave yet. Let me make you some lunch."

"No, I need to put your place back together and get moving." She looked at her watch and thought, *I can't believe it's after one, and I still need to get out to see the Bishops.*

It was a little past two o'clock when she drove by the tree up the road from the house. She felt an unease when it dawned on her that it was the spot where Candy had her last glimpse of home. She walked up on the porch, knocked, and Tom came out. Maddy smiled and asked how Judy was doing.

"Not very well," he said. "Some of the women from the church brought her to a prayer meeting. I hope it will help."

"That's a good thing," Maddy said.

They took the same seats on the porch as the night before. Tom said, "We read about what happened to Detective Abbott. How tragic." Then, hesitantly he added, "We're worried about how it might affect our situation. Has there been any progress locating Candy?"

"Allison's death has not deterred us from anything we're doing. And yes, we do have some new information we're following up on, which leads me to some questions I have for you. What can you tell me about Dr. Albright?"

"Only that he is an outstanding art teacher."

"Mr. Bishop, his specialty is photographing nude women." If Maddy could have avoided telling him what she had to say next, she would have. "He is particularly fond of using girls Candy's age as subjects and..." she hesitated, cleared her throat, and added, "...he has a sexual assault conviction in Britain." Tom grabbed his stomach. He looked like he'd been hit with a bout of food poisoning and was about to vomit. "We were tailing him last night when he evaded us. It looks like he's taken off for Buffalo, and we are working with law enforcement to track him down. Right now, we're operating on the assumption that locating him is our best chance of finding your daughter." Maddy pulled out her notebook. "Is there anything else you can tell me about him?" In the back of her mind, she couldn't shake the image of Albright's face, thinking that he was the man who killed her father and had come to kill her.

Tom began restating conversations he had had with Albright. Maddy wrote as fast as she could, and when the lead in her mechanical pencil ran out, she asked him to hang on, reached in her pocket, and pulled out another pencil. "Okay, please continue." There was silence. When she looked up, Tom was staring at her hand.

"Where did you get that?"

"This? This pencil?"

"That's Candy's pencil. Can I see it?"

She handed it over, and he scrutinized it. "Come with me," he said. When they walked into Candy's room, Tom reached under the bed, pulled out a highly varnished wooden box, and opened it. Inside, dozens of colored pencils were tightly held in place in slots and ordered by color. The array of pencils looked like a rainbow, deconstructed into hundreds of different shades. He took the pencil from Maddy and placed it in the only open slot. The color was slightly redder than the one above it and bluer than the one below it.

"These are expensive drawing pencils, and this one belongs to Candy. Not many people here have this set. I had to send away for it. Where did you get this?"

"In the kitchen of the Friendly Bean."

"What was it doing there? Candy has never been in the kitchen." He paused a moment and added, "Unless it was when I left her alone."

Not sure what to say or think, Maddy stumbled over her words. "I need to follow up on this and will get back to you as soon as I know more." She rushed from the house, pointed her car toward town, and floored it. Black clouds and strong winds whipped themselves into a frenzy, and within a quarter mile, a deluge broke loose. She was unable to see more than ten feet in front of the car. As she tried to finesse her way through the storm, she searched her mind for a logical explanation for how Candy's pencil made its way into the kitchen of the Friendly Bean. It was incomprehensible to Maddy that Candy's disappearance had anything to do with Rusty. She didn't even want to call Zep until she knew more.

The rain forced her to move slower and slower, giving her time to think. An occasional inkling escaped into her consciousness of how she might feel if Rusty was Cupid. The word that best described it was "betrayal," but she ignored the thought each time it entered her mind.

The lights inside the Bean were off when she finally arrived. The wind blew hard, and the rain fell at a slant; someone was parked out front in a Ford Pinto, but she couldn't tell who it was. She got out as rain spattered her face. Placing her hand over her weapon, she knocked on the driver's side window. When it opened, she saw that Artie sat behind the wheel.

"What are you doing here, Artie?"

"I'm trying to figure out what's going on. I told Rusty about you finding that fancy pencil, and he went berserk. He made me kick out all the customers and close the place up. I don't get it. It was just a pencil."

Maddy's senses suddenly ceased to work; she felt like she was in a vacuum. The wetness and sound of the rain were pushed to the background, and Artie's face appeared frozen, as though it was a picture, framed and hanging on a wall. The words, "It was just a pencil," kept reverberating around in her head. Her brain was on full alert.

It's not just a fucking pencil, she thought. *It's the missing piece to the puzzle of my life.* It was as though someone had put a spotlight on the man on the ship. *Rusty is Cupid!* For the first time, the monster who had haunted her since she was twelve showed himself. Rusty killed her father, and he had come to kill her. Like a fox dressed as a chicken, he pretended to be her friend for the sole purpose of destroying her.

"Are you all right, Maddy?" Artie's voice broke through her fog. She realized that she was standing unprotected in the downpour. She asked him if he had a key. "I have one for the back door, but Rusty said to never use it unless it's an emergency."

"This is an emergency. Get it out."

The rain beat down, and the wind howled as they walked through the alley behind the Bean. Drenched while waiting for Artie to hunt through dozens of keys, Maddy grappled with the enormity of her situation. *Rusty must have been planning to kill me for years.* His desire for her death was so deep that he had opened a restaurant where she lived and befriended her. She struggled to fathom such hatred.

When Artie finally put the key in the lock, she took out her weapon and thought of Bob Bennett's words: *Don't give him any chances, kill him at your first opportunity. When it comes to this guy, fuck the law.*

Artie slid open the steel door and turned on a light. The storeroom was empty save for boxes, cans, and cooking utensils that were scattered on the floor.

"What a mess," Artie said.

Maddy and Artie stepped around the debris and walked through the storeroom to the restaurant. "It looks like Rusty trashed the place looking for something," Artie said.

The dining area was empty, and the pleasant aromas that usually filled the place had turned to sickening smells of food going bad. The Friendly Bean had become anything but friendly. It was dark, damp, messy, and it stank. Half-filled cups of coffee and dirty dishes sat on top of tables. The only thing missing was the people. It was as if they had evaporated. Chairs stood askew, and pieces of bread, scrambled eggs, and bits of bacon from half-eaten meals smeared the floor. Maddy pointed at a picture on the wall in an area where she had never sat before. Emblazoned on the print of an old-time detective were the words "Rozzer's Roost." "What's that?" she asked Artie.

"Just some old picture Rusty had hanging in a Friendly Bean restaurant he owned in London."

For the second time in twenty-four hours, something tugged at her memory, like an itch that couldn't be scratched, and it gnawed at her. "What does it mean?"

"It's a place where cops hang out."

"So, rozzer means cop, right?"

Artie nodded.

Mason Charles! That's it. The day that she had stopped Mason Charles coming out of the hardware store, he had asked her, "Are you a rozzer?" Then another lost memory came crashing through to her consciousness. *The attic! I never checked the attic.* Pieces of experiences that were lost the day Maddy killed Benny Bowls had lingered in her memory, waiting to be found and placed in the puzzle.

"Am I in trouble, Maddy?" Artie asked.

"No, but you're going to have to be questioned. You can leave. I know where you live and can find you. Don't contact anyone about this."

Alone, Maddy stood in the middle of the Friendly Bean, a place she had once adored. It was a sweet façade Cupid had created to mask his nefarious intentions. She recalled friendly conversations with him, and it made her feel dumb and gullible. *I actually thought he was a friend.*

Filled with self-doubt, she walked out the back door. The rain had stopped, and heat thickened the air and made it sticky. A garbage can blew over in the storm and spilled coffee grounds and remnants of food into a puddle. Drowning maggots squirmed in the filthy water; it smelled putrid and made her gag. *This is how I will remember the Friendly Bean,* she thought as she walked away.

Chapter 32

Maddy drove to Donald Charles's house dazed, as though she had been punched in the head and was trying to find her sea legs. Yet, for the first time ever, her life made sense. Knowing the identity of her father's killer, as painful as it was, gave her a sense of freedom. In her mind's eye, she saw the girl that she was when she was twelve, sitting in an intensive care unit next to her dying father, and her heart broke for the child. With the Cupid saga finally in focus, Maddy was more alarmed than ever. She pulled out her father's badge, and it was as though he was sitting right next to her.

She called Zep with no intention of telling him what she'd learned. "A lot has happened that you don't know about. You're going to need to trust what I am about to tell you. I believe Candy Bishop is at Mason and Donald Charles's house. I'm headed there now and will explain everything when you arrive." She hung up.

Maddy parked down the street from the house, crept up to a window and peeked in. Empty rooms and no car in the driveway led her to think no one was there, but when she went to the back, she saw light shining in the basement, and Mason standing at a table, painting a model airplane. When she tapped on the window, he looked up, and she yelled for him to come to the front door.

"Where's Donald?" she asked when he opened up.

"I...I don't know," he stuttered.

"You must know."

"He's probably with Nigel."

"Who is Nigel?"

"He's the guy that Donald's always taking off with. Sometimes he calls him Rusty. They never let me go with them."

"Show me the attic." Maddy knew she was throwing protocol out the window, but time was running out on a child's life and for her, at that moment, protocol be damned. Mason's body stiffened, and his eyes, filled with fear, glared at her. Maddy knew she'd hit a nerve.

"I can't."

"You have to."

"I am not allowed to go in there. It has a special lock. No one can get in. If I try, Nigel said he'd kill me."

When Maddy put her hand on her gun, Mason recoiled, then turned, and started walking up to the attic. It looked like any other attic, except that half of it had been converted into a room. It had a steel door and a hefty lock.

"What's in there?" she asked.

"I've never been in it."

Maddy tried to open the door by shoving and kicking it, but it wouldn't budge. "Stand back," she told Mason and shouted for anyone inside to stand clear. She fired three slugs into the lock, and the door swung open a few inches. She kicked it the rest of the way, turned on the light, and walked in. "Jesus."

She stood in Cupid's den of horrors. Trophies of his conquests were everywhere. Pairs of little girl's underwear lined one wall, and newspaper clippings hung like diplomas on another. Among them were Sarah Benning's and Nancy Miles's newspaper articles, the three cases from Chicago, and several from Britain, revealing a long history of Cupid's thirst to ravage prepubescent girls. Most grotesque were photographs of victims in bondage, still alive, and pinned next to them the photos of the same children dead. When Maddy walked to a desk near the bed, she found a sheet of paper. On it, scribbled in red crayon, were the words, "Maddy Reynolds must die."

I've walked up to the gates of hell and am looking in, Maddy thought, remembering the words that Mary Thompson spoke to her. Mason's mouth hung open. "I didn't know anything about this," he said.

"Don't touch anything, Mason. Just turn around and walk out."

She heard Zep's voice calling out to her from downstairs. "Maddy, where are you?"

"In the attic," she shouted. When he came up, she said, "In there, it's all in there," and gestured toward the room.

He walked in. "Holy Mother of God!" he cried out. Zep turned back to Mason and said, "I'm going to handcuff you. If you don't resist, it won't hurt. With Mason secured, he moved toward the wall and examined the photos, then the news articles and underwear. He walked to the table where Cupid had written, "Maddy must die," looked over to Maddy, his face white and his eyes filled with disbelief."

Maddy drifted around the room, gazing at its contents, astounded by how perfectly arranged it all was, as if its creator had taken great pride in his work. *It's a cesspool of wickedness,* she thought. She felt a palpable presence of evil in the room as she looked at the tortured faces and the suffering of children who made up the exhibit. She opened a bottom desk drawer and pulled out shackles and ropes. Zep opened the closet door, where woman's clothing and different colored wigs hung on hooks. Taped to the back of the door was an old front-page newspaper article from the Chicago Tribune with the headline, "Veteran Detective, James Reynolds, Murdered by Child Serial Killer."

"Maddy!" Zep shouted; his eyes fixed on the headline.

"I know, Zep. I just found out that he killed my father. And there's more." She leaned against a wall, her body limp, gazing down at the floor. "I found out Rusty is Cupid."

Zep's face turned to stone. His lips grew taut, and a cynical grin crept over his face. "That explains how he stayed one step ahead of us all this time. He probably eavesdropped on cops having breakfast in his cozy little restaurant, where he learned everything he needed to know. That son of a bitch." Then, as if someone had hit him with a baseball bat, he looked at Maddy and said, "My God, Maddy, he's come here to kill you." He took off his glasses and let his hands dropped to his side. "I can't let him get to you.

You're my responsibility, and I can't let him get to you." It was as though at that moment, he saw Maddy in a new light, not as a comrade but as a responsibility. A chill ran through her.

"I want you back at the command center," he said. "Now." He seemed more frightened than pissed. "I'll be there when we finish. And no more going rogue. I mean it."

As she drove back, Maddy thought how she had pushed Zep beyond his limit and feared how hard he might push back. When she approached Forestport, it was just after nine p.m., and only a few cars were in the parking lot. With nothing to do but hang around and drink coffee, she tried to get information about what was going on at the Charles house from an old-timer cop doing paperwork. He told her Zep had ordered Al and Bud back from Buffalo. "With the Bishop kid running out of time, he wants to organize a big push before it's too late."

"Do you have any idea when he'll be back here?"

"They're going through the Beam Street house with a fine-tooth comb," the old-timer said. "It'll be hours."

Exhausted, emotionally spent, and bored, and knowing that Amber was safe with Jack, Maddy lay down on a cot to rest for a few minutes but fell fast asleep. When she sat up and looked at her watch, twelve hours had passed. She felt groggy from a sleep hangover and walked out to the main area. The place was nearly empty. Marcia, the new assistant, handed her a note. It read, "Don't be upset, but I'm taking you off the case. It's for your protection. It would be grossly irresponsible for me to do otherwise knowing what I now know."

Maddy's kneejerk reaction was to be pissed, but after a few hours of thinking it over, she realized that she had gone to a dark place and had abandoned the better part of herself. She had become willing to break the very law that she had sworn to uphold when she considered killing Rusty on sight.

The note went on to explain that in searching Donald Charles's house, they found documentation proving he had recently purchased a cabin in Chenango County, south of Utica. There was every indication, he said, that Rusty, Donald, and hopefully Candy Bishop, were headed there. "It's in a heavily wooded area. We're afraid he'll kill the girl if he hears us approach by helicopter, so we're assembling a team to hike in."

Finally, he added, "I know you're close with Mary Thompson. My wife knows her from the church. She told me this morning that Mary is dying. If you want to pay her a visit, she's at St. Luke's Hospital."

Oh, Mary, sweet Mary. Can there be anything sadder than losing you? The thought was almost too much to bear. Now that Maddy was disengaged from the investigation, while everyone else was on their way to Chenango County for the final showdown with Cupid, she decided to visit her dear friend.

She stopped by home to shower and change before driving to St. Luke's. Everything along the way seemed filled with life, but when she pulled into the hospital parking lot a queasiness began to grow in the pit of her stomach. *I hate hospitals,* she thought. *It's a place where people go to die.*

When the doors of the elevator opened on the eighth floor, she asked a nurse where Mary's room was. She walked in and saw Mary in a bed, tilted up, facing a window, and looking out, deep in thought. Before Maddy could say anything, Mary turned with a smile and said, "Why hello, child." The light from her smile was gone, and her eyes seemed sunken. Though her voice was soft and weak, Maddy could still feel the love pouring out from her spirit.

"I've been thinking about you," Mary said. "I read in the papers about that poor girl. So sad. Come, sit next to me."

"You're the one in a fight this time, Mary," Maddy said.

"It's my time, dear. It's my time. I'm ready for the good Lord to take me home." Mary sighed, lay back in her bed, and explained how she had gotten so sick one day that she fell and couldn't get up. "I was stuck in the house until Deborah, my neighbor, came by and called an ambulance. I have the cancer, and they told me I won't be going home again." Mary was worried about her tomato plants, bird feeders, and a stray cat that came around for food. Maddy assured her that she'd check in on them.

Then, with some difficulty, Mary shifted position and looked directly into Maddy's eyes. "Tell me what's going on with you."

Familiar with Mary's powers of discernment, Maddy didn't try to sugarcoat anything. "I have lost my compass. I've always known where true north was, but now, when I look up for the North Star, I see only clouds. I am lost, Mary."

"Don't look up there for your true north, honey, you're not traveling in the heavens yet. You're still on earth. You need to look deep within yourself, that's how you'll find your way. Trust that."

"Who am I?" The words spilled out of Maddy's mouth like they'd been dangling on the tip of her tongue for a long time, but now, unrestrained by pretense and sitting with a true friend, she set them free.

"You're different from the rest of us," Mary said. "Unlike most people, who avoid fear, you've always lived with it. For you, running away is not an option. If you do, you'll drown. That makes you stronger than most, and as strange as it may sound, your fear is your strength."

Maddy knew what she meant. She remembered that at the peak of her anxiety as a teenager, she had to choose between hiding herself or fighting back. Learning to shoot, for her, was fighting back.

"But I'm tired, Mary...I'm so tired."

"So am I, dear." Maddy moved up close, and they leaned on one another for a long while before Mary finally said, "There is something I want to tell you. I think it might be important." Maddy moved to a chair across from her.

"I had a dream. You were a mountain lion pursuing a wolf through a forest at night. The wolf was as strong as a tiger and as cunning as a serpent. You were trying to save a kitten he carried in his mouth to devour. As the wolf was about to kill you, the kitten became an eagle and stopped him." With that, Mary's head turned toward the window, and her eyes closed.

Maddy didn't understand the dream but just sat while Mary slept. She knew it was the last time she'd see her and reflected on how the old woman had helped her find a better way of seeing things. Maddy had few friends but knew she would always consider Mary among them. She got up, walked to the bed as Mary slept, leaned over, and whispered, "Thank you for all you've done for me." She kissed her forehead and walked out of the room with her head low.

Chapter 33

As Maddy drove from the hospital, the afternoon sun was getting low in the sky. The heat felt more like mid-July than June. She was thinking of Mary with a heavy heart when a call came through on the two-way radio. "Detective Reynolds. A woman in Forestport reported that her kids are lost in the woods. Can you respond?"

"Affirmative," Maddy said. She opened her notebook, which lay on the passenger seat. "Okay, shoot." She repeated the words aloud as she wrote them down. "The mother is Nora Novak and the address, 312 West Road, Forestport. Got it." As she headed north on Route 12, she thought, *Novak? Forestport? That sounds like Jodi.*

When she arrived at the address, a woman pacing on the front lawn ran up to the car and indignantly shouted, "Where have you been? I called you people over an hour ago." Maddy knew it had only been thirty-five minutes, but the woman seemed so unhinged that instead of reacting, she spoke in a soft, disarming tone. The woman pulled out a pack of cigarettes, lit one up, and seemed to calm down. "I'm Nora Novak," she said nervously. "My two kids, Jodi and Leon, and their friend Toby, rode their bikes to a place called The Deep Woods this morning. They were supposed to be home by four o'clock. It's now almost seven, and I know they're in trouble. Jodi's fourteen, very dependable, and if she could be here, she would. Something must have happened. I think they might be lost."

So, it is the Jodi I met at Mary's, Maddy marveled to herself. She didn't say anything about it to Nora, however.

Nora took a couple more drags from her cigarette, then added, "They may have gone as far back as the old Winfield place. It's an abandoned, turn-of-the-century house, deep in the woods. A lot of bad things have happened there, and people stay away from it."

"Is there anyone nearby who knows their way around the Deep Woods?" Maddy asked.

"Clyde Baker. He grew up around here and lives just up the road." Maddy took down the address and started out for Clyde Baker's place. She glanced in her rear-view mirror as she drove off and saw Nora standing in the road, arms folded, watching. Nora's face reminded her of the empty gaze she'd seen on the faces of Sarah Benning's and Candy Bishop's mothers when their daughters went missing.

Maddy pulled into an opening among a wall of trees that lined the road. A small cottage, nestled in among Hemlock trees, was the only structure in the area. *This must be it*, she thought. It looked more like a camp than a home. She heard the sizzling sound of meat cooking when she walked up to the screen door, and the succulent aroma made her stomach growl. A tall, slender man in his seventies, wearing a green t-shirt and suspenders to hold up his blue jeans, came out.

"Clyde Baker?" she asked.

The old man nodded. Maddy introduced herself and said that Nora Novak thought her kids were lost in the Deep Woods. "I am going there now. Do you mind coming along to help me find them?" Without saying a word, he turned, went back inside, and returned wearing a green brimmed hat and holding another in his hand.

"What's that for?" she asked.

"It's for you. You don't want to get your hair full of blackflies, do ya?"

Blackflies? They never bother me.

Clyde walked to his truck and Maddy to her car. "Can we drive together?" she asked.

"Sure, but that thing you're driving won't get fifty feet into where we're going. Get in." Maddy got in Clyde's truck. On the way, she asked him how much danger he thought the kids were in. "Well," he said slowly and calmly, "if Jodi's with them, they'll be fine."

"I met her once. She seems like quite a kid."

"She's not your average fourteen-year-old, that's for sure," Clyde said, as his hands wrestled to control the bouncing steering wheel.

"I saw her catch a fly right out of midair."

Clyde laughed. "She can do a hell of a lot more than that."

The truck slowed to a near stop, then turned onto a barely visible road, lined with high weeds and low hanging willow tree branches. They blocked out the sun, and when the old heap finally broke through a minute or two later, it filled with blinding light. Before them stood a vast open space. "We're here," he said. Clyde got out, walked up, and looked out at tall trees several hundred yards on the other side of a large field.

"Are those the Deep Woods?" Maddy asked.

"That's them, alright. I sure hope those kids didn't try to go all the way back to the Winfield place."

"Nora said bad things have happened there. What did she mean?"

"Oh, that's a lot of poppycock," Clyde said. "People like to make up stories to entertain themselves. But I'm concerned about what I saw out there last spring. Someone had been trying to cut a trail to the house from the Black River. It runs about a half-mile behind the house. I can think of no good reason why anyone would want to do that," he said.

Maddy wasn't sure what to make of Clyde. He was gruff and distant, but considering the circumstances, she was grateful to have his help. The height of the trees on the other end of the field seemed daunting, and she doubted she'd have any chance of finding the kids alone.

"Over here," Clyde called out. He stood by a clump of bushes where three bicycles leaned against a tree. He turned and pointed to a swath of bent grass in the field that led to the woods. "There. There's where they walked in, and that's where we have to go." Clyde began following the path, and Maddy went after him.

It was late afternoon, still hot, and the sun beat down on the back of Maddy's neck as she trudged through the untamed vegetation. The smell of moisture being drawn from the earth reminded her of Mary Thompson's newly tilled garden back in the spring. When she finally reached the other side, overheated and out of breath, it felt like she'd jumped into a refreshing spring-fed pond when she stepped into the shade of the woods. She and Clyde stood for a moment to catch their breath and to let their eyes adjust to the darkness of tall trees. They began to shout, "Jodi, Leon, Toby," but in return heard the rustling of leaves and warbling of birds.

Moving further back into the trees, at the crest of a hill, they came upon red, purple, and orange knapsacks that sat on a fallen tree. "What do you make of it, Clyde?"

"They probably had no intention of going beyond this point, but started playing, got lured into the woods and lost their way."

Trees blocked any breeze from entering the woods. The air was suffocating, and tiny gnats started to swarm around Maddy's face. *Now I know why he wanted me to wear a hat,* she thought, laughing to herself. The notion of hiking through the woods at night seemed overwhelming. She felt like a ridiculously small minnow in an enormous lake.

Before they started off, Clyde handed her his canteen, and she noticed a tattoo on his forearm of soldiers raising an American Flag. "Were you at Iwo Jima?" she asked. Clyde gave a slight affirmative nod and turned away with a look of painful aversion. Maddy asked no more questions but realized there was a lot more to the old man than met the eye.

"I need to call in," she said, as they were about to leave the area. She pulled out her mobile unit, and when she got through, the connection was terrible. Zep's voice sounded crackly and, though barely audible, she understood enough of what he said to know that he had gone with the others to Chenango County after Rusty. She tried to tell him that she was looking for three kids lost in the woods, but he seemed distracted and simply yelled through the bad connection, "Just go ahead."

It was after eight thirty when Maddy and Clyde started hiking. The night began to cover the woods like a blanket. "What are the chances of finding them in the dark?" she asked.

"At this point, we'll probably meet up with them at the Winfield Place. There's a stream a half-mile ahead that will eventually pass near the house. They'll probably follow it and hole up there."

Clyde seemed to prance over and around roots, rocks, and puddles like a deer. His knowledge of the Deep Woods gave Maddy the impression he wasn't only familiar with the forgotten place but had a deep affection for it. When they reached the stream, he stopped and said, "The water here is fine to drink." He knelt and scooped handfuls into his mouth before he filled the canteen. "You should do the same. You don't want to get dehydrated."

The water tasted sweet on Maddy's tongue and felt unusually refreshing as it went down. "How do you know your way around these woods so well?" she asked.

"I used to hunt here with my brother as a kid." She looked at the old man's face and, in the moonlight, saw beyond the wrinkles in his skin and his stubbled beard. She realized she had misjudged him. At first, she thought he was a redneck, probably crude and unsophisticated. But he had a sophistication of a different kind, a practical sort, one that could help a person find their way through a dense forest at night. Maddy knew of no one else who could do that.

She noticed Clyde looking out beyond the treetops with a sullen expression. "Are you okay, Clyde?

"It's that looks like a Gibbous moon," he said. He shook his head, looked away and under his breath added, "I don't like it." "What was that you said?" she asked, unsure of what he meant. When he didn't answer, she looked up and saw an odd-shaped, lop-sided moon. Her stomach rolled. Instantly, she was transported back to Halloween night when she was twelve. *That's the same moon that followed Bob Bennett and me the night Dad died.*

Top of Form

When they left the stream and started moving again, it became steep, and the hills came one after another. Maddy worked hard to keep up with Clyde, especially when the terrain changed and the banks left no space to step, forcing them to walk in the water. After a quarter mile of sloshing through the stream, their feet and pant legs wet, they came to a large, flat rock, and climbed up. "Let's wait here a bit," Clyde said. While catching her breath, Maddy looked up, and through an opening in the trees, saw stars shining brighter than she had ever seen stars shine before. *How beautiful.* In that brief moment, she decided that someday she'd like to live surrounded by such splendor.

"Ready," Clyde said as he prepared himself to start barreling forward again. They followed the stream to a place where the land flattened out into an opening with no trees. It was a small field, and the moon shed a blue hue on the grass. Clyde stopped suddenly. He seemed startled.

"What's wrong, Clyde."

"Quiet!" He pointed to an area beyond the open space. "Look. It's the Winfield house," he whispered. "Someone's in there, and it's not the kids. This can't be good, Maddy."

She looked carefully into the blackness of the trees beyond the open space but didn't see anything. "What am I looking for?" she asked, moving her head from side to side, squinting.

"Lights. Over there," he said, pointing.

"I see them," she said.

Then, out of nowhere, a voice said, "Mr. Baker, is that you?"

"Who is that? Is that you, Toby?"

"Yes. It's Leon and me." The two boys came out from behind a clump of trees. They looked scared and cold.

"Where's Jodi?" Clyde asked.

"She went up to that house to see if the people inside would help us find our way home. She made us hide here until she knew for sure that it was safe. Two men came out. One grabbed her by the hair and dragged her inside. That was an hour ago."

Maddy's heart raced. "Can you describe what they looked like?" The descriptions fit Rusty and Donald to a T. "We have to move these boys further back away from that house," she said.

As Clyde led them over the hill, Maddy's mind stirred, thinking of how destiny had taken control by leading her to Rusty. There was no doubt in her mind that before the night was through, one of them would be dead.

When the house was out of sight, Maddy called Zep. Sounding exasperated, he said, "We hiked all the way back to the damn cabin, and the place was empty. No one's lived there for years. It was another well-crafted ploy, and we took the bait. Son of a bitch."

"Listen carefully, Zep. I am within seventy-five yards of Rusty and Donald right now. They are in an old house in the woods outside of Forestport and have taken one of the three lost kids, a girl about fourteen. I have two boys and Clyde Baker, a neighbor. He knows the woods very well and helped me find the boys. I think Candy Bishop is probably in the house too."

After a long silence, Zep's voice, high pitched, and sounding almost comical in his disbelief said, "Did I hear you right? Cupid and Donald Charles are where you are?" The terrible irony didn't escape him, and almost sarcastically, he said, "I took you off this case to keep you safe from that monster, and now you're facing him alone?"

During the long silence that followed, Maddy looked over at the boys, who had heard everything, including the name "Cupid." Their faces were frozen with fear. Then Zep's voice rang out clearly and slowly as he said in a monotone, "What are you planning to do, Maddy?"

"I'm going in there."

"Maddy!" he shouted.

"Zep listen to me. He's going to kill both of those kids unless I do something."

He didn't respond, and Maddy thought, *He knows I'm right.* "I'll leave the boys with Clyde about a hundred yards from the house. He'll have my hand-held unit. If I don't come out in thirty minutes, Clyde will call, and you can send in help. But no helicopters before then. Agreed?"

"I don't like this...I do not like this at all."

"What else can we do?"

Zep sighed, and in a low, barely audible voice, filled with resignation, said, "Okay." Before Maddy headed back up the hill, she gave Clyde instructions on what to do, shook his hand, and said, "Wish me luck."

The tall old man stood up, looked down into her face, put his hand on her shoulder, and said, "You're one of the brave ones, Maddy Reynolds."

Chapter 34

Maddy walked up the ravine and felt Cupid's presence grow with each step. The tortured faces of the girls on the wall in his den of horrors flashed through her head. All she could think of was the kind of monster capable of doing such things. *It has all come down to this*, she thought. *A whole lifetime, and it's all come down to this.* Light from the abandoned house flickered through the trees, coaxing her to come closer. She pushed all thoughts from her mind except one; *the man who killed my father is inside.*

The pale light of the moon helped her navigate fallen tree branches, roots, and rocks. When she was within fifteen yards of the house, Maddy saw movement inside. It sent her off into the shadows, where she waited for it to stop. Crouched down, she scooched her way to the house, and when she reached it, leaned back against an outside wall. As she slid along the wall to a window, she heard Donald Charles's voice, looked in, and saw Jodi tied to a chair. She looked like she had been roughed up—hair messy, face red, and her left eye swollen. A missing pane of glass allowed Maddy to hear what Donald was saying.

"You are a pretty one, different from the others." His big belly hung over his belt and sweat dripped from his face. "You seem so sweet. I can make things easy for you if you're nice to me. Cupid is very rough with his girls, but I promise to be gentle." Aroused, Donald didn't try to hide the bulge in his pants while Jodi, expressionless, kept her eyes locked on his every move.

Where the hell is Rusty? Maddy wondered, not wanting to make a move until she knew where he was. On the ground, near her feet, a light from a basement window shined. She crouched down and looked inside. Candy Bishop lay on the dirt basement floor, not moving, face down. Her eyes were closed, and Maddy couldn't tell if she was alive. She returned to the window and heard Donald say, "Cupid doesn't understand me. I try to get him to be nice to the girls, but he wants to be so brutal."

"If you free me from this chair," Jodi said, "I'll go with you into the woods where we can be alone and away from Cupid." Donald's face lit up, and his excitement grew larger. He smiled tenderly and reached out to unbutton her shirt.

"Not here," Jodi whispered sternly. "Cupid might see us."

"Just a little taste," he said after he loosened her top button. He began rubbing her chest with his fingers. Revulsed, Jodi turned her head. He loosened a second button, and this time he rubbed her skin closer to her breast. *How far do I let this go?* Maddy thought as she pulled out her weapon.

When Donald loosened the third button and placed his hand on Jodi's breast, she lunged her teeth into the flesh of his wrist, clamping down hard. He screamed and pulled his arm away. Blood dripped down his hand, splattering on the table. His face was crimson with rage, and his eyes bulged out of their sockets as he reached for a baseball bat that leaned on a wall near-by. As the bat descended toward Jodi's head, Maddy's first shot entered over his right eye, popping his head back. He stood frozen in place, eyes blank and staring into space. The second shot tore a hole in his throat, and his large body crashed on the table. Blood gushed from his mouth.

Rusty still didn't enter. *He's watching from the other room, that son of bitch*, Maddy thought. She saw an object flying through the air. It crashed into the lantern, and the room went dark, except for a small fire on the floor where the lantern broke apart. All Maddy could see was the shadow of a man who seemed to run into the room, but it quickly disappeared when the fire went out. She waited a moment and was about to go to the front door when she saw two shadows exit toward the back of the house.

Maddy pushed her way around the side of the house through prick-ly bushes to the yard. By the time she got to the back, she only caught a glimpse of two people disappearing into the trees. Her instinct was to follow, but because Candy Bishop might still be alive, she returned to the house.

As she walked down the stairs to the basement, the smell of urine and feces was strong, and she covered her face with her hand. She walked over and knelt next to Candy. *She's alive. Thank God!* Placing her face close, she whispered, "You're safe now. We're going to get you home to your mom and dad. Just be calm, sweety."

Maddy went back upstairs to the front of the house and shouted for Clyde to come quickly. "There's a girl in the basement barely alive," she told him when he walked in. Clyde acted quickly. After he covered Donald's body with a blanket to keep the boys from seeing it, he carried Candy upstairs to a cot where Leon and Toby waited. While he and the boys attended to the child, Maddy tried contacting Zep again.

"Maddy, what's going on," he shouted, panic just barely concealed in his voice.

"I had contact with Donald, Rusty, and the girl. I shot Donald. He's dead. Rusty took off into the woods with Jodi. Candy is alive but not in good shape."

"I'm sending a unit in right now," Zep shouted.

"No! Damn it. Don't do that! If he hears them coming, he'll kill Jodi," Maddy said emphatically. "I'm going after him myself."

"Son of a bitch." Zep's shouted. "Let me talk to that, Clyde, guy."

Maddy handed Clyde the phone. He nodded every few seconds as he listened to Zep and finally said, "He's headed toward the Black River. It's about a mile back in. He could have a boat there."

There was another pause, then Clyde continued, "If you're asking me what I'd do if I were him, I'd head downstream to the reservoir. If he's smart, he'll have a car hidden somewhere around the shoreline." Clyde handed the phone back to Maddy.

"Maddy," Zep said. A long silence followed that seemed like an eternity. "Don't get yourself killed. We'll find a way to be nearby but out of sight. Keep the phone with Clyde. Once you are far enough away, he'll have to guide a medevac unit in to take Candy, Clyde, and the two boys out."

"If anything happens to me, Zep," Maddy said, "Promise you'll try to explain all this to my daughter."

"I promise," he said softly.

The two boys seemed to be distracted from their physical discomfort by helping Clyde care for Candy. When Maddy was ready to set out after Rusty and Jodi, Clyde looked at her and said, "Godspeed, my friend." Maddy reached out her hand, gently grasped his arm, looked at him warmly, turned, and hurried off into the darkness.

Chapter 35

The moon shed enough light for Maddy to follow a path of broken tree branches and bent-over grass for a short distance, but it soon disappeared into the marsh. She had no choice but to advance in a straight line and hope that Rusty and Jodi did too. It was hard to believe that she was actually chasing the man who killed her father; she felt electrified. Never before had Maddy known the power of purpose the way she did at that moment.

A guttural sound echoed in the distance. She stopped and stood perfectly still. When it didn't repeat, she continued. *I'll move in as close as I can to get a kill shot,* she thought. *But Rusty will kill the girl for sure if he hears me coming.* Her brain was in high gear. If a fish jumped, she'd snap around. If the crickets stopped chirping, she'd stop and listen for footsteps. Everything mattered; her and Jodi's lives were on the line.

An open area lay just ahead. Maddy moved into it, slow and silent, hoping to get a glimpse of her prey. *Nothing.* A hundred or more yards ahead, the Black River moved purposely, glittering in the moonlight. She stayed in the open, but near to the trees.

Maddy was startled by another loud noise. This time she recognized the sound of a motor straining to start. "Shit," a man's voice echoed across the open space. *That's him. I'd know that voice anywhere.* She followed just inside the treeline toward the sound, keeping the river in sight. The images of a boat, a man, and a girl emerged in the darkness and she edged in as close as she could. *There he is!*

A chill ran through Maddy as she watched Rusty move about in the small space in the front of the boat, bullying the controls, shoving a throttle and slapping at some buttons. *He looks like he's losing it.* Jodi sat very still in the back of the boat and Maddy realized that she was probably tied up.

Each time the motor moaned, Maddy's heart skipped, knowing that if it started, Jodi was a goner. *If he takes off, there'll be nothing I can do to help.* He was too far away for a good shot, and Maddy knew she'd have only one chance, so she waited. After a short time, she felt helpless and considered making a charge, but the forty yards of open space between them was too risky.

When Jodi began squirming about each time Rusty's back was turned, Maddy shouted to herself, *What the hell is she doing? She's going to get herself killed.* Jodi seemed to stretch out her leg, push down on something several times, then snap back into a sitting position before Rusty turned around. Then he caught her. "What the hell are you trying to do? I'll crush your head like a plum if you're not careful." He locked his gaze on her, then turned back to the console.

The motor moaned more slowly each time Rusty tried to start it. To Maddy's amazement, Jodi kept up the strange movement. The motor would almost start up but coughed as though it was flooded. *Damn, Jodi found a way to flood the engine.* Maddy marveled at the girl's cleverness and courage.

Apparently overwhelmed with frustration, Rusty finally let the starter run continuously until the battery was nearly dead, but a loud backfire, followed by an erratic sputtering, brought the motor to life, and it started.

"All right!" he shouted.

Alarmed, Maddy stepped out of the woods, ready to charge the boat. She waited for Rusty to look away, but when he went to the bow to untie a rope, the motor stopped running. She stepped back into the cover of the woods.

"Fuck!" he yelled out. He hurried back to the console and tried to revive the motor, but the battery was dead. He ran to where Jodi sat, pulled her up by the hair, and pushed her to the shore. He tied the rope around her neck, and the two disappeared down the river.

Maddy thought how the sweet girl was now in the hands of a child killer. She had found her way into Maddy's heart when she shared her story, and the thought that she might be headed for a horrible fate turned her stomach. Mary's words came back to her: "Jodi has a lot of interesting abilities," as well as what Clyde had said, "She can do a hell of a lot more than that," referencing how she caught a fly in midair. Maddy hoped they were right.

Maddy let several minutes pass before she started out down the shoreline. A mist began settling on the river as the night air cooled, and, despite her constant movement, she felt cold. *I'm probably dehydrated. I wish I'd brought Clyde's canteen.* As she moved forward, the sound of feet trudging through mud just ahead startled her, and she stopped. *Shit, I'm too close.* She waited, then continued.

A fallen tree blocked her way. She crawled over its branches and noticed a light glowing in the mist about a hundred yards ahead. Cautiously, she moved toward the glow. The muddy, fishy smell of the river and the strange, shining moon created an almost surrealistic feeling. She felt as if she were entering an alien world where nothing was familiar, and anything could happen.

She neared the illuminated mist and saw what seemed to be an open area ahead. Moving within the cover of a thicket, she approached the lighted area. A stone quarry lay before her, empty, without a soul in sight. The substantial open space had dirt hardpan and several forty-foot piles of stone scattered about. Amber lights on top of four telephone poles cast a dull glow on the dirt, and the Black River flowed off in the distance. Front-end loader machines were lined up near a building in the center of the quarry. It was made of blue steel sheeting, had two entrances, and no windows. Nearby, six white portable toilets stood side-by-side like tiny houses.

An empty parking area and two sets of wet footprints that led to the building made it ominously clear to Maddy that only Rusty, Jodi, and herself were there. She broke into the open and ran to the shadows of the building. Sweat beaded up on her face as she leaned her back against the building and extracted her Beretta from its holster. She slid toward the door. On the outside of the door, a red plastic sign with white letters read "Closed Until Further Notice." Maddy turned the knob, and stepped inside.

The room was thick with gasoline fumes. It was a machine shop, and in it stood two partially disassembled earthmoving machines. Holding the gun with both hands, ready for anything, Maddy inched her way around the enormous contraptions. Something moved to her left, and instinctively she snapped around, prepared to shoot. Nothing was there. *Man, I'm jumpy.*

When she was sure the shop was clear, Maddy moved toward double glass doors on the other side of the room. Beyond them was a hallway. It had offices on both sides and a gray steel door at the far end. Although the office lights were turned off, the florescent lights in the hallway illuminated the rooms, and Maddy safely checked them out. Then she stood at the gray door, and thought, *I can feel him.* She quivered and once again called on her father for courage. Using the weight of her body to nudge the door open, Maddy slipped inside. Except for a dim light on the opposite end of the large room, there was darkness. Unable to see the floor, she slid her feet along it to avoid bumping into something.

The room reeked of body odor, and when her eyes adjusted to the darkness, she saw rows of tall thin metal cabinets and realized that she was standing in a locker room. She moved toward the dim light, and when she got near, she was stunned to see two bodies sitting on the floor. *That's fucking Rusty!* she screamed to herself. Rusty held a rope and the other end was tied around Jodi's neck as she leaned back against a wall. Rusty sat across from her, appearing deep in thought. *He's trying to figure out a way out of the mess he's in*, Maddy said to herself.

Maddy released the safety on her weapon. She took aim but did not have a clear shot at Rusty's head. As she moved to a different angle, her foot hit something hard. The sound of a breaking glass cracked the silence. Rusty jumped up, pulled Jodi close, and put a knife to her throat. "Who's out there?"

Maddy stood frozen in the shadows and knew her options were gone. Rusty moved the knife to Jodi's nose. "I'm cutting this pretty nose off if you don't come out where I can see you." Maddy saw blood drip onto Jodi's shirt and moved into the light.

"Oh my, my, my, look who we have here," Rusty said in a high-pitched voice. "I guess this isn't such a bad day after all." He centered Jodi in front of him, blocking a clear shot.

"Let the girl go, Rusty. The entire Oneida County Sheriff's Department is almost here. You can't get away."

"Maybe so, but I know two people who won't be alive when they get here. Now put that gun down and kick it over before I damage this pretty bitch."

Rusty had cleverly covered a clear shot to the vital parts of his body with Jodi. *Damn, I can't get a clear shot in*, she thought before she kicked the gun over. When Rusty picked it up, he put the knife in his back pocket and Maddy noticed Jodi watching his every move as though she were analyzing the situation. Rusty began talking rapidly in the third person like a madman, and Maddy had to strain to understand what he was saying. "Everybody wants the big prize. Cupid is the big prize. But all you people are too small to have such a big prize as Cupid."

With the gun in his right hand pointed at Maddy, he put his left arm around Jodi's neck and held her to his side. As he rambled on, Jodi, with both hands still tied behind her back, managed to slip the knife from Rusty's back pocket and slid it into her own. Hardly believing what she had just seen, Maddy said, "You're pretty good at hurting helpless children, but let's see what you can do with someone who can fight back. Let the girl go, then it'll be just you and me."

"Very clever. There's nothing more I'd like than to rip you apart with my bare hands, but the answer is no. I kind of like this girl, and when I'm done with you, I'll be having her for dessert." He pointed the gun at Maddy's heart and said, "Before you die, there is something I want you to know. Your father killed my father, so I killed him. But that doesn't make everything even, not by a long shot. I'm going to wipe his seed from the face of the earth. After I kill you, I'm coming back to kill your precious Amber."

Maddy filled with rage. She was about to lunge at him when the words from Mary's dream popped into her head: "As the wolf was about to kill you, the kitten became an eagle and stopped him."

Jodi jerked the rope just as Rusty pulled the trigger. The bullet went off its mark, smashed into Maddy's left shoulder like a sledgehammer, and knocked her to the floor. She lost consciousness for a few seconds, and when she opened her eyes, burning pain in her chest was radiating to her ribs. Blood had splattered in her eyes, and when she wiped them clear, she watched Jodi break free from Rusty's grip, twist her body in a circular motion, and thrust her left knee into his groin. He screamed, squatted, and held himself. His face contorted with pain. Then Jodi whipped her body in the opposite direction and used her momentum to drive her right knee into his kidney. Rusty collapsed with a thud, rattling the lockers. His face contorted in agony. In a flash, Jodi disappeared into the shadows.

When he fell, the gun flew from his hand and slid far beneath a steel cabinet. Maddy saw Rusty watch it vanish out of sight. He dragged himself over to where it disappeared, reached, and unable to extract it, slammed the metal locker doors with his fists and yelled "Shit, shit, shit!" Maddy had all she could do to slip out of the room into the quarry. Deterred by pain, she was barely able to hobble across the yard. Blood dripped into the dirt and left a trail to the high grass where she hid, waiting for Rusty to appear.

Within minutes, he limped into the yard screaming, "Cupid is going to unleash hell on both of you bitches." He followed the blood trail into the high grass and thrashed about haphazardly. When he turned his head, Maddy grabbed a stone and hurled it at the steel building. It hit with a "clank." He snapped around, dragged himself back into the quarry, and began checking anywhere a person might hide. He examined the earthmoving machines, then the stone piles, and finally, he headed over to the portable toilets.

Maddy wondered where Jodi was hidden. She crept closer to the quarry and found a baseball-size rock to use as a weapon. *The tables are turned now, you bastard. I can see you, and you can't see me.* She thought of the years he had stalked her without her knowing it. *It's him or me. One of us is going to die tonight.*

Rusty checked the portable toilets. Maddy hid behind each one he finished with. She hoped to get close enough to crush his head. She watched him sneak up on each toilet and rapidly open its door, and looked as though he was ready to destroy whoever might be inside with his hands. A wave of wooziness caused Maddy to stop and collect herself. She put her head low to the ground and waited for a moment when she heard, "Got you!"

She looked up and saw Rusty at a portable toilet with his hands around Jo-di's neck. "You little bitch! Cupid has enough of your shit." Jodi turned her head from side to side, gasping for air. Maddy was only fifteen feet away, but it felt like a mile. She used her good hand to prop herself up, hobbled along the ground, and prepared to deliver a crushing blow to the back of Rusty's head.

Jodi was losing the battle against Rusty's grip, but when she saw Maddy, she seemed to regain strength, arched her back, twisted her body, and with both hands still tied behind her back, flung the knife from her back pocket in Maddy's direction. It fell halfway between Maddy and the killer. Rusty saw what she did, turned, looked at Maddy, and smiled. He whipped around back to Jodi, smashed her face against the portable toilet, and knocked her unconscious. "Now it is just you and Cupid," he said, grinning.

Maddy stretched for the knife. A bolt of pain arced across her chest. She grabbed its handle and held it with all her strength, knowing it was her only hope. Rusty stood over her, trying to take it, and in the struggle, the knife was kicked several feet away. As he raced for it, Maddy, still on the ground, stuck out her hand and hooked his toe with her fingers. He stumbled beyond the knife and landed on his stomach.

Maddy tried to leap for the knife, but Rusty grabbed her leg and reeled her to him. He had her in a headlock, and she felt a vicelike grip tighten around her neck. In desperation, she reached in her pocket for her father's badge. She freed the pin with her thumb and jammed its spike into Rusty's elbow. He screeched out in pain and immediately released her. Barely conscious when she hit the ground, nearing despair, she whispered, "Dad, please help me."

She forced herself to get up, turned, lowered her good shoulder, and like an offensive guard, smashed into Rusty's stomach, driving him backward. He fell into a slippery pool of leachate from an unmaintained toilet. The stink was horrendous. As he tried to get up, slipping and falling, Maddy grabbed the knife and lunged, shoving the blade deep into his lower back. Rusty let out a groan and fell back into the sludge. She climbed on his back to finish him, but he bucked violently and shook her off. She landed on her back and nearly lost consciousness, but still clutched the knife.

Covered with blood, Rusty struggled to get to his feet while in the sewage, but Maddy got to her knees first, leaned over, and stabbed the only body part of his body she could reach—his calf. He jolted, and in agony, screamed, "Cupid is going to fuck you while he cuts your head off, you bitch!" She climbed on his back a second time, and under her weight, he collapsed. As if he was aware that he was losing the battle, Rusty made a last-ditch effort to shake Maddy off. She shifted her weight and used her legs to keep him pinned down.

For an instant, Rusty's stamina waned. In his weak moment, Maddy thrust the knife into the back of his neck. She felt the steel rub against bone and vertebrae. Like a pig being slaughtered, a high-pitched squeal resounded throughout the open yard. Rusty's body stiffened, then collapsed into the sludge.

Maddy rolled off, and although barely conscious, she felt an overwhelming sense of relief. *Thank you, Dad.* She crawled several feet away from the reeking body and collapsed on her stomach. Exhausted and in pain, she looked up from the ground and began scanning the quarry for Jodi, but there was no sign of her. As she looked, the shadow of a man moved over her.

Oh, my God! He's still alive! Maddy tried to get up, but she could not, so she rolled over. Rusty stood before her, his pained-filled face was covered with black filth and blood. *He looks like a demon from hell,* Maddy thought. Rusty reached around, trying to pull the knife from his neck. With all of her remaining strength, Maddy lunged the heel of her foot upward into his groin. His eyes, filled with disbelief, looking at her with unmitigated hatred. He turned his head to the sky and released a thunderous roar that seemed filled with a lifetime of pain. His body drooped, and helplessly he staggered backward, glaring at Maddy as he collapsed into the leachate. The weight of his body forced the knife all the way through his neck, leaving the blood-covered blade shining in the moonlight.

Maddy staggered to her knees and gazed over. Rusty's eyes were wide opened, and even in death, they seemed filled with contempt. Barely conscious and with great effort, she slurred out the words, "Cupid is dead!"

The man who had brought so many people so much suffering lay sprawled out in reeking filth. Her thoughts went back to how he had left Sarah Benning and Nancy Miles. He had killed her father and best friend; he was the destroyer of more than ten girls; but now, finally, he had found his reward adorned in sewage.

Maddy tried to get up, but trees and lights converged into a blur, and she collapsed. Dizzy, she lay on her back with her eyes closed and heard a sweet voice. "It's me, Jodi." She looked and saw Jodi, with her face swollen and bloodied. The young girl applied pressure to her wound as she faded in and out of consciousness. A loud chop, chop, chop sound of helicopters vibrated through the ground, and in moments, shadowy figures hovered over.

She heard Zep's voice. "Thank God you're alive."

Maddy drifted between black silence and swirling light, and her head spun like she was on a carnival ride. Before she was lifted onto the helicopter, all sound and smell muddled together, and she nearly vomited. When Maddy was whisked away into the air, a soft hand found hers. She knew it had to be Jodi's. With her other hand, Maddy clutched her father's badge, then everything went black.

Chapter 36

"Good morning, Ms. Reynolds." the young nurse said as she walked up to the bed, holding a tray in her hand.

"Breakfast?" Maddy asked.

"No, not yet. More meds."

"Again?" She gulped down a cupful of pills. "The doctor said he thought I might go home today. Have you heard anything?"

"No, but I'll ask."

"Thanks."

The nurse leaned over and helped Maddy prop herself up with pillows. "Would you like me to help you clean up?"

"No, I think I can handle it."

"Ok, just be sure not to get your wound wet."

The nurse walked out for the room. Maddy held a mirror in her hand and looked at herself. *Oh my God*, she thought, trying to push her hair in place with her right hand, her left shoulder bandaged, and all the time wondering how her scarred body might look when she finally healed.

"Hey, Maddy." She looked at the doorway: it was Zep and Al.

"Hey guys, come over and have a seat. Sorry, I look a giant hairball." They laughed. Zep held up a bouquet of yellow lilies. Al clutched a box of chocolates.

"How are you feeling?" Al asked.

"Still a little sore, but I might be going home, so I feel great."

"You've been through quite an ordeal, Maddy," Zep said.

"I still haven't put all the pieces back together. I think it's going a take some time."

"Take all the time you need," he added.

The nurse walked back in, saw the flowers, and commented on how lovely they were. "I'll find something to put them in," she said, and carried them out of the room.

"I got your favorites," Al said, holding up the box of Godiva chocolates. "I thought you might need a fix."

Maddy knew the two men well enough to recognize that there was something more going on than met the eye. "Aren't you two supposed to be out catching bad guys?"

"You caught them all. Now we don't have anything to do," Al said with a chuckle.

She noticed a heaviness in Zep's eyes and finally came right out with it. "Okay, what's going on with you two."

They looked at each other, then Zep said, "It's the noise lady."

"Tonya? What about her?"

"She's dead."

It was like being kicked in the gut. Maddy grimaced. "What happened?"

"Breaking and entering gone bad," Zep said. Some kids got in her place, and when she tried to call for help, they shot her. The boy who did it is fifteen."

Maddy looked down, shook her head, hardly able to speak. "Did she suffer?"

"No. She went quickly."

"She was so happy to be rid of that annoying noise. If it weren't for her obsession with it, who knows how long it would have taken to connect Rusty to Cupid. I'm not sure I can do this anymore," she blurted out as she looked up at Zep and stared.

"You've been through a lot. Take your time, think about it," he said.

Maddy reached out her hand. When Zep took it, she said, "Thank you."

Al pointed to a blue and pink card with an unusual design of a dragonfly on it. "Wow, that's really beautiful. Who's it from?"

"Jodi."

"She was amazing that night," Al said.

"She saved my life," Maddy said, as she fixed her gaze on the card. "She said in her note said she needed facial surgery, and the plastic surgeon thinks there will be no visible scars when she heals. She also made sure I knew the two boys, Leon and Toby will be okay. She has been giving them a lot of her time to help them recover from that fearful night. Childhood psychological trauma is something Jodi knows a lot about."

"What about Clyde?" Al asked.

Maddy laughed. "Jodi passed along a message from him saying I forgot my hat. He found the hat that he gave me, and I lost, intended to keep black flies out of my hair. He will be sending it to me. He's quite a person."

"By the way," Zep said, sadly, "I spoke to Tom Bishop about Candy. She's in a special hospital unit at Albany Medical for traumatized children. He said it's going to be a long and difficult recovery for her. Right now, they are focused on her physical rehabilitation but it's the emotional and psychological trauma that will be the most difficult. Tom said that they aren't really sure everything she endured, because she can't talk about it."

The nurse returned with the flowers. They were in a plastic water pitcher, and she placed them on the table next to the bed. "That's the only thing I could find to put them in," she said, "but they're still beautiful." She turned to Maddy with a smile. "It looks like you're going home today. Your husband called a few minutes ago and asked how you were doing. I told him he will need to speak with you."

"He's my ex-husband."

When the nurse left, Maddy turned to the men, smiled awkwardly, and said, "It seems like everyone wants us to get back together, but that's something that'll have to go on my long list of things to think about.

Amber has finally come to a good place with our divorce and need to think long and hard about bringing her into more turmoil. She was here today, and thank God she's adjusting to all that happened as well as she is. Maddy looked directly at Zep and said, " I know you're not going to want to hear this, but she doesn't want me to go back to police work."

Zep seem to try to make light of her statement. "By the way," he said, "you won't have a problem making a living if you decide not to come back. I've gotten calls from publishers who want to talk to you about your story. Just remember, there are two 'Ls' in Zepatello."

As Maddy laughed, a man in blue scrubs walked in, looking at a chart.

"We better get going," Al said.

Zep got up to leave, started for the door, stopped, and turned. "Remember, take all the time you need to decide about what you want to do."

"Thanks," she said, thinking that she'd never go back.

When Zep and Al walked out of the room, Maddy looked over at her father's badge, where it lay on the table next to Jodi's card. She smiled and was filled with an indescribable joy as she felt her dad smiling back.

The End

Acknowledgments

I want to thank my wife, Jean, and granddaughter, Alexis, who sacrificed their time with me for many months while I labored over this novel. A special thanks to Megan, my writing coach, without whom I could not have written *Cupid* and who endured many long telephone calls. Maria, your excellent proofreading help was enormously helpful.

To the beta readers, Susan, Donna, Lori, Molly, Mike F., Joyce, Jean-Marie, and Mike S., your feedback and insights helped to significantly improve the story.

My family and friends, who gave me the encouragement to go on when I needed it most, especially Pat, Pam, Tom, Maria, John, Gary, Jolie, Darla, and Dick, thank you for listening.

I want to give a special shout out to Jodi, whose name I borrowed for the character Jodi Novak. To my colleagues in my writer's group, The Scrivener, your wisdom and experience helped me know that it could be done.

Finally, thank you, God, for a new beginning.

Made in the USA
Middletown, DE
24 December 2020